STUCK ON YOU

PORTIA MACINTOSH

Boldwood

First published in Great Britain in 2020 by Boldwood Books Ltd.

Copyright © Portia MacIntosh, 2020

Cover Design by Debbie Clement Design

Cover Photography: Shutterstock

The moral right of Portia MacIntosh to be identified as the author of this work has been asserted in accordance with the Copyright, Designs and Patents Act 1988.

All rights reserved. No part of this book may be reproduced in any form or by any electronic or mechanical means, including information storage and retrieval systems, without written permission from the author, except for the use of brief quotations in a book review.

This book is a work of fiction and, except in the case of historical fact, any resemblance to actual persons, living or dead, is purely coincidental.

Every effort has been made to obtain the necessary permissions with reference to copyright material, both illustrative and quoted. We apologise for any omissions in this respect and will be pleased to make the appropriate acknowledgements in any future edition.

A CIP catalogue record for this book is available from the British Library.

Paperback ISBN 978-1-80048-102-2

Ebook ISBN 978-1-80048-097-1

Kindle ISBN 978-1-80048-098-8

Audio CD ISBN 978-1-80048-103-9

MP3 CD ISBN 978-1-80048-100-8

Digital audio download ISBN 978-1-80048-096-4

Large Print ISBN 978-1-80048-538-9

Boldwood Books Ltd
23 Bowerdean Street
London SW6 3TN
www.boldwoodbooks.com

For Aud - You're an amazing lady

1

It doesn't matter how many times you break up with someone, it never gets any easier, does it?

While I'm not actually sure whether or not there is a good way to break up with someone there are, without a doubt, a million terrible ways to do it.

Dumping someone by text – that has to be the worst one, right? Text, WhatsApp, Facebook Messenger, or any other kind of written digital communication is about as low as you can go. The absolute coward's way out. And, sure, a phone call is better than a text but only in a similar way to how a broken finger is better than five broken fingers.

Break-ups must always be done in person, that's just the way it is – they should probably make it the law, which might sound extreme, but I'm sure it would cut down on a whole host of angry follow-up crimes. I know a guy who got his car windscreen smashed after breaking up with a girl over e-mail – and I'd be tempted to say he deserved it.

Still, it's not enough to simply say it to a person's face, you have to say it right. If you're wanting to do it as gently as possible there are many little sayings you can reach for. A classic 'it's not you, it's me' is a fine example. It's a way to take full responsibility without saying anything negative about your dumpee – of course, we all know if it were true you wouldn't be breaking up with them in the first place, but still, it's a way to do it without actually telling the other person what you think is so wrong with them that you don't ever want to see them again.

'I think we're better as friends' or 'I don't want to ruin our friendship' are other ways to try and edge away from things being romantic. Who the hell stays friends with an ex though, seriously? I honestly can't think of anything worse than trying to stay buddies with someone who has seen me naked. While we're making these break-up laws, perhaps we should draft something about how exes have to cease to exist, or at the very least move to a different country, after a break-up. I'm sure the world would be a much better place if we could all agree on that.

If I ever decide to get out of the art business and wind up in politics, I'll start some kind of Ex-it movement where, if you want to leave a romantic union, one of you has to go and live abroad or something.

'Hi, Sadie.' I hear a bright, excitable voice coming from behind me. It snaps me from my thoughts. I was miles away. I guess I'm so used to sitting in noisy bars these days I don't find it all that hard to let my mind wander.

I turn around to hug someone who clearly has no idea they are about to get dumped. This one is going to be an Ex-it Remoaner, I can tell.

'Hello,' I say with an equal, although completely put-on, enthusiasm. 'Take a seat, I'll grab us a couple of drinks.'

As I gently push my way through the crowd in the busy Belgravia bar I've been drinking alone in for the past thirty minutes it does cross my mind whether or not I'm doing the right thing, but the more I think about it, the more I don't feel as if I have any other option.

So I buy our drinks, I sit down at the table, I take a deep breath and I give one of my break-up speeches – perhaps my best one yet. I allow myself to think this might actually be a straightforward break-up, until...

'But things were going so well.'

Oh, God, I can't handle those sad eyes. I was deluded to think this would be fine, because there's always a 'but'...

'I know they were,' I lie. I shift uncomfortably in my seat. 'It's just, you know, things are so busy with work, as I said – no one has time for relationships at the moment.'

'But we have to *make* time, otherwise no one would have relationships at all, no one would have kids, the human race would die out!'

I mean, what can I actually say to that? I'm kind of over a barrel. On the one hand, things *are* really hectic at work. On the other hand, working in the art industry is hardly comparable to people like doctors and firefighters who work crazy hours and still find time to have families. I'm going to have to change strategy.

'It's not you,' I insist.

'Oh, come on, don't give me that. How often do we women have to hear that bullshit?' she replies with a roll of her eyes.

Once again, she's got me there.

I take a deep breath and psych myself up for my next play.

'Listen to me, there is nothing wrong with you,' I insist. 'You are a beautiful, caring, intelligent young woman.'

'If I'm so wonderful then why is he having you break up with me instead of doing it himself?'

I don't have the heart to tell her it's because he's started having me break up with all of his short-lived relationships.

'You can do so much better,' I tell her honestly. 'Seriously.'

She sighs, as though she's resigned herself to what's happening. Well, when someone sends one of their employees to break up with you, they clearly don't care that much about you, do they? She seems more frustrated than she does upset, and I totally feel for her. When you're dating, and things don't work out, it's always disheartening, even if you aren't head-over-heels in love.

'Yeah, well, so can you,' she replies. 'I highly doubt it is in your job description that you have to break up with women for your boss.'

And she's right again. It's a shame he's dumping this one; she really is intelligent. He usually dates models, and while the stereotype that they're all dumb isn't exactly true, it isn't always exactly false either.

'I'm really sorry,' I tell her. 'And he is too. I'm here because he didn't want to upset you.'

While it may be the case that I have to do whatever my boss demands of me if I want to be able to keep paying my bills, it has crossed my mind whether or not I should be protesting against having to break up with women for him, but I soon realised that I do a much better job of it than he does anyway, so it's probably for the best. It was my boss who got his car windscreen smashed by an angry ex, in case you haven't guessed. At least I can be tactful and gentle. And if I ever do get lucky enough to meet a man I like, and a time comes when I might need to dump someone for myself, at least I'll be well-practised.

'There's something wrong with him,' she tells me. 'He has intimacy issues.'

I'm absolutely certain he does.

My boss is the famous portrait photographer, Damian Banks. Well, he's famous if you know portrait photographers. So, while he's definitely met and hung out with Harry Styles, I doubt their fanbases are going to have any crossovers any time soon.

Damian is thirty-five years old. I'd say he was newly single were it not for the fact that he probably wouldn't have considered himself taken during the time he was dating this woman anyway.

If I were to speak ever so slightly in defence of Damian, his high-profile job has left him wondering who he can trust. On the other hand, he does lap up the attention.

Damian has models constantly throwing themselves at him, bombarding him with risqué pictures, showing a keen interest in him. He doesn't know who is an opportunist hoping to be shot by the great Damian Banks and who is actually genuinely interested in him, but the fact they are all models isn't lost on him. Eventually, he decides all of his dates have an ulterior motive and that's when he dumps them. Or that's when he gets me, his assistant, to dump them anyway.

'Are you OK?' I ask.

'Oh, I'll be fine,' she says. 'It's you I worry about, Sadie. Damian doesn't value you. He doesn't value anyone. The only person Damian Banks cares about is Damian Banks.'

What can I say? She isn't wrong.

'Stay and have a drink with me?' she asks. 'I'll get us a bottle of something. I can start the healing process right now.'

I smile. This is always so much easier for me when they don't cry. Some girls will cry, beg me – as though I can do anything about it – one of them even flirted with me once. No idea where she thought that would get her.

'OK, sure,' I reply. 'I'll just nip to the loo.'

I fight my way through the crowd to get to the other side of the bar where the toilets are. It's busy here tonight – as always. The place is overflowing with a mixture of cool arty types and high-flying business execs. It seems like a weird combination, but the two crowds aren't all that different. You're not going to find some creative, fresh off the train, who has come to London hoping for their big break in the art world. Any arty type in here is already a big deal. Already a businessperson. They just don't have to wear a suit. And then, of course, there are people like me, who work for the kind of person who belongs here, and the occasional girl who would get to come here with people like Damian. It only feels right to me that I give them their marching orders here, allowing them one last taste of the Damian Banks lifestyle. Plus, this is Damian's local, sand-wiched somewhere between his apartment and his office, so it's the easiest place for me to complete my unorthodox overtime.

As I wash my hands, I look at myself in the mirror – I mean *really* look at myself. How the hell have I ended up here? How is this my life? Something must have gone so wrong, somewhere, if the closest thing I have to a love life is dumping people for my boss.

I did everything I thought I was supposed to do, to land myself my dream career as an art curator, and everything had been going so well. I left the tiny northern seaside town where I grew up, I went to university where I got my BA in art and history, then I moved to London to try and bag myself a job. The problem was that it is such a competitive industry, so I had to work my way through a variety of jobs, some only loosely related to what I wanted to do, but it all felt like progress. Still, I didn't feel as if I was getting anywhere until I saw the job listing seeking an assistant for 'the great Damian Banks' – to give him the full title people so often refer to him by. I was blown away when I got the gig. Little did I know back then that I would only be assisting Damian with his private life, because his working life has been very much absent recently.

I look into my own eyes in the mirror, narrowing them as I mentally tell myself I can do better. I can find a better job. If I had more time I could probably try and have a love life too. I'm only thirty-three, that's still young, and I take pride in my appearance. My long, slightly wavy, honey-blonde hair passes my waist, in a sort of arty, boho way. As for my style, well, I'm just a bumpkin managing to pass as a cool wanderling. I fit right in here, with the cool art kids, but only in the sense that everyone looks so individual, so no one looks uncool. Everyone here looks as if they travel the world, for fun, probably on their parents' money. Of course, I know that's not true for me, but I do my best to have my own look. My eccentric outfits are mostly pulled together from items I picked up in vintage or charity shops. I'm no stranger to an Oxfam, with a keen eye for spotting a rare work of art, whether it be a loud pair of trousers or a delicate lace dress. I've also, over the years, curated myself one hell of a chic wardrobe from items of clothing that my mum and gran were about to throw out because they were old-fashioned. It's hard, doing what everyone else does on a much smaller budget, but by the time I make items my own, and load myself up with accessories, I feel as if I've created something truly unique. I am my own walking piece of art... although I suppose to everyone else I just look like a bit of a weird hippie.

I can do better. I need to do better. But not tonight. Tonight, I need to have a drink with the girl whose heart I just broke, and then tomorrow I need to be up bright and early to turn up for work, for the man who made me do it.

I used to think that each day was a blank canvas, when I

was young and naive, but these days I feel as though I'm aimlessly completing the same dot-to-dot puzzle, just going through the motions, following a path I can't deviate from. Still, at least I didn't just get dumped, hey? I'd have to have a love life for that to happen...

2

I used to think that working in a creative industry would make every day a little brighter, that the world would seem more beautiful, that each day would be different.

I grew up 'up north', with a dad who used to command soldiers for a living and a mum who used to (even worse) teach children; routines and rules were always at the heart of every-thing I did. I reckoned, in that way you do when you up and leave your home town, that I was moving to somewhere better, to live something different. I thought that art was creative, that artists were such free-flowing people who moved in whatever direction life took them, that I would be the same if I could just surround myself with them.

With Damian I have the worst of both worlds. I have the routine *and* the chaos, because somehow Damian is both impulsive and unpredictable, all the while still being so completely boring to work for. I always know what my days will look like. Other than a handful of occasional events, I know that most of the time we work out of Damian's apartment, or wherever he wants to go, apart from two days a week when we work here, at his office. The days that I'm here, I am bored beyond belief, because lately Damian isn't actually doing all that much work.

I pull myself up the stairs to Damian's loft offices, meaningfully grabbing at the wooden bannister, yanking myself up as though my life depends on it. This strange old building is a real labyrinth, a complicated mashup of corridors and staircases, far too complicated for a lift to have ever been installed. It doesn't even have one main stairwell, meaning you have to cross the building from one set of stairs to another about halfway up.

Damian's studio is made up of three rooms. There is his private office, the small room I work in right outside his room, and then there's the general office where the actual studio space is, the rest of the staff work, visitors are greeted, etc.

As far as staff goes there aren't that many people working here on a daily basis. There's Karen, the office administrator, and she really is a Karen. A middle-aged boomer with a can-I-speak-to-the-manager haircut who has lots of opinions about lots of things but none of them feel all that well thought out. At the other end of the scale, we have Ollie, the ultimate millennial, who handles the more techy side of the business. Then we have Colin, a chap in his forties who handles the business side of things – including planning trips and schedules (jobs I assumed would be mine when I started). Most other employees are only here as and when, for photoshoots or business meetings, and Damian does have a manager/agent-type person, but I don't see much of her.

I'm glad that I'm only here two days a week, and that I work in a small room on my own, because Karen, Ollie and Colin have Damian pegged as this nightmare boss and they see me as an extension of him. So, they don't make me coffees when they turn-take making the hot drinks, they don't show me photos of their kids or tell me about their holidays. I don't suppose I mind too much, but it does make my in-office workdays very boring.

I say hello to everyone as I pass through the room, heading for the kitchen area where I make myself a coffee. I don't ask if anyone else wants one because, not only can I see that everyone already has a mug in front of them, but they barely look up when I speak to them anyway.

You've probably already worked this out for yourself, but Damian is not a popular boss – not with me or with anyone else in the office. You would think this would create a sense of solidarity amongst the staff but, with me being Damian's right-hand woman, they treat me with a similar level of coldness. Except it's worse for me, because I'm not their boss, so they don't even have to pretend to respect me.

I head for my private office and plonk myself down at my desk. I mean, I say it's my private office, but it's purely circumstantial. It's not *my* office, it's just *an* office that no one else happens to be sitting in whenever I'm here.

I know that Damian is here – he's always the first one here, on the days when we're working in the office. There's post on my desk waiting for me to open it. I can see the little light blinking on my phone, alerting me to the voice messages – and there are always lots of voice messages. But despite all of that I do what I always do first. I open my desk drawer and see what's waiting inside for me.

Sure enough, there's a Twirl chocolate bar there for me, and there's a bright yellow Post-it Note stuck to it that says:

I THOUGHT YOU MIGHT NEED THIS.

He's absolutely right – I do need this. I'm starving, and there are few things on this earth I love more than chocolate.

When I say 'he's right' I'm not talking about the Post-it. I'm not so lonely and overworked that I've reached a level of delusion where I think the Post-it is a man. I'm talking about the person who wrote the note. I'm talking about Adam.

Adam is the person I share my desk with. I've hot-desked before, in other jobs, and I've always found it so strange. When you have your own desk, you have your own space, everything is always where you left it, but when you hot-desk you never know what you're going to find when you open a drawer – someone else's work, their half-eaten lunch, their anti-diarrhoea medication (which no one ever owned up to, unsurprisingly).

It's a little different here though, because here I only share my desk with Adam.

I remember when I first started working for Damian. My very first day on the job was working here in the office. I'd met Damian at my interview and he seemed great. So cool, so charming, so undeniably handsome. And, of course, I was such a huge fan of his work, so I was completely in awe, pinching myself every few seconds because I couldn't believe my luck. I remember sitting in Damian's office across the desk from him on my first day, chatting about his work and his plans for the future, and it all seemed great until I went and sat at my desk, opened the drawer and found a Post-it Note stuck to a stapler.

THE BOSS IS A NIGHTMARE. GOOD LUCK.

I just closed the drawer, putting the note to the back of my mind, going about my business, getting set up for my first day on the job. Then I noticed the framed photo on the desk, of a tall man with dirty-blond hair, big muscular shoulders, and an arm wrapped around a woman next to him. Going by the age gap, and the family resemblance, I knew that it just had to be his mum. That was when I realised I was sharing a desk. The picture, the various other personal items, the note. This wasn't just my space, it was someone else's too. I was sharing a desk with someone, someone who was looking out for me, someone who thought Damian was such a nightmare that they left me a note to warn me about him.

When Damian called me into the office, to give me my very first assignment, I was so excited. I figured it was going to be something to do with his next project, whatever it was, because the art world was waiting with bated breath for what Damian was going to do next. What he actually gave me was a list of errands. Personal errands. Picking up dry cleaning, moving a dental appointment, trailing around Harrods for a very specific pair of shoes, which, you'll know if you've ever been to Harrods, isn't a quick process – the place is like a maze. By the time I got back to him, way after I was supposed to finish work, I was knackered. Not only was the work tiring but it was mind-numbingly boring. I was so disheartened that I grabbed my wad of pink Post-its from my bag and wrote back to my desk mate. Nothing too controversial. I just wrote:

He certainly is.

And I stuck it on top of the original note, to make clear that it was a reply.

So I worked my first couple of days in the office, then I had a few working out of Damian's apartment with him and it became very obvious that my job as Damian's assistant wasn't so much assisting him with work, it was mostly just managing his life for him, practically babysitting him most of the time. The following week I found a reply to my Post-it Note. It said, 'We need to stick together. I'm Adam.' and just like that a weird, Post-it-based friendship was born. It felt strangely exciting but mostly I was just happy to feel as if I had a friend.

During my first couple of weeks I tried to talk with my fellow employees – that was when I realised they were lumping me in with Damian, keeping me at a distance, so I couldn't ask them about Adam. Eventually I asked Damian. He said Adam worked for him on the days he wasn't in the office, managing the place in his absence, which meant Adam also only worked the days that I wasn't in the office. So, I haven't actually ever met Adam, despite months and months of swapping notes. I waited a month or so to subtly add a framed photo of myself to our desk, so that Adam could see who he was talking to. Not just a photo of myself, that would seem at best unsubtle, or, at worst, incredibly narcissistic. I opted for a photo of me and David Attenborough, who I met when he popped into a museum gift shop I used to work in. I am such a huge fan of his and it's actually a really great photo. I was so nervous when it was taken that I was convinced I was probably making a weird face, but it turned out perfectly. It's one of my favourite things.

The funny thing about my friendship with Adam is that I feel close to him, even though we've never actually met. I feel as if we know each other pretty well though, and I feel as if he knows what I'm going through. Adam has worked for Damian for far longer than I have, and for him to feel as if he needed to warn me on my first day, he must have known exactly what I was letting myself in for.

It's going to sound weird, given that we haven't met face to face, and all of our interactions have taken place over Post-it Notes, but Adam is my best friend at work, the thing that keeps me sane, the person who gives me something to look forward to when I know I'll be in the office. I just wish we could be in the office at the same time, or that a reason would come up for us to meet – that wouldn't make me seem creepy – like a work Christmas party, but we're not even having one this year. Not enough people were able to attend. That speaks volumes, doesn't it? And I'm certainly not the kind of girl to just ask out someone I've never met. That sounds absolutely terrifying.

I maybe, just maybe, have a slight crush on Adam. I mean, obviously I can tell from his photo that he's completely gorgeous but it's not just that. His notes to me are so sweet. I feel as if we've been slowly getting to know each other. I really feel as if he cares about me too, but don't think for a second that I don't know how delusional this sounds, because I do.

I pen a quick thank-you note, asking Adam if he's had a good weekend, telling him about mine. The best thing about writing on Post-it Notes is that you only have so much room to work with, like an old-school text message. When I was at school, and terrible at flirting, I really had to take my time with text messages to boys I liked. Well, with limited space, and at (what seemed like) a whopping 10p a go, there was always pressure to make sure that the message you sent was perfect. I feel like that with my limited Post-it space. Someone really should develop a dating app around the concept because it might make people think twice about what they say. If my brief stint on Matcher is anything to go by, people really don't think all that hard about the messages they send on dating apps, and they really, really should. Adam made a better first impression on a Post-it than anyone did in their opening message to me on Matcher.

I grab a bag of peanut M&M's from my bag – Adam's favourite desk snack – and stick the Post-it Note to them before returning them to the drawer. Time to stop daydreaming about Adam and get on with my work.

I open up my laptop as I bite into my Twirl. I'll just take a couple of minutes to enjoy it, before firing up my emails. The calm before the storm. This will probably be the only peaceful part of my day.

The phone on my desk rings, making me jump, just a little.

I glance down and see that it's Damian, calling me from inside his office.

'Hello?' I answer, after quickly swallowing my chocolate, washing it down with my coffee.

'Morning, Sadie, can you pop in for a minute?' Damian asks.

'Sure, I'll be right there,' I reply.

I make a point to quickly finish my chocolate and chug a few mouthfuls of coffee before I go. Damian's minutes are rarely actual minutes.

So much for thinking I could enjoy my poor excuse for a breakfast for a couple of minutes. Time to see what fresh hell Damian has in store for me today…

3

I always hesitate before I open the door to Damian's office. It's only ever for a second but, with each day I work for him, I'm feeling as if I need to psych myself up more and more. I usually tell myself something before I open it – a different thing every day, but the sentiment is always the same. I remind myself how lucky I am to have this job, how well connected Damian is, how he can open doors for me. I am on the road to my dream job and, as far away as it seems, to stop moving would be a big mistake. And Damian does have the fastest cars, as he is always reminding me. Of course, I'm speaking metaphorically now; he usually means it literally. He's very materialistic, for someone so artsy.

It's not that I don't like him – we have a really unique professional almost-friendship – it's more just that every time he calls me in here he gives me something to do that I know is going to be either boring or completely weird. There is no in between.

'Good morning,' I say with a brightness that does not reflect the mood I am currently in.

'Morning,' Damian says. 'Take a seat.'

Damian is sitting at his ridiculously large desk, smack bang in the middle. His desk is absolute chaos, littered with a sea of papers, photos, miscellaneous camera bits like lenses and straps. His laptop is open in front of him. He pats it shut as I sit down opposite him to reveal a glass with a splash of bourbon in the bottom. Given how messy Damian is there is a chance this could be from another day but, given what a rock star he thinks he is, it could be from this morning.

'Bit early for that, isn't it?' I say. I can say things like that to Damian. I could probably say anything I wanted, none of it would matter, for two reasons. The first is that Damian does whatever he wants, doesn't care what anyone thinks, and doesn't listen to criticism. The second reason, which really does feel like a double-edged sword, is that Damian is absolutely, completely dependent on me. I'm sure he could live without me, and God knows I could live without him, but he doesn't think so. He believes that, to allow him to be fully 'open' creatively, he needs someone to bear the burden of, well, day-to-day life, I suppose.

'I was just on a call with Australia,' he says by way of an explanation. I'm sure he's joking but he doesn't let his serious expression slip. 'How did last night go?'

Ah, straight down to business. Not actual business, obviously. He just wants to know how the dumping went.

'Awful,' I tell him very matter-of-factly.

'Yeah, breaking up with someone is never easy,' he says with a sigh.

'Would you know?' I ask with a laugh. I don't wait for an answer. 'She was a nice girl. I stayed for a couple of drinks with her. Lord knows what you thought was wrong with her. I couldn't find anything.'

'Well, Sadie, you have my blessing, if you want to go for it,' he says, still straight-faced.

'Yes, because I have time to have a love life,' I reply sarcastically. 'I'm seeing my friend tonight for a drink, for the first time in weeks. I definitely don't have time to go on dates.'

'Really?' Damian replies, narrowing his eyes at me for a second. 'Because it sounds like you're saying you're going out drinking two nights in a row...'

He leans back in his chair, smiling smugly. As handsome as Damian is, smugness is not an attractive look on a man, as far as I am concerned. Luckily for him there are women (usually much thinner ones who wear way less clothing than me and have far looser morals) who find his arrogance really attractive.

He's dressed down today, which I envy. It's not that I think Damian would ever tell me what I could or couldn't wear, but I've never been one for going out of the house in my sweats. Damian looks good no matter what he wears. He's very stylish, even when he's dressed down in a pair of trackies and a hoodie – I don't suppose it hurts that they're always designer – which means that, no matter what he wears, he looks as if he should be on the cover of *GQ* magazine. His style is very much his own, which makes him seem all the more attractive, and then there's that certain something he has...

Damian has long-ish brown hair, which he always blows back, designer stubble and big brown eyes. He looks like a movie star – in fact, people often mistake him for Jake Gyllenhaal, but that might have something to do with the fact that he's treated like a celebrity. A lot of people have no idea what he's famous for but assume he must be a star.

'Let's talk work, shall we?' I say, changing the subject.

'Yes, let's,' he replies. 'I've got a list of jobs for you to do today.'

Damian pushes a piece of paper towards me. Skimming it confirms the usual list of boring jobs he often gives me. I sigh subtly.

'You've reminded me about Christmas gifts – I've done all your Christmas shopping,' I point out.

'Not all of it,' he says. 'I need a present for you.'

I smile but only for a second.

'You want me to buy *myself* a Christmas present?'

'Look at it this way, at least it will be something you want,' he says.

'Well, there's that,' I reply.

'I do have some work-work for you today,' he continues.

'Oh?'

It's been a long time since Damian's last exhibition and people are starting to wonder what's going on. Apparently, he's got some sort of creative blockage.

'I'm scrapping everything we've done so far,' he says. He's done this a few times already, for the new exhibition he's planning. The first time I was in shock – all that work! – but I don't bat an eyelid now. 'I need some new subjects. Some more worthwhile subjects.'

I gasp theatrically.

'The underwear models weren't worthwhile?' I ask in disbelief.

He frowns at me for taking the mick.

'Yeah, I don't know where I thought that was going to go,' he says. 'I thought they might have some depth.'

'So, what are you thinking now?' I ask.

Damian is a portrait photographer but his pictures have always said so much. They've packed powerful punches, hidden messages; he's made political statements, given voices to victims. He's putting a lot of pressure on himself lately but, I have to admit, his last few shoots have felt so empty, and the harder he tries to find or create worth in an image, the emptier it seems.

'Can you find me some prostitutes?' he asks with a bizarre yet not entirely surprising level of casualness.

'You definitely don't pay me enough for that,' I reply almost instantly.

'No, not *for me*,' he says with a scoff. 'Obviously not *for me*. For the exhibition. I want real, interesting women with real things going on, stories, darkness, struggles. I want to give them a voice.'

'We both know you can get girls to sleep with you for free, just promise to take their photo afterwards, before, during – whatever,' I can't help but tease.

Damian laughs, but only for a split second. He takes things so seriously sometimes.

'Come on, Sadie, this is serious. I'm struggling.'

I nod.

'I'll try my best,' I lie.

'Maybe search online?' he suggests.

'Yes, sure, I'll search online, that'll work,' I reply. It absolutely won't. Damian doesn't pick up on my sarcasm.

As we move on to chatting about what the day ahead looks like I secretly wrack my brain for alternative ideas for Damian's next exhibition. I mean, I doubt he would even accept one of my ideas but, if I could come up with something good enough, perhaps there's a way I could make him think it was his idea? I do that all the time with smaller things. Things like leaving parties early, stopping drinking, being fussy about who he gives his number to...

Of course, I have no idea what I could suggest, but I'll have to think of something. I suppose I could give it some thought while I'm buying myself a Christmas present. And I'll tell you what, the harder it is to come up with something, the better my present for myself is going to be. I've definitely earned it this year.

4

I was so excited for my first non-work night out in weeks that I spent ages getting ready.

It's December and it's bloody freezing. This suits me just fine though because, as far as I'm concerned, *more* is more when it comes to clothing. It's rare that I have much skin on show, and I'm not one for wearing tight-fitting clothing. I know it sounds weird, and aggressively feminist (and the fact I feel as if I need to justify it is exactly why we need feminism), but I like to keep my body relatively under wraps. I express myself through my outfits and my creativity, and I want that to be the reason people are drawn to me, rather than because I'm wearing a tight, short dress. Don't get me wrong, I have no problem with people wearing whatever they want, and I would never judge anyone for wearing what they want – how can I, when I'm wearing a trilby hat, as I am tonight?

Overthinking how I dress is yet another horrible side effect of working for Damian. He shoots a lot of women in their underwear – he's completely desensitised to it now – so if women want to get to him, they feel as if they need to compete.

For them, less really is more. And Damian being a man – a famous man with an endless supply of women to choose from – he's there for it. Briefly, of course, because it's always only a matter of time before I'm having to sit these girls down and tell them Damian doesn't want to see them any more. But I think that's largely why I like to wear lots of clothes. I don't want to compete.

I'm wearing my long hair down, which means it covers a fair bit of my long, floaty dress. I've teamed it with a black trilby hat, a black leather jacket and enough gold bangles to sink a ship.

My friend, Xara, looks absolutely fierce. Despite the icy cold weather outside she is wearing a bikini top under a pair of retro dungarees. Her hair is scraped up into a massive messy bun that seems to defy gravity on the top of her head. She looks fresh from painting someone's bedroom – although squeaky clean, with flawless make-up. Her workshop chic outfit is offset with shoes and a bag that probably cost more than my rent.

Tonight we're in a super trendy bar called BÆ – no, I don't know how to say it either – having our first catch-up in weeks. Xara and I met when we worked in the same museum gift shop. We actually quit a matter of days apart, to move on to different jobs, but she's made much more career progress than I have.

'We really should do this more often,' Xara says as she gestures at a waiter to come and replenish our drinks. 'It's insane, how busy we both are, *all the time.*'

'I know,' I reply. 'But it's so nice to see you doing so well.'

'Aww, thanks, doll,' she replies. 'I complain about the hours but I really am loving it.'

Xara is an audience development manager at the super prestigious Ashworth Gallery. It's her job to get people through the door and, while she is great at it, it's the Ashworth. People are *always* going to be walking through the doors. I would love to be doing something like that – especially in such an amazing gallery.

'I'm working on something at the moment that is going to knock your socks off,' she says excitedly.

We're interrupted by my phone lighting up on the table.

'It's just Damian,' I say. 'It won't be important. If it is, he'll text.'

'How are things at your work?' she asks.

'Oh, you know,' I reply. She does know. I whine to her about Damian all the time. 'Same old same old.'

'We need to find you a new job,' she says.

'I know but where am I going to find such a good job in the industry?' I reply.

Xara smiles smugly.

'What?' I ask.

'What if I knew about a job going?'

'Where?' I reply in an instant. 'Not at the Ashworth...'

Xara nods.

'No! Tell me more,' I insist. 'Tell me everything!'

'We're looking for an assistant curator,' she says.

My jaw drops.

'When were you going to tell me?' I squeak.

'Tonight,' she replies excitedly. 'I thought I was going to have to get you more drunk first, to convince you to apply.'

As I ponder why she thinks I might need convincing my face falls.

'They'll never hire me,' I say very matter-of-factly.

'See, I knew you'd say that,' Xara replies. 'Why not?'

'Why would they?' I reply. 'There must be so many people so much better suited for the role. People with more to offer than me. I'm basically a babysitter.'

'For *Damian Banks*,' Xara adds. 'Let me put you forward, I—'

'Excuse me, ladies,' a man's voice interrupts us.

We both look up, expecting to see the waiter, but instead we find a pair of twenty-something twin brothers standing there.

'Hello,' Xara says, lighting up. Well, these two are tall, skinny, gorgeous, ultra-cool-looking. They're identical in all ways apart from their hair. Their style is the same, but one has a bleach blond do while the other's is jet black.

'We were just wondering if we could buy you ladies a drink,' the blond says.

Right on cue the drinks we ordered previously are placed down in front of us.

'We already have drinks,' Xara says. 'But I'm sure we'll want more, if you'd like to sit and chat with us?'

It's only after Xara suggests this, ever so flirtatiously, that she glances over at me, silently asking me with her eyes if it's OK, although I'm not sure what I could do about it now.

I smile at her. I'm more than happy for them to join us, although I am slightly terrified. It's been a long time since I spoke to a man who wasn't my boss (or a man doing my boss's dry cleaning) without a Post-it Note to hide behind.

The twins are called Bry and Albi. Bry, the blond, has sat down next to Xara. Albi has taken the seat next to me. We all sort of chat together for a while before naturally pairing off.

'So, what's your story, Sadie?' Albi asks.

He's leaning in close to talk to me. So close I can smell his aftershave. He seems really interested in talking to me and that's just not something I'm used to these days, I guess.

'Well, I'm not from London, I'm a northerner,' I practically confess. I didn't have a strong Yorkshire accent to begin with (not in Yorkshire, at least) but, living in London for so long, working with people who all had the same accent, it wasn't long before I adapted out of necessity to try and remove all traces of it. I do feel like a bit of a fraud though.

'My brother and I are Italian,' Albi says. 'Well, a quarter Italian, on our mum's side. We were born here. You can probably tell by looking at us.'

My drink is more Italian than Albi and Bry, but I don't say that of course; I smile and nod.

'Oh, yes,' I start, but I don't get to finish. My bloody phone is ringing *again*. It's been ringing and buzzing constantly while we've been chatting. When it first rang, I pulled it out from my bag and quickly silenced it when I saw that it was Damian. I told him that I was out tonight so he shouldn't be calling me. But then he tried again, and again, and again.

'Do you need to answer that?' Albi asks. He sounds a little frustrated.

'No, no,' I insist. I leave it at that because I'm not sure the truth does me any favours.

'Anyway, you were saying?' he prompts.

'Yes, I was saying... what was I saying?' I wonder out loud.

As my screen lights up again, this time with a message, I look down at it almost suspiciously. Could something actually be wrong? As I lift my phone to see who the message is from, my Face ID unlocks it, revealing the message for both me *and* Albi, who is still sitting intimately close to me. It says:

Any luck finding us a prostitute?

I know Albi has read the message too because he instantly pulls away from me.

I just lock my phone and place it back down on the table, although I'm not sure I'm going to be able to style this one out. Well, I'd try to explain, but I'm not sure he'd believe me.

'Er, bro, let's, er, let's go get another drink,' Albi prompts his brother.

It takes a couple of seconds for the twintuition to kick in.

'Right, yeah, OK,' Bry replies.

'Well, that was weird,' Xara says once we're alone again, not realising that was probably my fault. 'What's their problem?'

'Put me forward for that job,' I say confidently. 'Do it. You're right, I should go for it. I can't keep working for Damian.'

'Yey!' Xara squeaks, doing a little dance in her seat. 'You won't regret this, Sadie. You deserve better.'

Yes, I do. I still can't imagine them choosing me – because it's such a competitive industry and I'm just, well, me – but I have to try. I feel as if I've sold my soul to Damian. This could be my way to get it back, to get my life back. That's got to be worth a shot, even if I am terrified. Things can't go on as they are. It's time something changed. Whether Damian likes it or not.

5

Sitting on a massive sofa, with a home-made porn star martini in one hand, a Hawaiian pizza on a plate on my lap, Netflix on the massive 150" screen in front of me – this is the life.

It isn't my life, of course, it's Damian's.

I was halfway home from work when he messaged me, saying he had an emergency, asking me if I could pop back and let myself into his flat, because he had to go out right away but had an important delivery coming. I sighed and immediately turned around. At least he pays me generous overtime, and it's not as if I have a thriving social life, is it? I'm sure you won't be surprised to learn that Albi, the guy I met last night, never came back.

I remember, six months ago, when Damian was looking for a new place to live. Of course, he needed me to help him, because he struggles to make any decision on his own these days. It's as if the longer he goes on without putting any work out, the more he questions everything he does.

We were flat-hunting between Knightsbridge and Belgravia. Obviously I knew that property was going to be very expensive, but I had no idea just how little your millions get you in terms of square footage in that area. After viewing all the places the agent had to show us in Damian's price range we both chose a favourite and, of course, we picked completely different places.

My favourite was the two-bed cottage, quietly situated in a quaint pedestrian mews in Knightsbridge. It was so spacious, boasting gorgeous oak flooring on the ground floor, a separate kitchen with large skylight – it even had a little garden. Upstairs it had two bedrooms and a bathroom. It was exactly the kind of house I would love to live in, if I could afford it, which, let's face it, is never going to happen. It's nice to dream though.

This property wasn't Damian's favourite. It was actually his least favourite. Damian wanted something modern, high up, with big glass windows and absolutely zero charm.

In the end he went for a contemporary two-bed corner apartment with an open-plan living space. Which is where I am now. It is gorgeous, with floor to ceiling windows, and views overlooking the River Thames. It's undeniably amazing, especially with all the tweaks he's made, and all the cool tech he's installed. It's not an awful place to do overtime consisting of nothing but enjoying the facilities and waiting for a delivery.

I was ever so slightly annoyed when the important delivery arrived and it turned out to be a new TV – God knows where for, because he only bought his living-room TV a couple of months ago – but I'm having a great time eating pizza and watching an absolutely gripping true crime documentary. Why are we all so obsessed with true crime TV at the moment, and why is it that, the crazier the story, the more we love it? Things like *Tiger King* and *Don't F**k with Cats* are the new water cooler talk – forget *Game of Thrones* and *Killing Eve*. No one wants to talk about fiction when real life is even wilder.

I'm currently watching *'Til Death Do Us Part*, a five-part documentary about a man called Terry Mackie. The show follows in his footsteps as he prepares to marry his fiancée, Joanna. Terry is in his late forties while Joanna is in her late twenties – but that isn't the most remarkable thing about their relationship. Joanna is actually Terry's fourth wife, because the previous three all met their grizzly ends shortly after tying the knot with him. There is no denying that, in each case, the deaths were incredibly suspicious, but despite it seeming as though Terry might have something to do with the demise of each wife (either because he killed them, or because he's some kind of jinx at the least), no one has ever been able to charge him with anything. Terry is a really interesting chap. He's a self-made multimillionaire, living in a monstrously huge house – he could give any woman the most amazing life... until they wind up dead, obviously. The documentary follows Terry and Joanna in the run-up to their big day, planning their wedding, going through the motions. It's such a compelling watch. You can't take your eyes off Joanna; you're just waiting until she has a skiing accident or falls down the stairs or has some other freak accident...

It's such a tense watch that, when Damian unexpectedly arrives home, the sound of the door opening gives me the fright of my life.

'Jesus Christ, Damian!' I say as I hurry to pause the documentary. I place a hand on my chest and take a deep breath. 'Are you trying to give me a heart attack?'

'You're jumpy,' he points out, hovering in the doorway.

I can't help but notice that he's dressed up.

'How was your emergency?' I ask him. 'Your TV arrived.'

I'm sure he's already realised that, given how massive the box is.

'Oh, sweet,' he says, hurrying towards it. 'It's for the bedroom.'

As soon as he moves away from the doorway, I spot the tiny brunette who has been standing behind him this whole time. She must be in her twenties; she's wearing a tiny pink dress but no coat – doesn't she know it's December? She can't be more than 5'4", which is probably why I didn't notice her in the first place.

Damian pushes his TV box towards his bedroom. The girl comes in and sits down next to me on the sofa.

'Hi,' she says.

'Hello,' I reply. I try to sound friendly, but this is so awkward.

We look at each other for a moment.

'I'm Kelsey,' she eventually says.

'Sadie,' I reply.

She wiggles awkwardly in her seat.

'I've never done it with a couple before,' she tells me.

'A couple of what?' I ask. I immediately know the answer. 'Oh.'

Oh my God, tell me he hasn't brought an escort home with him. And not even a good one, this one must be fresh out of escort school. And I think she thinks I'm a part of this.

'I just work for him,' I point out quickly.

'Oh, cool,' she says. 'How long have you worked for Damian?'

Too long.

'A year,' I reply. 'How long have you... erm...?'

'Oh, I don't work for him,' she says. 'I don't have a job at the moment. We were on a date.'

Thank God I didn't try to pay her to leave.

So, the reason Damian went out was to go on a date and the

reason I've been here all evening is because he was having a new TV delivered for his bedroom. Fantastic. And now I'm sitting here with one of his floozies. At least she invited me to join in, I guess. Pretty sure I'll pass though.

Right on cue Damian walks back into the room.

'Right, that's out of the way,' he says.

I hope he means generally, rather than because he has something weird planned that he needs the floor space for, because there isn't enough overtime in the world...

'Well, I'd better get going,' I tell them. I reach for the remote to turn off the TV.

'What's that you're watching?' Damian asks me curiously.

'It's just a TV show,' I tell him. 'You wouldn't like it – it's a documentary. No sex, no explosions...'

'Look at his eyes,' Damian says as he walks over, plonking himself down on the sofa between me and Kelsey. 'He's got such a darkness in his eyes. What's his deal?'

The TV is paused on a talking heads shot of Terry Mackie. He's looking into the camera, which makes it feel a bit as though he's looking right at you, and it's horrible. Throughout the series I've never been surer that Mackie killed his wives than I am right now.

'Basically everyone he marries winds up dead – always in suspicious circumstances,' I tell him. 'He's about to marry his fourth wife.'

'He's got *three* dead wives? He looks like a creepy boy.'

'He's a really nice guy – on a paper. Almost too nice, which just makes his niceness come across as creepy. He's friendly, generous, very softly spoken – all things that make him seem so unlike a murderer that it actually makes you start to think that he might be a murderer.'

'Absolutely fascinating,' Damian says. He continues to stare at the TV.

'Anyway,' I say, pulling myself to my feet. Damian grabs my hand and pulls me back down.

'We need to watch this,' he says. 'All of it.'

'What, us? Now?' I reply.

'Yes,' Damian replies excitedly. 'This is what I've been looking for. This is what I need. This is the kind of person I should be shooting – someone with something going on behind their eyes.'

'You said you'd take my picture,' Kelsey chimes in hopefully.

'Yeah, yeah, that's great, but this is work,' he tells her dismissively.

Kelsey pouts.

'You want to shoot Terry Mackie?' I say in disbelief.

'Like he's one of his wives,' Damian jokes. He turns to Kelsey. 'I'm really sorry, some work has come up.'

'You're... you're just going to watch TV,' Kelsey points out.

'Yeah, but for work,' he replies.

'Do you want to stay and watch?' I ask her. I don't really know what else to say.

Damian frowns. It's obvious now, to me at least, that he regrets bringing her here and wants her to leave. It's always business first with Damian.

'This is not what I thought we were going to be doing when I came back here,' Kelsey says. I've seen that disappointed look on many a female face thanks to Damian. 'I could've got on board with a threesome but I'm not watching serial killer documentaries with you.'

'Suit yourself,' Damian says, still staring at the TV. He can be so cold sometimes. 'I'll text you.'

He definitely won't.

Kelsey has a face like thunder. She sees herself out.

'Well, she seems lovely,' I say sarcastically.

Damian laughs as he takes off his shoes.

'Seriously,' I continue, because I'm pissed off. 'I think she's the one.'

'She seemed to like you too,' he jokes dismissively.

'Hmm, that's new,' I reply. 'Anyway, I'm going.'

'Wait, we need to watch this,' Damian insists.

'I thought that was just your excuse, to get her to leave?' I reply.

'Obviously I wanted her to leave,' he says. 'She was clearly just using me.'

Damian doesn't trust women at all. Mostly because they do all always seem to be using him, but he makes no real effort to meet regular people, he just keeps dating models in the hope that, one day, one of them will be sincere. I'm not saying sincere models don't exist, but obviously they all want their photo taken by the great Damian Banks, and his wealth and status are always going to make him London's most eligible bachelor.

'I really do want to shoot him. I think he's exactly what I need to get my edge back,' Damian insists.

'You won't get your edge back, you'll get murdered,' I point out.

I swear, I see his eyes light up with delight.

'Tomorrow, bright and early at the office,' he says. 'Get straight to work, trying to get in touch with him, or in touch with his people. Let's make this happen.'

I sigh.

'OK, but can you watch it without me?' I ask. 'I'm knackered, I need to get home, do things in my apartment, prepare for tomorrow, try to get enough sleep...'

Working for Damian involves lots of long days. I'm starting to try and put my foot down now and then because I'm so exhausted so often. I think he ploughs through on a combination of adrenaline and caffeine, but I suppose his job is his life, so he's always going to be fiercely passionate.

'Oh, OK, sure,' he replies. He seems a little disappointed that I'm not sharing in his enthusiasm. 'Well, maybe try and watch the end of it, if you haven't seen it. I'll take it from the top. Do you want a car?'

By 'a car' he means a lift from the chauffeur service that he uses. Imagine a really fancy Uber, but only for the super-high profile, with luxury cars, bottled water and – most importantly, to the clientele at least – discretion.

'No, no, I'm fine, I'll get the Tube,' I insist.

You would think it would be nice, to have a driver, to be chauffeured around in luxury – I thought I would love it, but I kind of hate it. I don't know, it just feels so awkward.

'You sure?' he asks.

'Yep,' I reply.

'See you tomorrow, then,' he says as he fumbles with the remote, skipping back to episode one.

'Yep, see you tomorrow,' I reply.

I thought sourcing escorts to have their photo taken was going to be tricky... now I've got to call a potential murderer. I definitely don't get paid enough for that.

6

It's been a long time since I had to do it, so I could be remembering it wrong, but isn't it nerve-racking, calling someone to ask them out on a date? It's that feeling of putting yourself out there, hoping and praying they say yes, that you don't embarrass yourself or, worse, that you don't get hurt.

Obviously I'm not calling someone up to ask them out today. That would be completely unrealistic. I'm calling a serial killer.

OK, so technically I'm calling his publicist, and he might not be a serial killer. But it's not dissimilar to asking someone out on a date. I'll be putting myself out there, hoping he says yes, desperately hoping I don't get hurt... *gulp*.

I'm transferred between a few people before I'm put on hold. I play with the Post-it Note Adam left for me yesterday.

It reads:

NO CHRISTMAS PARTY AGAIN THIS YEAR, HUH? THE BOSS IS A REGULAR SCROOGE. DON'T WORRY, NEARLY THE WEEKEND. HOPE YOUR WEEK IS GOING WELL.

I grab a Post-it and a pen.

*The week is really dragging. Re: Christmas party... Rumour
has it no one wants to hang out with the boss. Can you
blame them? Haha. x*

Oh God, I put a kiss. Why did I put a kiss? I never put a kiss.
At least it's an old-fashioned piece of paper and not a text
message that I can't rewrite. I can just toss this one in the bin
and write it again... but... you know what? I'm going to leave the
kiss. Screw it. Why not? It's just one of those things you do
when you message with someone. Totally normal – or as
normal as this abnormal situation will allow, at least.

'Hello, Ms Kirke.' A man's voice on the phone snaps me
from my thoughts. I decide to just stick with the kiss and shove
the Post-it in the drawer.

'Hello, yes,' I reply.

'This is Ken Foxton, I work for Mr Mackie – I understand
you're trying to arrange a photoshoot?'

'Yes—'

'Let me stop you there,' Ken interrupts me. 'Mr Mackie
doesn't do press.'

'It's not a press thing,' I point out. 'I work for portrait
photographer Damian Banks, and he's really quite captivated
by Mr Mackie, and his journey, and he'd love to shoot him for
his forthcoming exhibition.'

'What's the angle?' he asks.

'The angle?'

'The theme,' he continues. 'What's the theme of the
pictures?'

'Oh, erm... no theme, Mr Banks is just very interested in Mr

Mackie. Call it artist's intuition. He just sees something in him that he thinks will shine through the photos he takes.'

That sounds like bullshit, doesn't it? But that's how Damian describes it. He doesn't just take photos of anything, Damian takes photos that tell stories, that show something beneath the surface... perhaps that's why Ken is so worried.

'I'm going to be honest with you, Ms Kirke, because we are always honest here,' he starts. Sounds a little like he doth protest too much if you ask me. 'This sounds like another fishing expedition. Another thinly veiled attempt for people to get up close and personal with Mr Mackie, to pry into his personal life, to try and catch him out. Mr Mackie has complied with the requests of the authorities throughout a deeply tragic and unimaginably difficult decade. He has made statements to the press as well as giving full access to the *'Til Death Do Us Part* documentary team. He will not be hounded nor will he be made to feel like he's in any way responsible. The documentary was intended to put this all to bed so that Mr Mackie can get on with his life.'

Given the change in Ken's tone, and the clear firmness with which he is suddenly speaking, I'd hazard a guess he's reading me the official line drafted to shut down any calls from journalists.

'I do appreciate that, Mr Foxton, but I can assure you, Mr Banks is not a journalist. He just—'

'Ms Kirke, as I'm sure you can imagine, I am a very busy man. Unfortunately, it is a firm no from us.'

'I understand,' I reply. 'Well, should you have a change of heart, you have my number.'

'Indeed,' he replies. 'Good day.'

Oof, he hit me with a 'good day'. Is that a middle-aged man's verbal equivalent of replying 'K' to a message when you're moody and you want to shut the convo down?

I'm a little frustrated. I just want to do my job and, while no one is under any obligation to work with Damian, now we're going to have to go through the whole process of finding someone else, and believe me it isn't easy. Although I'm a little relieved. Terry Mackie gives me the creeps. The last thing I want to do is be in a room with him.

I puff air from my cheeks and grab another Post-it.

He's only got me calling possible serial killers for him. Not sure how much longer I can take this gig.

Damian sticks his head outside his office door. I quickly shove the Post-its under my notebook.

'You fancy going for lunch?' he asks.

Damian often invites me out for lunch, but I usually say no. For starters, I like my lunch break to be an actual break, rather than the inevitable work lunch it always winds up being if I go with Damian. Then there's the fact that my co-workers already think Damian and I are big buddies and hold me at arm's length accordingly. The last thing I need is for them to see me fraternising with the boss.

'I'm having a bit of trouble with your serial killer,' I reply. 'I'm going to look into other angles. I'm a bit busy for proper lunch today. I'll probably just pop out and grab something – thanks though.'

He looks a little disappointed.

'No worries,' he says. 'Can you grab me something? You know what I like.'

'Sure,' I reply.

You've got to love how things just shifted from Damian

taking me out for lunch to me going out to buy him something. I'm not complaining, it's my job after all, but so is working out how to woo a maybe-murderer.

'I'm starving, if you fancy going now?' he says.

'OK, erm, I'll go now and finish what I'm doing when I get back, then?'

'You're a star,' he says as he disappears back into his office, closing the door behind him.

I sigh, sulking for just a second, before springing into action.

I stick my note to Adam in the usual place, in the drawer, close my laptop and grab my bag.

As I walk through the main office my phone starts ringing.

It's a number I don't recognise so I answer it out in the hallway.

'Hello?'

'Hello, can I speak with Sadie Kirke, please?'

'Speaking,' I say brightly.

'Hello, Sadie, this is Robyn Young calling from the Ashworth Gallery. Do you have a moment to discuss your application?'

Oh, God. I don't know if I pushed it out of my mind because I didn't think I'd hear anything so soon, or if I just dismissed the concept entirely because I didn't think I'd hear from them at all, but I am so not prepared for this.

'Of course,' I reply, trying to keep my bright and breezy tone in place.

'We were very impressed by your CV and Xara told us all about you, and your work with Damian Banks. I can't wait to find out more! We would love for you to come in for an interview.'

'Oh, wow,' I blurt. 'Yes, certainly, I'd love to.'

Play it cool, Sadie, don't seem desperate.

'I know it's short notice, but do you have any availability on Monday?'

'I'll just check my schedule,' I lie, pausing for a moment to actually seem as if I'm checking something. 'I have some time around 1 p.m., if that works?'

Around 1 p.m. I'll be able to style it out as my lunch hour. It isn't too far away, so that would be perfect, otherwise I'll have to lie to Damian and tell him I have a dental appointment or something.

'Yes, 1 p.m. on the dot, that works for us,' Robyn replies. 'We'll see you then.'

As I make my way out of the building, I'm smiling so wide, I'm surprised I fit through the doors. Someone from the Ashworth actually wants to meet me – to interview me for a job. My God, I want this job. I want it so bad. My smile drops into something less comfortable as fear and feelings of inadequacy bubble to the surface. It's not enough to land an interview, is it? You have to actually get the job.

I'll have to call my sister over the weekend. This is her arena. I'm sure she can coach me, practise with me and help me prepare for the interview. She helped me prepare for my interview with Damian, which almost certainly helped me bag the job.

Then again, look how that turned out...

7

I have a large glass of white wine in one hand. The other is hovering above my laptop as I aimlessly scroll through the Harvey Nichols website.

Damian told me to buy my own Christmas present, and gave me a generous budget, so I'm looking at fancy moisturisers, something that will counteract how much this past year has aged me.

'Perhaps we should do some more practice questions,' my sister Selena suggests.

Selena, my older sister, works in recruitment. She commutes to York for work (from our home town on the Yorkshire coast), where she mostly finds jobs for engineers. While art might not necessarily be her field, Selena gives expert advice on how to impress potential employers. She's coached me through every interview I've had, and I've always found her advice so valuable. And then there's the helpful fact file Xara armed me with, so that I can swot-up on the gallery ahead of my interview, just in case they quiz me on how much I know.

'OK, shoot,' I reply.

'OK, some random tricky quick-fire questions... what is your least favourite thing about your current position?'

'Hmm, as much as I love it, it would have to be handling Damian's dirty drawers,' I say playfully.

'Oh, Sadie, tell me you don't have to do his washing?' Selena replies, seamlessly switching from interviewer back to sister.

'No, well, he has a laundry service. So, while I don't actually do his washing, I do round it up for the person who does. Someone comes to take it away, washes and irons everything, brings it back. I sneak my own stuff in, from time to time, if it's something with tricky washing instructions.'

'God, how the other half lives,' she says with a sigh. 'I wish someone would come and take some of my washing away – or Mark and Ben's, at least.'

Selena is only two years older than me but she's like a proper adult. She's married to a lovely man called Mark, she has a gorgeous six-year-old called Ben, she has a proper job and a good haircut, and she lives in such a stunning house.

'You love your family's mess,' I remind her.

'I guess I do,' she replies. I can almost hear her smile. 'By the way, you can't answer questions like that.'

'Selena, I was definitely joking,' I say. 'Real answer, here we go: the only real downside to my current job is being restricted to working with one artist. Damian's work is truly incredible but the variety that would come with working at a gallery, rather than with an individual, is what I want.'

'Perfect,' Selena replies. 'OK, next question. What's the best thing about your current position?'

'He just bought me triple digits' worth of skincare products for Christmas?' I offer up. 'Even if I had to pick them myself. I don't take offence though – after all, if I'm buying the presents to send to his family, he's not going to take the time to shop for his assistant, is he?'

Selena laughs.

'I mean, again, obviously you can't say that but... well, just out of interest, what is the best part of your job?'

'Honestly... it's my notes from Adam,' I say with a sigh.

'Oh my God, your Post-it boyfriend, seriously?'

'Selena, you laugh, but we've really got to know each other over our notes. We brighten up each other's day. It's the highlight of my time in the office, when I open up the drawer and see a little note about what he did over the weekend attached to a bag of chocolate buttons or something.'

'You two really should meet up,' she says. 'Unless... could he be married?'

'It did cross my mind,' I admit, slightly embarrassed. 'But he isn't wearing a wedding ring in the picture on our desk and whenever he talks about what he's been up to it always sounds like he's been doing things alone or in groups.'

'And you say he's hot?'

'He's definitely a good-looking boy.'

'Then you should definitely meet up – especially if you get offered this job, and you take it.'

In all of the excitement and the nerves it didn't actually occur to me that if I did give my notice, I wouldn't just be leaving Damian, I'd be cutting off contact with Adam too. We've spent so long swapping notes now that, I don't know, I almost feel as if I'd miss him.

'Well, we'll cross that bridge when we come to it,' I say. 'I'm hyped for Christmas. Can't wait to see you all, get out of London, get some sea air. Are things suitably festive there now?'

'Things are unrealistically festive here,' she replies. 'Even Santa Claus himself would describe it as "a bit much".'

I grew up on a small tidal island just off the coast of Yorkshire and I am not exaggerating when I say that almost everyone there gets really into the festive spirit. We have a winter festival, competing Christmas light displays – for God's sake, the Christmas shop is open all year round. Needless to say, I'm very excited about it.

'I am even more hyped now,' I tell her. 'OK, ask me another question. I need to nail this interview.'

'Serious answers only from now on, OK?' Selena insists.

'OK, promise,' I reply.

As Selena runs me through everything I could be asked I give her my best responses. Then Selena tells me what was wrong with my replies and gives me something better to say. This is great though, just what I need. I need to get this job. And if – by some miracle – I do, then, well, I guess the next thing to do is work out how to tell Adam.

8

Robyn Young must be in her late forties, but I want to be her when I grow up. I know, she's probably only about fifteen years older than me, and I – at thirty-three – am already technically a grown-up, but, given how immature I am, I think I can get away with saying it.

My interview – which is going really well, thanks for asking – is being conducted by Robyn and a man called Curtis, who I would also be working with, if I were lucky enough to land the job.

Robyn and Curtis are both so stylish. Both have a unique look, a little quirky, sure, but not your stereotypical arty types. You know the one: art-teacher-looking, hair scraped back, pencil behind the ear, paint down the fingernails. Robyn and Curtis (who I'd guess was in his sixties) look more as if they work for *Vogue*. Ultra-fashionable. Not a hair out of place.

I decided to play it safe for my interview. I straightened my long blonde hair, before winding it up into a tight, trendy bun on the top of my head. I'm wearing wide-leg black trousers (so wide they hide the black heeled boots I'm wearing on my feet) and a white shirt with lace ruffles down the sleeves. I look very much myself but the most clean-cut version possible. I guess, with this being such a prestigious gallery, everyone has to dress to impress.

'We're all such big Banks fans here,' Curtis says. 'How have you found it, working for him?'

Is it OK to lie during job interviews if it's for the greater good? I hate lying. It's not that I'm bad at it, I can lie my pants off in a pinch, but depending on what I'm lying about, and to whom, makes a difference. Guilt eats me up, which is probably why I let Damian take the piss sometimes, because I know it's my job, and I know he doesn't have anyone else he trusts, or anyone else he can rely on.

'It's been quite the challenge,' I say honestly. 'My days can look so different, from one to the next. My responsibilities have been far greater than I anticipated when I started but I have risen to the challenge. I have extended my list of skills, travelled to some amazing places, met lots of seriously talented people in the industry.'

'That's great,' Robyn says with a smile. 'Damian Banks has quite the reputation. It must be so completely fascinating, seeing the inner workings of his brain.'

Not as fascinating as reading his emails, that's for sure. What a lot of people don't seem to realise is that his 'personal' email address isn't actually his personal one. Damian has a separate address that he uses but external emails come through to an inbox that I manage. I'll be going about my day-to-day business when all of a sudden I'll be confronted with something that was probably intended for Damian's eyes only. Pitches from models, that's what we'll politely call them – not something you want to see when you're eating a cereal bar at your desk.

'And the parties,' Robyn continues. 'I'll bet you've seen some things.'

'It's been a very fascinating and eye-opening job,' I reply. Discretion is everything.

'Well, Sadie, I must say we're very impressed with you, with your CV – and for holding a job with the great Damian Banks. Everyone knows about his incredibly high standards so that speaks volumes. But do you think you might potentially be a little bored working here? Not that the work isn't stimulating, far from it, but it will certainly be a change of pace.'

They both look at me expectantly. It doesn't just feel as if they're waiting for my reply; I feel as if they're waiting to see what I say, to read me. Selena talked over questions like this with me – it's all about finding a balance. Suggest that you like things to be too hectic too often and you'll seem as if you don't consider how much you're taking on. Say that you don't like a fast-paced environment and you might seem as if you don't know how to handle any pressure.

'It's a change of pace that appeals to me. If it's a challenge, I'll rise to it. Working with Damian has allowed me to experience a range of different responsibilities and paces, which has allowed me to determine what my preferences are. I think working as an assistant curator is exactly the right balance for me.'

God, I sound like such a muppet. These are the sorts of things you're supposed to say in interviews, right? The buzzwords, the things they want to hear.

'Well, OK,' Curtis says. 'Thank you so much for your time. We'll be in touch.'

'Thanks very much,' I reply, pulling myself to my feet slowly, making sure I don't rush off before they give me something, anything to let me know if things are going to go my way. 'If you have any other questions, don't hesitate to call me.'

I leave the gallery, popping into the M&S next door to grab a sandwich, seeing as though this is my lunch hour. I thought that went well – really well, in fact. At least until they mentioned the change of pace. They're probably worried I'll quit if I find it too boring. If only I could be honest with them, tell them that almost all of the time working for Damian *is* boring. You would think the fact that he relies on me so heavily would give me lots to do but, honestly, I really am practically like a mum to him. Everything he relies on me for is completely boring.

I'm just leaving the shop when my phone rings. It's a private number. Oh my gosh, is this it? Is it about the interview? That's a great sign, right... or is it? To be calling me so soon they're either so sure I'm right for the job or so certain I'm wrong for it. Either way, I have to answer, and I'm glad it's sooner rather than later because I would have obsessed over it until I did hear from them.

'Hello?'

'Hello, is that Sadie Kirke?' a familiar man's voice asks.

I'm so nervous I feel the hairs on the back of my neck stand on end.

'Speaking,' I say. I need to get back into professional mode, otherwise the only thing he will hear is me throwing up my nerves.

'Ah, Sadie, hello,' the voice says. That's when I realise why I know the voice. It isn't Curtis from earlier. It isn't anyone I've been expecting to hear from. I know exactly who it is – it's no wonder his voice made me feel funny. Still, I don't let on.

'Hi,' I say, suddenly even more nervous than I was when I thought it was someone calling about the job.

'This is Terry Mackie, returning your call – I understand you work for Damian Banks?' he says. His voice is impossibly smooth, so gentle it tickles, but in a completely uncomfortable way. He almost sounds as though he sings his words, sometimes, with the way he strings his sentences together. It was one of the things that creeped me out about him the most, when I watched *'Til Death Do Us Part*. It almost felt as if he was trying to hypnotise the audience.

A shiver runs down my spine. Somehow Mackie is even creepier when he's talking directly to you. I hate that he knows my name, knows my job – has my phone number!

I don't know what to say to him. Luckily smooth-talking Mackie knows how to lead a conversation (and a jury, if you ask me).

'You called to enquire about Damian taking my picture,' he prompts. 'I understand one of my aides said no?'

'He did,' I eventually say. 'Not a problem at all. We respect your privacy, Mr Mackie.'

'Well, I think he might have been a little hasty,' he says. 'I think you and I might be able to come up with some sort of plan – a way to make things happen – if I tell you what I want, and you convince your boss it's what's best for all of us...'

'I thought you didn't pose for photos,' I say, perhaps a little unprofessionally. I don't want to sound as if I'm discouraging him, maybe... although I absolutely am, reminding him of his own rules.

'It's true that I don't pose for photos,' he says. 'But, as I also understand it, your boss doesn't take pictures at weddings...'

'He doesn't...' I say cautiously.

'Perfect,' he says. I hear him clap his hands together. 'Then let's talk.'

'He wants me to shoot a wedding?' Damian shrieks. *'Me?'*

I purse my lips and nod my head.

'He's not even killed this wife yet and he wants to book me for his next wedding?' Damian asks in disbelief.

'I mean, I'm not saying I disagree with your verdict,' I start. 'I absolutely think Murderous Mackie killed his wives, but he was never found guilty so we're not technically allowed to talk about him like he's guilty. You really need that to sink in, if you're going to spend any time around him. And anyway, it's not his wedding, it's his daughter's wedding.'

'Right, I don't want to sound like a dick – but I know I'm going to, so don't feel the need to point it out – but I'm Damian Banks. I'm not a wedding photographer.'

I don't think he sounds like a dick, not really. Hiring Damian Banks to shoot your wedding is a bit like hiring Banksy to paint your bathroom ceiling.

I shrug my shoulders.

'OK, just... hang on a minute,' he says. Gosh, he seems so frustrated. Whenever anything puzzles him, stresses him out, or gets him thinking, his brow furrows to the point where it looks uncomfortable. Damian massages his forehead, as though he can iron the creases out with his fingertips. 'Run this by me again.'

'Mackie says you can have your photoshoot with him... in exchange for you taking pictures at his daughter's wedding,' I explain again.

'Don't they already have a photographer?' he asks.

'Yeah, but it sounds like they want you for fancy wedding portraits, rather than being the person who snaps the relatives while they get hammered,' I explain.

'I do really want to take his picture, Sadie, but a wedding? What do you think?'

'I think...' I pause for a second. What do I think? I think I definitely don't want to be in a room with Terry-wife-murder-ing-Mackie. But I wouldn't be doing my job properly if I talked Damian out of it, would I? And after sitting in a job interview, talking about what a great employee I am, should I really be proving myself wrong less than an hour later?

'Look, sure, it's his daughter's wedding, but it's not exactly a trip to the village church before a reception in the function room at a three-star hotel. Mackie is one of the most famous people on the planet at the moment. This wedding is going to be something really special.'

'Go on,' Damian says curiously. His brow remains furrowed but it's a look of curiosity now, rather than stress.

'Angel Mackie, his daughter, is a socialite. She's marrying Ryan Sharpe – a premiership footballer, plays for England, the one everyone was going mad for during the last World Cup.'

I've heard Ryan's name in passing – there was a lot of hype around him during the World Cup – but I really don't care about football so I don't know much more than his name.

Angel is a lot more familiar to me because she's a popular influencer. Damian isn't interested in football and he meets so many influencers they all blur into one.

'Yeah, I probably care less about football than you do,' Damian says dismissively. 'But it sounds like there's going to be a lot of buzz around this wedding.'

'There is… There's going to be lots of celebrities there – not to mention how obsessed everyone is with Mackie. People literally follow him, keeping an eye on him, waiting to see if his reigning missus pops her clogs. It's a lot of attention for the wedding, for Mackie – for you and your next exhibition, if you play your cards right.'

'God, you're right,' he says. He sounds almost disappointed. 'You're always right.'

'I know,' I reply with a smile. 'Best of all, the wedding venue… it's on a disused sea fort just off the coast somewhere down south. It's like a tiny island with a five-star hotel built on it. They've hired the place out for a long weekend. Mackie says you'd be invited for the whole thing.'

Damian rubs his chin thoughtfully. I can practically see the cogs turning in his brain through his narrowed eyes. He stares at me for a couple of seconds before a smile spreads across his face.

'When is it?' he asks.

'It's this weekend,' I tell him. 'Honestly, you couldn't have asked at a better time. If you'd left it any later you wouldn't be in with a chance.'

'Right, OK, I'll do it,' he says. 'I need to shoot him. I'm at the end of my rope.'

'Erm, less talk of anything related to guns or ropes, please,' I insist. 'He makes my blood run cold.'

Damian laughs.

'I need this, right? This is the first idea I've had in ages that I've felt passionate about.'

And don't I know it? It's all he's been talking about for the last two days.

'You definitely seem passionate,' I confirm.

'OK, get him on the phone, tell him I'll do it,' he says confidently, although I'm not sure how confident he actually is.

'Sure thing, boss,' I reply with a playful salute. 'I'll get back to my desk.'

'You're an angel, Sadie,' he calls after me. 'Who knows, maybe we'll have fun if we're there together?'

I sigh ever so gently. I mean, of course I knew I would be going with him, as his assistant and general hand-holder, but still... no matter how cool the trip sounds – the awesome location, the celebrity guests – knowing that Mackie will be there is more than enough to put me off. I've watched the whole series of *'Til Death Do Us Part* now and, honestly, Mackie terrifies me. He's so overly charming, always making little jokes, seeming so sickly sweet that it just makes him seem all the more guilty.

'At the very least we can keep each other alive,' I reply. I'd be tempted to say I was kidding but you never know.

I plonk myself back down at my desk. So... I need to ring Mackie and make arrangements, get everything ready at our end – I probably won't be in the office again this week so obviously my top priority is to write a note for Adam.

We're only going to a disused naval fortress in the middle of the sea so he can take pictures of a potential serial killer. I definitely don't get paid enough for this. You might not hear from me until next week. If you haven't heard from me by the time you're in the office next Tuesday... well, I guess I didn't make it. I leave all my desk snacks to you. x

He'll know that I'm, kidding, right? God, I hope I'm kidding.

This is exactly why I need a new job, because at no point during my art degree did I imagine myself attending celebrity weddings with alleged serial killers, socialites and premier-league footballers. I have this feeling I'm going to wind up at the bottom of the sea, or as a talking head on some Netflix documentary, chatting about what happened on 'that day', people making memes out of me. I'm not sure which is worse...

10
_____

I've always been a nervous flyer. It's not that I'm not used to flying. I'm often jetting around with Damian (don't get too excited, they're not always glamorous locations – a lot of the time it's just because he'd rather fly to places like Newcastle than drive there), and I've been on a few holidays. Still, something about being in a heavy metal tube thirty-five thousand feet in the air doesn't sit well with me, despite knowing how technically safe it all is, and that millions of people do it every day.

I don't know how I thought we were going to get to Astern, the ex-naval fortress turned five-star hotel – I suppose I didn't think about it at all. I figured we'd have to take a boat from the coast, from a southern seaside town I could at least recognise by name, but that's not what has happened at all.

On the one hand, I can finally tick flying in a helicopter off my list. On the other hand, regrettably, I'm going to have to tick it off again to go home and I'm really not looking forward to doing it for a second time.

We are currently hovering above the naval base, about to

land. I'm holding my seat so tightly I can see my knuckles turning white.

Before we set off, when we were told our car was taking us to a helicopter, rather than driving us south towards the coast, I felt my usual pre-flight nerves, but flying in a helicopter feels nothing like flying in an aeroplane. The take-off is completely different. I was so nervous, but it happens in no time at all. All of a sudden, you're up there, and then you're going impossibly fast. You don't really feel the speed in a plane, not like you do in a helicopter. You lose track of the landscape so quickly, and then all at once you hear through your headset that you're almost there. It's completely disorientating.

As we prepare to land on what is essentially a tiny island, I take a deep breath. Damian must notice because he grabs hold of my hand and squeezes it – something I really appreciate. He does this whenever we fly anywhere together. He knows that the landing is always my least favourite part. I suppose, if you're nearing the end of anything, and nothing has gone wrong, then all the more reason to believe disaster will strike in the short amount of time that's left. I know that's wrong, but irrational fears are exactly that. Irrational.

I dare myself to peep out of the window next to me. I peer down towards Astern, watching as it grows bigger and bigger as it gets closer. It looks so peculiar, like a man-made island – which I suppose is exactly what it is. The large perfectly round island almost looks like a toy town, with a mini lighthouse, a grassy garden area, a pool. There are a few surface-level buildings, and a big glass atrium, but I'd imagine most of the hotel itself is deep down in the fortress, which, now that we've touched down on the helipad, appears to stand quite high up from the water, a bit like being on a cruise ship.

'You made it,' Damian tells me, in that reassuringly playful way he always does when we land.

'Thanks,' I say with a smile. 'You can let go of my hand.'

'Yeah, sure,' he says awkwardly. 'Damn, this thing is huge.'

'Huge and so weird,' I reply.

'Apparently there are four or five of them out here, just off the coast of Portsmouth,' he tells me. 'A few have been turned into hotels. Kind of cool.'

As soon as we're out of the helicopter, (reasonably) safe on (semi) dry land, I peer across the water, back towards the land.

'Oh, so that's Portsmouth?' I say as we walk down the few steps from the helipad.

Damian takes hold of me gently and turns me around on the spot.

'*That's* Portsmouth over there,' he tells me. 'It's a bit further away. That was the Isle of Wight.'

'OK, if you want to wait here,' our pilot instructs us. 'I've got more guests to collect, but someone will be here to greet you shortly.'

'OK, thanks very much,' I say, extra politely, you know, just to make sure he takes extra good care of me when he eventually flies me home.

It's mid-December, so naturally it's pretty chilly out here in the... I don't know. The Atlantic Ocean? The English Channel? I'm still not 100 per cent on where we are exactly, other than knowing we're south of England – assuming what Damian just said is correct.

Despite it being so cold, the... is it a deck? Honestly, this place is so surreal. Whatever it is, outside is quite busy with people all wrapped up, walking around, taking in the sea air. Many of them have Astern-branded takeaway coffee cups in their hands. Without drinks or movement to keep us warm I'm feeling pretty chilly, standing here with our bags, waiting to be greeted.

Of course, I tell myself that I would have happily waited much longer when I hear that silky-smooth voice coming from behind me.

'Damian, Sadie, welcome!'

I hear Mackie before I see him. His voice is practically iconic. It almost tickles my cold ears, to the point where I could happily itch them off.

I take a deep breath before turning around. And there he is. Terry Mackie. He's taller than I expected him to be – almost 6 ft, which is kind of intimidating – but build-wise he's just average. He's in his late forties but looks older. He has short, mousey-brown hair that sits sort of flat on top of his head, as if someone swept up the wispy bits from the salon floor and plonked them there. His rimless oval glasses make his eyes seem smaller, not bigger, which, coupled with the fact they seem to be permanently narrowed, gives him this chilling look. It's almost as though he's somehow simultaneously peering into your soul while putting up a guard so you can't look into his.

He's walking down the steps from the mini lighthouse next to us. Following close behind him is his latest wife, Joanna, the one he married in the documentary. She's smiling widely, until she loses her footing on the steps. It seems as though she's falling for ages, in super-slow motion, until eventually Mackie grabs her wrist just in time to stop her falling to the bottom.

'Whoa there, girl,' he says, yanking her back up. He looks over at us in a sort of playful 'did you see that?' kind of way.

I glance over at Damian. He has a low-key terrified smile on his face, as if maybe he thinks this was a mistake but, at the same time, he looks as if he's struck gold.

'Joanna sure does know how to make an entrance, doesn't she?' Mackie says as he extends a hand for Damian to shake.

It looked more as though she was going to make an exit than an entrance to me.

'Terry Mackie, nice to meet you,' he says, practically yanking Damian's arm off – a weirdly unnecessary power play, given how most of the world thinks he's a murderer.

'And you,' he says to me, pointing almost accusingly. 'You must be the one I spoke to on the phone.'

'Sadie,' I say as I offer him my hand to shake, instantly wishing I'd given him a fake name. I can feel my hand practically shaking as it hovers in front of me. The thought of Mackie's maybe murderous hand about to take hold of it has me petrified.

I'm expecting a warm, gentle hand to loosely take mine. Somehow, I get something far creepier. Mackie snatches my hand and brings it up to his lips, and as he plants a kiss on the back of my hand his razor-sharp stubble scratches my skin a little. Still, I'd take a world of that feeling over the horrible sensation of his soft wet lips. Surely only a murderous sociopath would kiss a woman on the hand like that, right?

'Wow.' Damian chuckles. 'You're quite the ladyki—'

He stops mid-sentence. I glare at him. He was going to say ladykiller, wasn't he?

Mackie stares at him blankly. Damian theatrically clears his throat, buying himself a little time.

'Excuse me,' Damian eventually says. 'I was just saying, you're quite the ladies' man, aren't you?'

'It's been said before,' Mackie says with a smile. 'Anyway, listen, we can't thank you enough for agreeing to take pictures at our darling Angel's wedding.'

'It's my pleasure,' Damian says. 'Thank you, for agreeing to feature in my work.'

'A fair exchange,' Mackie says.

'Hi, Sadie,' Joanna greets me as the men chat between themselves for a moment.

'Hello,' I reply. 'Joanna, right?'

'Call me Jo,' she replies.

Jo is gorgeous. She's wearing a pair of super-high heels, which, in addition to making her close to six foot tall, give her impossibly long legs. If I remember correctly, she used to be a model, until she became a kept woman/walking target. Her long blonde hair is perfectly straight, and intensely shiny, and her make-up is flawless. The only weird thing is her outfit. Jo, despite being in her twenties, is dressed more like someone in her fifties. She's wearing a navy pencil skirt and matching jacket, teamed with a white blouse – she's even wearing a pearl necklace, for crying out loud. She's not so much a sexy super-model any more, more like a matronly mother of the bride. Jo is not the mother of the bride, just in case that wasn't obvious. She's her stepmum.

Poor Jo, I'm not sure if, behind her big smile, her eyes are screaming for help, or if I'm just projecting my preconceptions after watching the documentary.

'Let's get you two to your room,' Mackie says. 'Get you settled in so you can dress for dinner later.'

'Rooms,' I correct him.

'What?' he replies.

'Rooms,' I say again. 'Our rooms. Two of them.'

'Ohhhh,' he says with a big grin. 'Are you two not...?'

I shake my head.

'Sadie is my assistant,' Damian tells him. 'We asked for two rooms, didn't we?'

He looks at me for confirmation.

'We did,' I say firmly.

'Well, you'll have two rooms,' Mackie says. 'I just assumed. Someone less presumptuous than me will have already booked them, don't worry. Do you need help with your bags?'

'Oh, no, we can manage,' Damian insists. 'We've only got these few.'

In addition to his camera bag, Damian and I packed an overnight bag each – well, I packed them both, obviously – with just enough stuff to get us through the weekend. I am definitely not sticking around any longer than I need to. I'd swim back to shore first.

Mackie beckons an employee over with a wave of his hand.

'Can we get these two checked in to their two absolutely separate rooms,' he says with a wiggle of his eyebrows. I swear, it's as if he doesn't believe us.

The employee nods before silently gesturing at us to follow him.

'See you at dinner,' Mackie says excitedly. 'Can't wait for us all to get to know each other better.'

There's something in his eyes that I can't quite figure out. A sort of manic excitement that terrifies me.

After checking in we are pointed in the direction of our suites – yes, there are two of them waiting for us, thank God. As we walk along a corridor, checking the numbers on the doors as we pass them, we finally have a moment alone.

'I can't believe you almost called him a ladykiller,' I point out, hardly able to control my smile. I shouldn't be laughing – it's not funny, is it? Except it kind of is. Just a bit.

'Oh, God, I know,' Damian replies. 'That was a Freudian slip and a half, wasn't it?'

'I don't *think* he noticed,' I say. 'But, if he's the evil genius everyone says he is, he wouldn't let his smile slip, would he?'

'At least we have an adjoining door between our rooms,' Damian points out. 'So, one of us can escape through the other's room.'

'Ah, but we'd still be on a tiny man-made island in the middle of the sea though,' I point out. I'm only playing along but it's enough to give me the creeps. Then something occurs to me.

'While we're on the subject, hand me that key,' I insist.

'What, the adjoining-door key?' he asks innocently.

'Yep, I'll take care of that,' I say, snatching it from him. 'I promise to let you into my room if, say, Mackie is hacking his way into yours with an axe, but otherwise that door is not opening.'

Damian just laughs.

'This is us,' he says, stopping abruptly.

'OK, so...' I glance down at the itinerary given to us at reception. 'Dinner is in a couple of hours, so, I'll meet you back out here about five minutes before?'

'OK, sure,' he says. 'See you then. I'm weirdly looking forward to it.'

'I guess I am too, now that I'm here,' I admit. 'Right, don't be late.'

'Yes, boss,' he says jokily before disappearing into his room.

The first thing I notice inside my suite is the adjoining door. I subtly check it, to make sure it's locked, careful not to make any sounds Damian might hear on the other side. Thankfully it is locked. Hopefully it stays that way.

Wow, this room is nice. I don't know what I was expecting, being so deep down in the fortress, but they are stunning rooms with arched ceilings – they even have windows. It's like being in a hotel on the coast. I can even see civilisation from my window.

I love the exposed brickwork, coupled with all the black and gold furnishings. The super-king bed looks so inviting. Then again, most beds look inviting when you're used to sleeping in such a tiny bedroom. To be honest, my bedroom in my flat isn't even a proper bedroom, it's behind a piece of semi-frosted glass. Just enough to make it technically a one-bed apartment, rather than a studio flat.

My absolute favourite thing about this suite though, by a mile, is the large freestanding bath over by the window. I don't know what it is about the idea of taking a bath not in a bathroom that sounds so luxurious. I do have a bath in my apartment – a small, not very comfortable one – but it's inches away from my toilet, which doesn't exactly encourage relaxation. I can't wait to jump into this one. In fact, I think I'll do it right now. Well, look at it this way – it's only a matter of time before Damian knocks on our shared door for something, right? I need to try and squeeze in some relaxation while I can. Especially because – call me over the top, if you like – something about sitting down to dinner with a man who women just can't seem to stay alive around makes me think I'll need to keep on my toes. Not that there's anywhere for me to run to out here...

11

I can't help but alternate between feeling exactly like I'm on a cruise ship and marvelling at how little this feels like a cruise.

On the one hand, the entire thing is man-made, so you're on the good side of the metal fence or you're in the water, but then there's the obvious fact that the fortress doesn't move, and moving was probably the feeling I hated the most on the albeit brief cruise I took from Cardiff to Dublin to Liverpool with my parents, years ago. It was spring when I went, and supposedly the Irish sea is one of the worst of chop, so I'm really relieved to feel so still right now.

The dining room, however, has a strong 'cruise ship' vibe. A large room with decadent decorations, big tables of mixed groups, serving staff doing the rounds with bottles of wine – there's even a seating plan. It turns out Damian and I are sitting at the same table as Mackie, Jo, their daughter, Angel, her fiancé, and various other members of the wedding party – people far closer to the happy couple than the photographer and his assistant, that's for sure.

Damian and I stare at each other for a second.

'Top table,' I point out with a grin. 'I wonder if it will be the same for the wedding. He must be excited about you being here, if he wants you to sit with him at his table.'

'I'm not sure if I should want him to love me or hate me,' Damian muses. 'Which one keeps me alive?'

'Not coming here at all,' I say emphatically. 'Coming here is how you get mur... Mackie! Terry Mackie, hello!'

Oh, God, he always rocks up when you least expect him. I think I got away with that – he looks positively charmed by my enthusiastic greeting.

'Sadie, Damian, hello – you both look divine,' he sings.

I shuffle on my heels awkwardly. It sounds strange but I hate that he can see me. Not just being in front of him, being in the same room as him, being in his eyeline – I mean he really sees me. He acknowledges me. He knows my name. He's complimenting me.

He's not wrong about Damian though, he does look really good. He's wearing a dark blue suit with a black shirt. When I met him in the hallway, he had a handful of ties in his hand, which he held out to me like a wilting bunch of flowers. I told him I didn't think he needed a tie, so he tossed them through the door, clapped his hands and said, 'Let's go.' It's a good job I don't get off on power because Damian pretty much always listens to anything I say. He says I've never led him wrong before. He trusts me. It's nice, to be valued like that. I just wish he didn't rely on me so much. I've almost made myself too valuable.

'I want you sitting with me and my family tonight,' Mackie insists. 'Tonight, you are my family.'

Well, that's pretty much the last thing I want to be.

'Great,' Damian says.

'Come, come,' Mackie instructs. He wraps an arm around

Damian, as if they're old friends, and leads him through the dining room. I follow close behind them.

It's weird, watching Mackie walk through a room; it's as though everyone always has one eye on him, just in case.

'Everyone, this is the great Damian Banks and his assistant, Sadie… Sadie… Sadie what?'

Mackie turns to me.

'Oh, don't worry about it,' I insist. 'I'm not important enough to have a surname announcement.'

I am *so* relieved he's forgotten my surname already.

Mackie laughs.

'OK, well, Damian, Sadie, this is my darling daughter, Angel, and her soon-to-be husband, Ryan – you'll probably know Angel from the papers, and Ryan for almost winning us the World Cup. He just didn't try hard enough, huh, Damian?'

Damian hates sport. He isn't really a manly man at all in a lot of ways. He doesn't like to get his hands dirty, he's terrible at DIY, and he hates watching and playing pretty much all sports. He won't even play FIFA games, and, given that Damian is a bit of a gaming nerd, a staple game like FIFA is a big gap in his gaming CV.

I watch as Damian makes a face – his best attempt at bro-ing down, I'd imagine. He just looks constipated.

'Right,' he replies. I swear his voice gets deeper.

Angel is gorgeous – exactly what you'd expect a socialite to look like. I don't feel as if socialites are a thing, not like they used to be, not without a stint on a reality show or something. I feel as if she would be right at home with the Kardashians, with her glossy dark hair, and that exact face everyone seems to have these days, courtesy of a combination of either filling things in or sucking things out.

'Jo, my darling wife, you already know – and no, you can't

have her,' he says with a theatrical laugh. Everyone at the table laughs. Are people too scared not to laugh at his jokes?

'This lovely little creature is Lottie,' Mackie says. 'She's one of those influencers.'

'Lottie Loves,' she tells us proudly. 'Influencer and model.'

She sounds extra squeaky.

Lottie is practically a clone of Angel. This is what I mean: everyone has the same face. The celebrity look that involves jaw fillers, lip fillers, nose jobs, Botox, etc. Though Lottie is on the edge of taking things too far. Everything is blown up just a little more than looks natural.

Each to their own, I guess. Everyone should be able to look the way they want to look; no one is obliged to look 'natural', just as no one should feel the need to replicate the 'extreme cosmetic intervention' look, but when you are literally an influencer, your job is telling people how to live their lives, encouraging them to be just like you. So when you've got millions of young women looking up to you, and you're telling them they need lips the size of scatter cushions, well, we're telling people not to look like people any more.

Sorry, I suppose I've just got a bit of a bee in my bonnet about Lottie because I have heard of her. She's always in the press, always in trouble, because she pitches herself as a lifestyle influencer, and talks a lot about clean living, but she works with 'skinny' shake companies, and pushes appetite-suppressing lollypops on her Instagram, and given that she's already in unrealistically good shape, it's not something she should be telling people to use so they can be just like her.

'Great to meet you,' Damian says warmly.

I can call it now. Lottie is going to be all over Damian. Models always are. People think that if he takes their picture they'll be on the road to stardom, and they probably would be, but Damian doesn't take pictures of just anyone. He takes a lot of pictures for fun – he almost always has two or three different cameras to hand – but the pictures he takes for fun are almost never of people.

'Oh, you too,' she replies, kind of casually.

'And this gentleman – this fine specimen of a man who could turn the head of even the straightest man – is Hunter O'Meara, male model. Hmm.' Mackie pauses for thought. 'I wonder why it is that we call women models and men male models. I suppose it's because all women are models.'

Eesh.

He's right about Hunter, he's a beautiful man. I'd be surprised if he wasn't modelling himself on Thomas Shelby, because almost everything about him screams *Peaky Blinders*. He's even got a bit of a look of Cillian Murphy, with his chiselled cheekbones and his bright eyes. He's got that iconic haircut, the disconnected undercut with no fade, the one that makes your hair look as if it's just sitting on top of your head. He's very sharply dressed in a three-piece suit – in fact, he'd look fresh out of the TV show if it weren't for one thing. Hunter is absolutely jacked. His arms are thicker than my thighs – and that really isn't something I get to say all that often.

'Ah, you're too kind, Terry,' Hunter replies. Oh, God, even his voice is sexy. He's got a deep voice and an Irish accent that I wasn't expecting.

'Damian, you sit here, next to me,' Mackie insists, which puts Damian in the space between him and Lottie. This leaves a space for me, on the other side of the table, between Jo and Hunter. Is it bad that I'm happy I get to sit next to him?

'Good to meet you, Sadie,' Hunter says as I sit down next to him. I feel all the hairs on the back of my neck stand on end.

'You too,' I reply.

'So, Damian, what do you do?' I hear Lottie ask him on the other side of the table.

It's practically a cutlery-clatter moment.

'There's no way she doesn't know who he is,' Hunter whispers to me. 'This is all part of her act.'

'I'm… I'm a photographer,' Damian replies.

'Oh, wow, good for you,' Lottie says patronisingly.

'Next she'll ask if he's ever sold anything,' Hunter whispers again. His face is so close to mine I can smell his aftershave.

'Have you ever sold any of your pictures?' Lottie asks.

'Erm… one or two,' Damian says. He looks bemused and, annoyingly, almost charmed by the fact she seemingly doesn't know who he is. Well, how do you make yourself appealing to someone who is terrified of being used for their fame? Pretend you don't know who they are.

'What do you like to take pictures of?' Lottie asks.

I can't help but roll my eyes.

'For work, I shoot people,' Damian replies.

'Oh, don't say that too loudly around me,' Mackie chimes in. 'People will think I'm paying you.'

I swear, everyone is flying so close to the sun, in so many ways, I'm surprised we're not all on fire. With Mackie and his murder jokes, and Damian falling for Lottie's act – surely he isn't?

'Everyone who takes my picture always tells me what a natural I am,' she tells the table. There's a look on Hunter's face as if he's heard this a million times.

'What do you model?' Damian asks.

'I do lifestyle-y stuff,' she says. 'I enhance products in catalogues and adverts.'

'Like what?' I ask curiously.

'You did that B&Q ad recently, didn't you?' Angel offers. 'Sitting on the patio furniture.'

'I did, yeah,' Lottie says. 'And I've modelled with plates, bike helmets, pens – all sorts. I'm hoping to branch out into much more.'

'Motor oil, draft excluders, Sellotape,' Hunter whispers.

I like having him in my ear, making me laugh, undermining Lottie who, so far, seems really unlikeable. I hate to see her trying to manipulate Damian.

'What do you model?' I ask Hunter.

'What do you think I model?' he asks playfully.

'Motor oil, draft excluders, Sellotape,' I reply, trying not to smile.

He laughs. God, he looks good when he laughs.

'I was thinking clothes,' I say genuinely. 'You're stylish but...'

'But...' he prompts.

'Well, male fashion models aren't usually built like Avengers,' I point out.

Hunter laughs.

'I'm a fitness model,' he says. 'Pictures of me rarely involve much clothing. I suppose that's why I like to make an effort when I'm not working.'

'Well, you look great,' I tell him.

'Thanks,' he says. 'You do too. I love this dress.'

He strokes the material on the sleeve of my vintage army-green velvet dress.

'Oh, thanks,' I say, just a little taken aback by the physical contact. 'I got this from a vintage boutique in my home town. I always raid the place, whenever I visit my parents. They sell men's stuff too – you'd love it, if you love fashion and vintage looks.'

'It kind of sounds like you're inviting me to meet your

parents,' he says with a cheeky smile.

'Oh, God, no...' I babble, until I realise he's just teasing me.

'Are you from near London?' he asks.

'Yorkshire,' I reply. 'So not really... They sell online though – I can give you the info.'

'Thanks, Sadie, I'd love that. We're stuck on this... well, whatever this is, boat, island, fort thing for a few days. Maybe we could look together?'

'I'd really like that,' I reply.

I look over at Damian and notice him staring. I smile at him until he smiles back.

'You OK?' I mouth to him.

An oblivious Lottie is still talking at him, at a million miles an hour.

He nods.

'Hey, did you hear that, over that side of the table?' Mackie asks.

We all look over in his direction.

'There's an indoor pool here. Why don't we all meet up there tomorrow morning after breakfast? We could play some games. I love water sports.'

I feel my eyes widen.

'Oh, yes, Damian, say you'll come, say you'll come,' Lottie whines.

'I'd love to,' Damian replies, still staring at me.

'Oh, yeah, me too,' I say. Well, I can't let him go on his own, can I?

'Well, I was going to try and get out of it,' Hunter tells me. 'But if you're going to be there, I think I will too.'

I smile about 50 per cent of the way, because I don't want to seem too keen, but I am positively buzzing with excitement.

Suddenly this trip is a lot more interesting...

12

It is on days like today that I wonder why I would ever want to quit my job. Put out of your mind my overly demanding boss and the fact I'm stranded on a sea fortress with a maybe-murderer (don't put it too far out of your mind though; we have to be vigilant) – this is actually a really cool perk of the job.

I'm in a five-star hotel, sitting by a pool in the atrium, in the heart of the fortress. It's really warm, as if perhaps they heat the place to make it feel like being poolside abroad, the cocktails are amazing, and I'm so happy I decided to bring my swimming costume just in case. Although, at the time of packing it, I jokily told myself it was just in case I needed to swim to shore... I say jokily but I'll never rule it out.

The perkiest perk of my job, though, has to be hunky Hunter. I was a bit annoyed the second we walked through the door, when Lottie rushed over and whisked Damian away to introduce him to 'some people'. I was just standing there, all alone, suddenly feeling really awkward and vulnerable in my swimwear. Damian said he'd be right back but what was I supposed to do until then? Sit and sip mai tais with Mackie?

And then I felt it, a gentle tap on my shoulder. I turned around and Hunter was standing there, in his teeny tiny trunks, soaking wet from swimming, pool water rolling down his abs. Think Daniel Craig in *Casino Royale*. He asked me if I wanted to grab a drink and have a chat, and here we are.

'So how do you know the happy couple?' I ask as I sip maybe the best pina colada I've ever had.

'I'm Ry's best man,' he tells me. 'Best friend, best man. I actually met him through Angel – we were friends first. We're all in the same circle.'

'Lottie too?' I ask nosily.

'Hmm, yeah,' he says. 'I'm not her biggest fan – I'm not sure anyone is. She's Angel's BFF.'

'What's her deal?' I ask. 'Do I need to pry her off my boss?'

'Ah, he looks big enough to take care of himself,' Hunter replies. 'What can I tell you about Lottie…? Well, she's unofficially blacklisted by most agencies. She can get the Insta ads and the low-paying catalogue gigs but that's about it. Before she was a *full-time influencer*…' Hunter says this in a squeaky Essex accent almost exactly like Lottie's '… she was a model. Specifically, a maternity model.'

I furrow my brow.

'I guess no one really talks about it,' he explains. 'But a lot of the time, maternity models aren't actually pregnant. A journalist wrote a big feature on it – and before you think I'm really into maternity fashion news, I'm not, but Lottie was just talking about it nonstop when it kicked off. In fact, she still talks about it nonstop. So, there was this article about it, saying it wasn't fair on models who were pregnant, taking work from them, and some talk about unrealistic body image for pregnant women. But while others were delicately explaining that sometimes shoots are long and strenuous – not what you'd expect a pregnant woman to endure – Lottie was tweeting about how people only wanted to see thin people modelling clothes.'

'Nice,' I say sarcastically.

'Yeah, so the industry turned on her, but she's had a few celebrity boyfriends. Footballers, popstars – one was from… now, was it One Direction or The Wanted? I forget. We didn't like him much. She picked up legions of follows via him though.' Hunter laughs to himself. 'Ry jokes that Lottie always lands on her back.'

Gosh, maybe I do need to get Damian away from her. But, well, is it my problem? I'm certain it isn't in my job description. Dumping girls for Damian is enough, I'm not about to start vetting them for him too.

'So, what's it like working for the great Damian Banks?' Hunter asks. 'I'm pretty sure that's the only thing I ever hear people refer to him as.'

I laugh. I do hear that a lot.

'Damian *is* great,' I say. Well, he is, so credit where it's due. 'Working for him is not so great, if I'm being honest.'

'No?'

I shake my head. Should I really be confiding in a stranger?

'It's just not what I want to be doing,' I say tactfully. 'Just between us, I've applied for a job in an art gallery. I've always wanted to be a curator. This would be my foot in the door.'

'You've got to do what makes you happy,' Hunter says. 'I love my job now, but I've had jobs that I hated, and it's a big part of your life. Too big to be unhappy.'

'You're absolutely right,' I reply. 'It's great that you love your job. I don't think I could hack it. I know that I should exercise but… I just struggle to see how people enjoy it. It's a necessary evil – one that I don't partake in nearly as much as I should. I have so much respect for you. Your hard work is all over your body.'

Hunter makes his pecs dance for me.

I know that I haven't had much of a love life for a really long time, so this might come across as kind of thirsty, and I don't mean it exactly how it sounds – Hunter's body really is a work of art.

'All the better for smashing everyone at pool volleyball with,' he says, nodding over towards the pool, where Mackie is attempting to assemble the players. 'You want to be on my team?'

'Are you any good?' I ask, as though there's a chance he couldn't be.

'I'm fantastic,' he says flirtatiously. 'My moves would leave you speechless. Are you any good?'

Suddenly I get the feeling we're not talking about pool volleyball any more… but I can't risk it.

'I am absolutely awful,' I confess with a smile.

Hunter stands up and offers me his hand.

'Come on, I'll give you a few pointers before we get started,' he says.

I reach out for his hand so he can help me up.

As we make our way towards the pool Damian stops us.

'Hey, Sadie, can I borrow you for a sec?' he says. 'Just a work thing.'

'No worries,' Hunter says. 'I'll see you in there.'

Like something out of a movie Hunter makes a move towards the edge of the pool and dives straight in.

'Did you just bite your lip?' Damian chuckles.

Oh, God, did I?

'No!' I quickly insist. 'What's up?'

'Oh, nothing,' he says. 'I thought you might need saving from him.'

'Saving?'

'Looked like he was talking your ear off,' he says.

'Oh, no, it's fine. He's really nice,' I reply. 'Sorry, was I supposed to save you from Lottie?'

'Nah, she's harmless,' he says. 'She just introduces me to people, talks about herself, and keeps saying how odd it is that she's never heard of me.'

I nod thoughtfully, minding my own business.

'What?' He laughs.

'Let's pretend, for a second, for argument's sake, that she could be a model and have never heard of you. Fine. But Mackie has made such a huge deal about you shooting Angel's wedding – it's everything she wants – and, what, she's not mentioned this to her best friend? Hunter says this is all part of her act.'

'You know I'm not falling for it, right?' he says plainly.

I hate it when I get overly invested in Damian's personal matters. I guess, when I manage all other aspects of his life, it's hard not to take care of him across the board.

'Well, we've got more important things to worry about,' I tell him. 'Pool volleyball. Hunter says he'll make sure I'm on his team. You want in?'

'Why?'

'Erm, because he's good at it,' I point out. 'And we're not.'

'You've never seen me play pool volleyball,' Damian insists.

'Yeah, Damian, that's kind of my point. I've never seen you play any sports. You hate sports,' I pointlessly remind him.

'Damian, Sadie, come on,' Mackie calls out. 'Time to play!'

'We really should be getting on with some prep work,' Damian says seriously.

'Come on, live a little,' I insist.

'Fine, fine.'

There's a net hovering across the shallow end of the pool. On one side – team one – there's Damian, Mackie, Angel and Lottie. Over on my side – team two – there's me, Hunter, Ryan and Jo. Jo is being pretty girly about it all, trying not to get her hair wet or pop out of her bikini, but Hunter and Ryan are big, buff sporty men. Even with me and Jo holding them back, they should be able to win easily.

Lottie serves and of course she's amazing at it. She sends the ball flying over in my direction and – of course – I don't know what I'm doing so I get the fear and try to dive out of its way.

'It's not dodgeball, Sadie,' she calls over.

'Wow, Lottie, you're really good at this,' Mackie tells her.

'Oh, well, at boarding school, you get really good at all the girls' sports – volleyball, netball, hockey,' she replies. 'I'm terrible at other things.'

The game gets going again. The ball goes back and forth a few times until Hunter smashes it over the net, sending it hurtling towards Damian who, as I did, instinctively moves out of its way.

'Sorry, brother,' Hunter shouts to him. 'I can get a bit competitive.'

Damian shrugs. A sport was never going to make him feel emasculated; he just doesn't care. He's too cool for that.

'Nothing's worth taking a ball to the face,' Damian says.

I snigger to myself.

'I can give you a few easy ones, if you want a bit of practice,' Hunter suggests.

I know the look on Damian's face. It's the face he makes when he thinks someone is being a dick.

'It's just a game, mate,' Damian replies.

I don't think Hunter likes being made to look bad. His face falls.

'You're pretty chilled out for someone with such a bad-boy reputation,' Hunter says.

'Oh, are you a bad boy?' Lottie says excitedly. As if she doesn't already know.

Damian just stares at him. Sure, he might have a bad-boy reputation, but I know that isn't exactly the reality. He definitely doesn't like confrontation.

'OK, come on, let's keep this game moving,' Ryan demands impatiently, his sportsman's competitive nature fully kicking in.

The game picks up again. I do my best to keep out of the action – because I'm as terrified as I am useless – but Hunter effortlessly picks up my slack. He hits the ball hard, sending it flying up in the air. Mackie seems to have a few seconds to ready himself for it, to get into position, to line up his response. As the ball reaches him, he jumps up in the air and hits it with all his might, sending it flying at full speed towards Jo.

Poor Jo, she just stares at it. Despite Hunter's best efforts to get to her in time, the ball hits her in the face. Jo falls back and disappears under the water.

A series of 'oh' and 'oh my Gods' echoes around the room.

'Oh, don't worry, she's taken balls to the face before,' Mackie tells us, borrowing Damian's words but somehow making them sound much worse.

Not only does Jo not immediately pop back up, but there's a reddish tinge to the water.

Hunter reaches into the water to grab her, pulling her up, dragging her towards the side of the pool. Ryan rushes along-side him, jumping out of the water to help him lift her out.

Jo coughs and splutters until she gets her breath. Her nose is bleeding so Ryan grabs a towel for her.

'Are you OK?' Hunter asks.

Jo nods from behind the towel although her eyes look wide with fear as she holds the towel tightly to her face.

'Ah, there we go, she's OK,' Mackie casually announces to everyone. 'Shall we play on without her for a bit?'

I exchange a look with Damian, who raises his eyebrows at me.

'Actually, we'd better go get ready for our shoot,' Damian says. 'Right, Sadie?'

'Oh, gosh, yes,' I reply. 'So much to get ready.'

We set everything up earlier, but I want to get out of here just as much as he does. It's weird – there's this awkward, horrible, uncomfortable vibe. Jo is like a time bomb; you can tell everyone thinks that way.

'OK, well, I'll get ready too,' Mackie says. 'Looking forward to it.'

I follow Damian's lead, heading for the side of the water. We grab our things and head for our suites.

'Did he... did he do that on purpose?' Damian asks me quietly.

That's the question, isn't it? Either everything people have accused him of is true and it's only a matter of time before something bad happens, or it really was just a genuine accident, and no one is going to cut Mackie an inch of slack for the rest of his life. Either way, he doesn't need to worry about it. It's not like anyone is brave enough confront him about it, is it?

13

'Maybe I'm going soft,' Damian says as he messes with the settings on his camera. 'But I'm feeling bad for bringing you here.'

'Well, the great Damian Banks doesn't usually feel bad for anything,' I tease. 'So you must be.'

'Oi, I do feel bad,' he insists.

'Just not about things like having me dump women for you or making me give up my evenings so you don't have to sit in and wait for deliveries, to name a few things,' I point out semiplayfully. I mean, I'm not trying to have a go at him, but those things are true.

'Sadie, I'm sorry, did you have plans?' he replies.

Now I'm not sure if he's teasing me or not.

'Not the point,' I reply with a smile.

Damian abandons his camera to come and sit next to me on the sofa in the room we're using for the shoot.

'Sadie, listen, I know I'm a highly strung creative – I can't even imagine what it's like to work with me – but, you'd tell me if I were having a negative impact on your life, right? I don't want you to be unhappy.'

I feel my eyebrows shoot up. This is new. Damian doesn't usually talk about things like this; he's usually too busy obsessively looking inward to worry about what's going on outside his head. I think for a second. Let's just say there's a chance I get the assistant curator job – then none of this will matter. Sure, I'm not happy at work now, but if there's a chance I could change my job soon, it doesn't seem worth airing my issues, only to quit after he makes moves to resolve them, *if* he makes moves to resolve them. Up until now I've kept my mouth shut because I needed this job. Now it makes more sense to keep things to myself just in case I don't need this job any more. And, well, if I don't get the gig, at least he seems like he's open to fixing things,

'It's fine,' I insist. 'I'm just teasing you.'

'Phew,' he replies as his serious expression dissolves into something softer. 'You had me worried there for a second. I need to keep you happy – I don't know what I'd do without you. I'd probably lose my mind – if I haven't already. I am about to take pictures of someone who most people believe murdered three women.'

Right on cue there's a knock on the door. I open it to find Mackie standing there. He's clearly made an effort to look good and dress nicely for his big moment.

'Sadie, here I am,' he sings. 'About to give your boss the chance to do what millions dream of – shooting me.'

I laugh politely.

'Come on in, he's all ready for you,' I say.

'OK but, before we get started, Hunter is outside. He wants a quick word,' he tells me, looking over my shoulder to get a look at the set.

'Oh, OK, I'll be right back, then,' I reply.

Sure enough Hunter is standing there, leaning back against the wall. He looks fresh out of the shower, dressed casually in sweats and a vest, but somehow he still looks fashionable.

'Hello,' I say brightly. 'Terry said you wanted to see me.'

'Yes,' he says as he approaches me. 'So, tomorrow is the wedding day, so everyone is having a quiet, chilled evening.'

That makes sense. It would be too on-brand for something big to happen, resulting in something going terribly wrong the night before the wedding.

Hunter takes me by the hands.

'Do you have plans this evening?' he asks.

'No plans,' I reply. I can't think of a joke quick enough – something about there being nowhere to go on the fortress, that probably wouldn't have been that funny anyway – because the second he touched my hands fear surges through my body, taking hold of every part of it.

'Would you like to have dinner with me?' he asks. 'Ordinarily I'd love to cook for you but, with that not being an option, I thought I could order us something special from room service? But... I was going to invite you to my suite, but Angel has had a change of heart about seeing Ryan the night before the wedding, so he asked if he could crash in my room. Do you have a dining-table area in your suite? I could bring everything to you.'

I blink as I stare at him. Is this real life?

My relationship with my confidence is a tricky one. I'm not shy; I don't mind speaking in front of large groups of people; meeting 'celebrities' doesn't faze me. I'm happy with the way I look too – I'm not perfect, but the people I meet who look perfect are always deeply flawed in other ways, so I'm pretty happy with how I've turned out. Where my confidence fades is when I think about how other people value me. Am I good enough for my dream job? Do I deserve to be asked out by the hottest man here? Whenever anything good happens to me, I always worry someone has made a mistake. It doesn't make a lot of sense but these things rarely do, do they?

'I do have a dining table, yes, sure, I'd love that,' I say enthusiastically. The fact that this seems like a dream almost emboldens me. Well, if I wake up, none of this matters, and, if I don't, guess who has a dinner date with a hunky fitness model who, as well as being gorgeous, with a dreamy accent, has a great personality too? Well, that's if it *is* a date.

'Great, it's a date,' he says. 'I'll let you get back to work.'

'OK, sure, what time shall I see you?'

'Does seven work for you?' he asks.

'Perfect,' I reply. 'See you then.'

I save my enormous smile – and dorky happy dancing – for when I'm back inside the room with the door closed behind me.

'Sadie, there you are,' Damian says. 'Ready to start?'

He pulls a face, as if he can't wrap his head around why I look so excited.

'Yep, all ready,' I reply.

'If you're both gentle with me, I'll be gentle with you,' Mackie says with a wink.

I just need to survive this now.

14

The last thing I expected, when I was packing my bag to come here, was that I would need an outfit for a date. And not just any date, a date with an insanely attractive model – and one that is currently taking place in my hotel suite, on a sea fortress, in the middle of the sea. Pinch me, I'm still convinced this is all a dream. Not just because of how surreal this situation is. You could strip all that back and I would still be surprised because, I cannot stress this enough, I don't ever get asked out on dates and, even if I did, I don't usually have any free time anyway.

I'm all dressed up, hovering around the door in my suite, waiting for Hunter to turn up. Usually, when I lurk excitedly behind the door like this it's because I'm waiting for a takeaway to arrive.

I'm nervous, because I haven't been on a proper date in a long time, and because I'm so certain Hunter is out of my league and... oh my God! I must be wound so tightly right now because the sound of my phone ringing causes my whole body to jolt with surprise. I hurry over to the table and, even though it doesn't say who it is, I know. It's about the job.

'Hello,' I say, trying to sound bright and breezy but not quite masking the terror in my voice.

'Hello, Sadie, it's Robyn,' she says.

'Robyn, hello,' I reply. 'How are you?'

I just need to keep things calm and casual.

'I'm very well, thanks. And yourself?'

'Oh, yes, I'm great,' I reply.

'Great,' she says before pausing for a second.

Oh, God, this is what I do when I'm dumping birds for Damian. I have this moment of hesitation where I pause to psych myself up, because I know I'm about to break someone's heart.

'I wanted to call you now, to let you know about the job, rather than leave you wondering all weekend,' she starts. Ergh, honestly, I really would have preferred she do this on Monday, when I'll be back in London, and it won't be so tempting (or so easy) to throw myself into the sea. Also, I'd really rather not spend this date in tears. That wouldn't be a good look.

'OK,' I say. Let's get this over with...

'Sadie, the job is yours if you want it,' she blurts, finally letting the professional tone slip, just a little.

I scream.

'Oh my God!' I reply. 'Oh my... wow, that's... that's amazing!'

So much for playing it cool.

'Well, I take it from that reply this is good news, but it's a big decision, so take the weekend to think about it. I'll call you back on Monday and you can let me know if you'd like to accept – sound good?'

'Sounds amazing,' I reply.

'OK, Sadie, have a great weekend.'

'You too,' I practically squeak back.

I got the job. *I* got the job. I hoped I would, but I didn't think that they would want me, but they *do*! I have until Monday to decide what to do but it's a no-brainer, right? It's my dream job – and I already have a fancy dinner arranged to celebrate. What a wonderful evening this is shaping up to be.

There's a knock at the door. I hurry back over to it and fling it open, suddenly not all that nervous. I'm just too happy.

'Hi,' Hunter says.

He's looking amazing, in another snappy three-piece suit – and he's brought me flowers too.

'Hello,' I say.

'These are for you,' he says as he hands me the flowers, kissing me on the cheek.

It's a small, kind of strange-looking bunch – but beautiful none the less.

'Wow, thank you. Where do you get flowers from, in the middle of the sea?' I can't help but ask.

'Honestly, they're wedding flowers,' he admits. 'I didn't want to turn up empty-handed so I stole them. Don't worry though, I only took one flower from a handful of different arrangements, so you can't even tell anything is missing.'

'That's so thoughtful,' I say. 'And so sneaky!'

'What can I say? I'm a bad boy,' he jokes.

I realise we're still hovering in the doorway.

'Sorry, come in, let's get some food ordered,' I say. 'And some drinks!'

I hope I don't seem too eager, as I practically drag Hunter through the door, but not only am I starving, I'm suddenly a little worried about Damian spotting us together.

We order our food and it arrives pretty much straight away – and my God, it's good.

I've gone full Italian, with mozzarella Milanese to start, pasta primavera for the main event, nicely finished off with creamy rose panna cotta. Hunter naturally went for the manliest options available to him – all heavy on the protein. For his main course he had chicken arrabbiata. It was so spicy I felt the smell of it burn my nostrils. Hunter didn't even flinch as he ate every last bit.

'So are you a vegetarian?' he asks me as I finish my dessert.

'I'm not strictly a vegetarian, but I'm trying to cut down,' I tell him.

'I get a lot of stick online from vegetarians and vegans – vegans are the worst. They come down on me pretty hard because I have to eat a lot of meat and dairy to stay in shape,' he explains. 'They're all on some moral crusade. I was worried you might be the same...'

'Oh.' I feel a little taken aback. 'No crusade, you're not going to get a speech from me. I'm just cutting down. Everyone cutting down, even just a bit, will make a difference. At the very least it will offset all the bonus stuff you have to eat.'

I always make terrible jokes when I'm trying to ease tension. We've been having such a lovely evening, I don't want to start getting into controversial territory.

Hunter laughs.

'I guess that's true,' he says. 'It's nice to see a girl with a good appetite. I'm used to Angel and Lottie and Jo, all competing to see who can survive the longest on the least calories.'

I suppose I should be freaking out, worrying that I ate too much in front of him, when everyone else he knows potentially has an eating disorder, but I'm not. I know that I'm fine.

'I'm bulking,' I joke.

Hunter laughs.

'I like how fun you are,' he tells me. 'You're so smiley. It's a pleasure to be around you.'

'If I'm being honest, I do have an extra reason to be happy today,' I tell him. I'm desperate to tell someone my good news.

'Oh, really?' he replies, his eyebrows shooting up.

Ohhhh, I think he thinks I mean because I'm with him.

'It's a double good day,' I tell him, covering all bases. 'I got a call earlier, offering me my dream job.'

'Sadie, congratulations,' he says. He seems genuinely pleased for me. 'I'm guessing you took it.'

'They're going to call me back on Monday, to ask if I'd like to accept it,' I reply.

'Is your mind not made up?' he asks. 'You don't sound so sure.'

Am I not sure? This is everything I want, right? There's no time for pause now; we're way past that stage.

'I'm pretty sure I do,' I reply. 'Yeah. I mean, I'll think about it, it would be stupid not to but... yeah...'

Hunter smiles.

'Shall we sit on the sofa?' he suggests.

'Sure,' I reply. I am kind of desperate to sit on a comfortable chair, especially after all the carbs.

As I make my way over to the two-seater sofa at the bottom of the bed, I notice my phone vibrating on the desk. I grab it, taking it with me. It's Damian. There's no way I'm answering it.

'Do you need to take that?' Hunter asks as he takes off his waistcoat and loosens his top shirt buttons, making himself more comfortable.

'Oh, no, it's not important,' I say, placing it down next to me.

We sit on the sofa, our bodies angled slightly so we're facing each other. We're only silent for a few seconds before Hunter starts up the conversation again.

'How long did it take you to grow your hair?' he asks. 'I love how long it is.'

'Oh, God, years. It's always been long. My sister always tells me it's an immature hairstyle for an adult,' I tell him. 'She says grown women shouldn't need to worry about sitting on their hair. She says she lives in fear of me trapping it in a lift door or something. I think she just likes to worry.'

'Well, you don't have to worry,' Hunter says. 'It's gorgeous.'

He takes a small section of my hair in his hand and strokes it with his thumb. Right on cue my phone starts ringing again.

Hunter drops my hair, sits up straight and clears his throat.

'Do you need to get that?' he asks.

'It's just Damian,' I tell him.

'Does he know I'm here?' Hunter asks seriously.

'No...'

'Is... is something going on between the two of you?' he says. 'I've been getting a vibe.'

'Oh, God, no,' I say firmly. 'Never. He's my boss. He's just kind of needy. He calls me a lot. It's never important. In fact...'

I switch my phone to silent.

'Oh, OK, sorry,' he says. 'You just seem really close.'

'We are but – as friends, at best,' I tell him. 'I am single. I am *really* single. Totally available.'

Hunter laughs and relaxes again. He grabs the remote from the bed and puts some music on.

'Available is good,' he says softly. 'Available is just what I want to hear.'

Hunter reaches out and gently moves all of my hair to one side of my head. He takes it in his hand and twists it around before wrapping it around his fist like a rope. With me exactly where he wants me, Hunter pulls me close, bringing my lips to his. I don't know if it's the kiss or the spicy food he's just eaten but it makes my lips tingle like crazy. He's got moves, you've got to give him that.

It's been so long since I kissed anyone like this – I'm relieved I still know how to do it.

With a swoop of one of his big strong arms Hunter has lifted me up and laid me back on the bed. Our lips lock together again as he runs his hand up my leg. Everything feels so smooth and effortless – until we're interrupted by a banging sound. For a second we just hover in position, waiting to see if it happens again.

'Sadie,' Damian shouts as he bangs on the suite door. 'Sadie, let me in.'

'Is that Damian?' Hunter says in disbelief.

'Yes,' I reply. It's hard to even pretend I am surprised.

'Sadie, I know you're in there. I can hear your music. Come on, it's an emergency,' Damian rants.

'Will he give up?' Hunter asks.

I wince because I don't think he will, but it's worth a shot.

'I'll get rid of him,' I say as I wiggle out from under Hunter. 'Stay there.'

I hurry to the door, which is thankfully around the corner from the bed, and open it up just enough to speak to Damian without letting him see inside.

'What's wrong?' I ask, skipping pleasantries.

'I've been trying to call you,' Damian says. He looks me up and down before narrowing his eyes. 'Were you in bed?'

'Erm... yes,' I say, because I must look as if I was, and it's not technically untrue.

'Can I come in?' he asks, edging towards the door.

'Can this wait until morning?' I ask. 'Or just... later? I can't really talk right now.'

Damian looks taken aback. I don't think he's used to me saying no.

'Sadie, please, I really need to talk to you,' he says. I can see it, something in his eyes that makes me think this really is important, that he does really need to speak to me.

'Just, wait here for a minute,' I tell him. 'I'll be right back.'

By the time I'm back by the bed, Hunter, who obviously heard all of that, is gathering up his things.

'I'm so sorry,' I tell him. 'I think something must be really wrong.'

Hunter purses his lips and nods.

'It's always going to be something with him,' he tells me softly. 'He's always going to need you for something. You want my advice? Take that job. Take it and don't ever look back. If you don't, he's always going to be there, always in the background, and people like Damian – I've seen them before – they don't settle down, and if they don't, you don't.'

I'm momentarily stunned. I mean... is he wrong? He isn't, is he?

Hunter gives me a peck on the lips before heading for the door.

'She's all yours,' I hear him tell Damian as he passes him. It isn't long before Damian is in my suite with me.

'Erm... sorry, have I interrupted something?' he asks as he edges towards me. He clocks the plates on the table. 'Sorry, were you having dinner?'

'It's fine, we had already finished. What's wrong?' I ask as I plonk myself down on the bed.

Damian grabs a biscotti from the table before sitting down next to me.

'It's just...' He pauses, freezing on the spot. 'Oh my God, this bed is warm – were you having sex? With *him*?'

Damian is a combination of baffled and amused.

'Nope, you put a stop to that,' I tell him, unable to hide my frustration.

'Sadie Kirke, you surprise me,' he teases. 'I didn't think he'd be your type. A big meathead like that. He's so intense, and he dresses kind of weird...'

'No one is asking you to sleep with him,' I point out. It might have been nice if he'd left me to it though.

'Are you actually upset?' he asks me. 'Because I ruined your date with Creepy Blinders? Come on, Sadie, you can do better than that.'

'This emergency is starting to sound less urgent,' I tell him. 'Come on, tell me what was worth ruining my date for.'

'It really is important,' he says, getting back to business. 'I was processing my pictures of Mackie and, well, they're just awful. He doesn't look like a wrongly accused man, he doesn't look like a murderer. He just looks like some middle-aged bloke in his Sunday best. Just empty, boring images. They're no use to me at all. I'm going to have to go back to the drawing board. Find a new subject.'

I lie back on my bed and quietly laugh to myself.

'Of course, you are,' I say. 'Of course, you are.'

'OK, but time is running out,' he says. 'And there's so much pressure on me, and the deadline is looming for the show...'

Because we don't cancel shows when we decide to abandon our projects, apparently, we leave them booked in and just start from scratch – even when they're only *two months* away.

'Can we have a brainstorming session?' he asks. 'Obviously I still have to do the wedding tomorrow, but we can catch the helicopter back as soon as possible after, get straight on with it. But if we could just come up with something...'

I sigh.

'Sure,' I say. 'Why not?'

'Sadie, you're an angel,' he tells me. 'Let me order us some more biscuits, we'll see what we can come up with. I am so relieved we're always in this together.'

That's just the thing – although I can't tell him yet, not until things are official – I don't think we are in this together any more. I might have had a few doubts earlier but now I am absolutely sure I am doing the right thing. I need to take this new job and give my notice ASAP because Hunter was right: I'll never have a normal life if I don't.

15

I am both pleased and incredibly relieved to report that Angel and Ryan's wedding went ahead without a blip, a blunder or a bloody murder. Well, so far anyway. With our plates cleared and the speeches taking place now, we're about to transition from the formal sit-down to the more casual evening do. You never know, perhaps as people drink more, and start dancing, things might liven up – not that I want them to. A peaceful party suits me. I was a little worried that Hunter might say something to me or, even worse, say something to Damian, but he's completely blanked me all day. Don't get me wrong, I am upset that my work life is affecting my personal life, but, now that I've had a little time to think on it, I'm not all that bothered things didn't work out between us. Well, other than a bold sense of fashion, I'm not sure how much we had in common. I doubt it would have worked out in the long run, but I was down for the short run. So to speak.

I'm glad we didn't wind up sitting on the same table today, and that the wedding is well under way now. This will all be over soon; we just need to keep going through the motions until all the wedding formalities are over and done with.

Because everything is basically the Terry Mackie Show, you had better believe this wedding has been engineered around him being the headliner – there's even a camera crew here, which makes me think they might be filming another instalment of '*Til Death Do Us Part.*

Tradition be damned, even the order of the speeches has been rejigged to lead up to Mackie giving his 'father of the bride' speech last, so he can well and truly steal the show, I'd imagine.

'Ladies and gentlemen, if I could have your attention, please,' he says into his microphone.

Mackie wasn't famous before all the, y'know, dead wives business, but he's so completely at home with it now. He holds his mic like an old pro, with all the swagger of a Frank Sinatra tribute act, and he speaks with such self-assurance. It's almost as though, if he says things with enough confidence, or insists things are true, then how could anyone possibly think he was lying?

'Here we go, the main event,' Damian whispers to me with a cheeky grin.

I raise my eyebrows in response, turning straight back to the top table, not wanting to miss a moment of the action. Every second of this man is great TV.

'I won't waste any time introducing myself. I'm sure everyone here already knows who I am,' Mackie starts. 'If you don't, well, congratulations on sneaking into such an expensive meal, and maybe pick up a newspaper once in a while.'

That polite wave of laughter you always get during speeches crashes around the room. Well, it's rare speech jokes are actually funny, isn't' it?

'I want to thank you all for coming to my Angel's wedding today,' he continues. 'It's been such a wonderful day so far, welcoming Ryan into our crazy little family, handing over my little girl to him, threatening him with unthinkable things if he doesn't take good care of her.'

Hopefully a joke. Everyone is laughing at least. The happy couple seem more than pleased with the show Mackie is putting on, and Jo isn't cringing, as I imagine I would be.

'What can I say about my Angel?' Mackie rubs his chin thoughtfully as he pretends to wrack his brains. 'She's always brightened our lives – although that's mostly because she never remembers to turn any lights off. Funny, intelligent, kind, good-looking – these are all traits I have passed on to her. And then there's Ryan, my new son. I thought it might be good to give him a little advice – because I have been married four times, so that makes me a bit of an expert, I'm sure. First of all, a few ways to keep the peace... In any argument it is important to remember that one person will always be right – the other person will be *you*. And, you know, the wedding anniversary, that's a big deal, especially to women, right? Well, the best way to remember it is to forget it once. You forget it once and you'll never forget it again.'

More laughs. What is it with speeches and the terrible, cliché jokes everyone feels as if they have to tell? They're usually pretty old gags that rely on tired stereotypes, and they're not actually that funny, but everyone feels obligated to laugh at them.

'I'm glad you're all enjoying my jokes. They say that brevity is the soul of wit – something I'll get into further on page fifteen of my speech.' Mackie pauses for his not-so-hard-earned laughs. 'Now it's time to put the jokes to one side, it's time to get serious. Angel and Ryan, you are perfect for each other, a match made in heaven. You've found each other, fallen head over heels in love and, here you are, about to embark on the rest of your lives together.'

The laughs have turned to awws now that Mackie has switched to something more sincere. Angel smiles widely as she squeezes Ryan's hand. I swear, this moment, right now, might be the most honest and genuine Mackie has seemed.

'It's a rare thing, to find the right person for you,' he continues. 'And for them to love you back and, well, if you find someone like that, love them with all of your heart, love them to death!'

The room falls deathly silent. I feel my eyes widen. Damian and I shoot each other a side glance. Suddenly he seems quite intense.

'So, if you'll all join me in raising a glass to Angel and Ryan,' Mackie says, picking up his own glass of champagne. 'To Angel and Ryan – may they be happy together. Until death do they part. Angel and Ryan!'

As we all pick up our glasses and drink to the happy couple a cold shiver runs down my back.

Now that the speeches are over, we're all allowed to go back to talking amongst ourselves. With everyone free to move around it's just me and Damian at our table.

He turns to me excitedly.

'OK, do you think he was threatening or advertising?' Damian asks quietly. 'Because that was absolutely wild.'

'It was definitely close to the bone,' I reply.

'Oh, I forgot to tell you, you know when you let Mackie in yesterday, and you went out into the hallway?' Damian says, leaning in as if he's got something juicy to tell me. 'He walks up to me, gives me one of his trademark handshakes. Then he pulls a knife from his pocket!'

I feel my eyebrows shoot up to the ceiling.

'A knife?'

'Yep. A Swiss army, multi-tool kind of knife, and he flicks a tool out...' Damian pauses for dramatic effect. 'I swear, my life flashed before my eyes, but it was just a USB drive. He was asking if I could put the photos we took on it. I thought it was seriously cool that it had a USB drive in it but, get this, he tells me it's got biometric security – only his fingerprint can access the data on the drive. How cool is that? I want one – no, I need one. It would be more secure than carrying around any old thumb drive.'

'It does make me wonder what he needs one for...' I muse. 'Honestly, I can't wait to get out of here.'

And I can't wait to tell Adam all about this. He's not going to believe it!

'First thing in the morning,' he reassures me. 'I'm sorry about all this. I don't know what I was thinking.'

'It's OK,' I reply. 'Art is a funny thing. But, well, you're supposed to be delivering at the end of the year, ready for your February preview, so... is that going to be possible?'

I don't want to freak him out but that is one hell of a tight turnaround. If there's one thing I've realised it's that the more talented you are, and the more famous you get, the more people will let you do whatever the hell you like. Lowly workers like me have to do everything asked of them, on time. Whereas people like Damian will be cut miles and miles of slack. Thing is, he doesn't want it; he wants to stick to his deadlines, he wants to put things out when he says he will. He just feels all this pressure to be beyond amazing, which petrifies him into slow motion.

'I've got one last try in me,' he says. 'Over Christmas, I'll see.'

'Well, just let me know what you need,' I tell him instinctively. Then I remember that I'm quitting. Still, this will continue to be my problem while I work my notice, which thankfully is only two weeks. I did comment that this was quite short, back when I signed my contract, but apparently, it's mostly for Damian's benefit. If he can't work with someone, he doesn't have to wait long before he can swap them out for someone else – that way it doesn't derail his work.

'Ladies and gentlemen, the bride and groom would like you to join them on the dance floor,' a voice booms through the PA system.

As I glance over at the dance floor, which is fast filling up with people, I notice Hunter dancing with a leggy brunette, her arms locked tightly around his neck as he holds her close. He doesn't waste any time, does he?

'You wanna dance?' I hear Damian say.

I don't know why I assumed he would be talking to anyone but me. He's looking at me though.

'What, me?'

'Yes, you,' he says with a laugh.

'We don't dance,' I tell him, not that he doesn't already know we've never danced together before.

'Well, I'm sure Jo would let you cut in with Mackie,' he jokes. 'Look at her face. She almost looks like she wishes he'd kill her.'

It's true, Jo doesn't look all that at ease in Mackie's arms. Then again, he doesn't look like a very good dancer. His smooth charm does not extend to his feet – not that it's a competition, and not that I can do any better.

I shudder at the thought of taking her place.

'Come on, dance with me,' he insists. 'Let me take a night off from annoying you.'

'Someone You Loved' by Lewis Capaldi is playing, which is exactly what I would have guessed cool, young people like Angel and Ryan would choose for their first dance... That said, it's not exactly a romantic song, is it? Still, with Lewis Capaldi's gorgeous voice, the twinkling white lights from the disco ball hanging high above the dance floor, and just the general atmosphere of everyone taking to the floor with the person they love, it's hard to resist joining in, basking in the romance – even if it is with my boss.

'OK,' I say. 'Let's do it.'

Damian hops to his feet with a real spring in his step and extends a hand for me to take. He really looks the part today, in his black suit, with his hair neatly slicked back and his beard trimmed.

'May I have this dance, miss?' he says with a wiggle of his eyebrows.

'Why, yes,' I reply as I take his hand.

Damian leads me into the centre of the dance floor. I reach up to place my arms on his shoulders, keeping him at arm's length, but he pulls me close with his hands on my hips. It's strange, being so close to him. Not bad, just not usual.

'You know, I really can't thank you enough for coming with me,' he says.

'It's literally my job,' I point out.

'I know,' he replies with a laugh. 'But don't think I don't notice that you always do it all without complaining.'

'Did my predecessor not do that?' I ask.

'He wouldn't dance with me,' Damian jokes. 'It's weird, but I guess you're the closest thing I have – or that I've had in a long time – to a stable relationship with a female. Just, please don't think your hard work goes unrecognised. I know I must be a nightmare but, I don't know, you just get me. So... thanks.'

Damian doesn't give me chance to say anything, he just pulls me close and dances with me. With my head pressed into his chest I can feel the warmth of his body and smell his delicious aftershave. I can't resist snuggling in closer to him – probably just a combination of the mushy music and the free-flowing champagne but... still... it's nice.

But as I move with him to the music, smiling to myself at his touching, heartfelt thank you for all my hard work (even though I know he'll be driving me mad again tomorrow), reality hits me: I'm quitting my job. I'm not only leaving Damian in the lurch but I'm leaving him full stop. It's going to be hard, and I feel so guilty now – it's practically going to be like a break-up. As always, it's going to be me pulling the trigger, calling time, breaking the news that things are ending. I just have no idea how I'm going to do it with Damian, especially when he's going through such a hard time. I have to put myself first though – how often do dream jobs come along?

'I couldn't imagine doing stuff like this with anyone else,' Damian whispers into my ear and his embrace gets tighter, just for a couple of seconds, but I really feel it.

I try to say something back, but the guilt is catching in my throat.

'I... I need to—'

'Mind if I cut in?' Lottie interrupts us.

'Oh, erm, well,' Damian babbles.

'Sure, go for it,' I insist.

I don't know why, because the last thing I want to do is hand him over to someone who is so clearly trying to manipulate him, but I feel as if I have to put a bit of distance between us.

'Sadie,' Damian starts, taking me by the hand as I try to walk away.

I quickly pull my hand back.

'Don't worry, we'll talk later,' I assure him. I smile, to let him know everything is OK, even if it isn't.

I hurry back to my seat. Our table is still empty so I sit down on my own, scanning the table for my glass so I can top it up with the almost empty bottle of white wine that's been sitting on the table for a little too long.

I watch Lottie wrap herself around him like a snake, pushing herself up against him so she can whisper into his ear. I wonder what she's saying to him. Bragging about an ad she did for gardening shears? Offering him some work experience maybe? Being a model and pretending not to have heard of Damian Banks doesn't make you seem attractive; it makes you seem as though you don't know the industry you work in. I don't even know why I care.

A loud clatter snatches the attention of the room – myself included. I'm not watching Damian and Lottie any more, I'm glancing around to see what's happened. The music stops and the lights get a little brighter.

'Is she OK?' a very worried-sounding DJ asks.

'She's fine, she's fine,' I hear Mackie's not all that reassuring voice reply.

I lean across the table to get a better look, only to see Jo on the floor, covered by a tablecloth, surrounded by plates and glasses.

'Aren't you clumsy?' Mackie teases her – loud enough for everyone to hear – as he pulls her to her feet. 'Sorry, everyone, please, get back to having fun.'

I move my glance from poor Jo and Mackie back to Damian and Lottie, who are still holding each other as they stare.

Thank God we're going home tomorrow because I don't know how much longer I can handle this. Any of this.

16

Oh, how great it is to be back in London. Cold, chaotic, Christmassy London.

There are so many things about Christmas time in London that I never grow tired of, even now that I live and work here.

Having grown up in a coastal town that loves all things Christmas, I am more than used to being submerged in the most wonderful time of year, but there are many massive differences between Christmas on the coast and Christmas in a big city like London. The lights, the music, the Christmas shoppers. It's so frantic and somehow just so peaceful to walk amongst it all. It's hard not to feel as if you're in a movie, especially when you visit festive favourites like Hyde Park's Winter Wonderland, and basically any part of Harrods. Damian is always asking me to 'just pop to Harrods' for something – I even had to pop in for painkillers once, though I know that he knows there is a pharmacy just down the road. I think he secretly just wanted a cronut too.

For the full pretending-you're-in-a-movie effect you're going to want to walk down a busy street – ideally with bags, if you have them, weaving in and out of busy passers-by, having a few near misses, and all while Michael Bublé's Christmas album plays through your headphones, to add some necessary non-diegetic sound to your Christmas scene. In an ideal world you'd bump into a movie star who's just in town for the holidays (but who you will fall madly in love with) or your drink will be knocked out of your hand by some handsome but frazzled businessman who is being forced to close down a toy shop – and right before Christmas too! Of course, life isn't like a movie at all though, so I manage to make it all the way to work, a sausage and egg McMuffin and a latte in hand, without so much as a hint of eye contact. That's probably more London than any of the above.

'Good morning,' I say brightly as I walk through the main office. There are murmurs of greetings from the troops but, honestly, I could burst into flames and the most they would probably do is move their plants and crack a window. I will *not* miss this bunch of miseries at all.

Damian's office door is closed, which always means he is in it, so I sit down at my desk and unwrap my breakfast. With my McMuffin secure in my left hand I open my desk drawer with my right, ready to see what my Post-it from Adam says today. Is it weird that I've kind of missed talking to him (even though I don't actually talk to him) while I've been away for a few days?

There isn't a Post-it today though – there's an envelope instead. I quickly put down my breakfast and wipe my hands, opening the envelope faster than I've maybe done anything in my life. I can't help but smile. It's a Christmas card... a Christmas card with the Mona Lisa on the front, except someone has pulled her face into a smile, wrapped her in Christmas lights and plonked a Santa Claus hat on her head.

Inside it reads:

DEAR SADIE, I HOPE THIS CHRISTMAS CARD FINDS YOU WELL – AND ALIVE. I SAW IT AND THOUGHT ABOUT YOU, BECAUSE I KNOW YOU LOVE ART, AND CHRISTMAS, SO THIS FELT LIKE A COUPLE OF YOUR PASSIONS COMBINED. I'M ONLY SORRY IT'S NOT MADE OF CHOCOLATE. ALONG WITH CONFIRMATION THAT YOU MADE IT AWAY FROM A POTENTIAL SERIAL KILLER ALIVE, I'D LOVE TO HEAR ALL ABOUT IT. I KNOW WE'LL SPEAK AGAIN BEFORE WE BREAK FOR CHRISTMAS BUT, THIS IS A CHRISTMAS CARD AFTER ALL, SO... MERRY CHRISTMAS! ADAM XXX.

Three kisses? *Three kisses?* And in a Christmas card? I don't want to sound nuts, even though I am absolutely going to – do keep in mind that this relationship has been entirely Post-it based – but surely this is the next step, right? This is the first step towards kicking things up a notch.

I jump up and head over to the other side of the room where I know the leftover Christmas cards are. Damian always has Christmas cards made to send out with a photo he has taken for the occasion – usually something tongue-in-cheek. This year it's a naked Santa Claus striking a weirdly seductive pose, his modesty only just about hidden by his epically long beard. It's my job to write Damian's cards for him, so I know there are a couple left. I realise that using one of Damian's cards isn't anywhere near as thoughtful as going out and buying one that I think Adam will like, as he did for me, but this is all I have to hand right now, and I'm so excited to reply. Anyway, I think he'll find it funny that I've used a company card.

I tap the top of my pen on the card as I think about what to write. With all things considered, there's only one thing for it...

Dear Adam, I am happy to report that I am alive and well – although it was just as nightmare-ish as you would expect, being stranded on a sea fortress with a murderer (I am almost certain of it now) and – even worse – the boss. I'm sad to say it but I think this job might be too much for me now. I've actually been offered another job and… I accepted it this morning! It's going to be weird, not swapping notes with you any more so, what the hell – would you like to go for a drink with me? It can be our own staff Christmas party and my leaving do combined (but we won't tell the others). What do you say? It would be so great to finally meet you. Sadie xxx

I glance over at Adam's photo on my desk. I love his big, beaming smile, and the way he clearly adores his mum – it's just so cute. I would love to meet him, even just to say that I had, but as hard as I try I can't imagine being in the same room as him. It did cross my mind, from time to time, to try and bump into him here. I figured I could just forget something that I absolutely had to pop back in for, but the one time I tried it he wasn't even in the office. I later found out he was on holiday, but everyone else found it so weird that I was in on a day when I wasn't supposed to be – to collect a notebook that I *needed* (the best I could come up with on the spot). I think they all thought Damian had sent me in to check up on them, and I didn't want it to become a big, embarrassing thing, so I left it after that. It did feel low-key stalky, which I didn't feel great about. I mean, what kind of weirdo orchestrates bumping into someone because they sent her a few Post-its? We do have a connection, but better to do things properly, and ask him if he wants to hang out, right? If he feels like I feel, I'm sure he's going to be just as nervously excited as I am.

17

It's beginning to look a lot like Christmas. After a few hectic weeks of working for Damian – and doing all of his Christmas stuff like sending out cards and buying presents for his family, which should hopefully arrive at his parents' house in time for Christmas – I've finally had a couple of days free to do some Christmas prep of my own.

Given that I always go home for Christmas, I don't exactly go hard on the Christmas decorations in my flat. I always get a small, real tree on the first of the month and find a little corner to put it with a few lights and a few baubles. The decorations are just a few random cheap ones I've picked up over the years. The Christmas decorations I have that actually mean something to me – my sentimental baubles – are safely at home with my mum and dad, and seeing as though I do always spend Christmas there, I'd rather see them on their tree, at least until I have my own proper home and a family to share them with. Which, come on, does not seem likely any time soon.

What I have done over the last couple of days is my Christmas shopping. While I know that I could do it online, I much prefer to trail around the shops picking up things for people. Well, it's so easy to just click a few buttons and wait for something to arrive, right? Somehow, knowing that I braved the Christmas madness, queued and then carried everything I bought, it makes it feel as if I've really put in the effort, and my parents, my gran, my sister, her husband and my nephew all deserve it.

This is not only my last day in the office before Christmas, but my last working day of the year completely. Well, when you work almost the whole year without taking much holiday, you can give yourself a really generous Christmas break, and while Damian did try and convince me on a couple of occasions that he needed me to help him work between Christmas and new year, I had to put my foot down because it's the only time I get to see my family properly.

The office has a weird last-day-of-school vibe to it today. I don't know if Karen and Colin have collaborated but they are both dressed as Mr and Mrs Santa, in outfits so similar that I'm sure they must have come as a set. Ollie is wearing a plain black jumper with small, simple white lettering on it that says 'Error 404 – Christmas Jumper Not Found', which is exactly the kind of thing I'd expect from a geeky millennial like him. But while it might seem Scroogey, this is definitely him playing along. Of course, I'm only wearing my regular clothes because no one told me about the Christmas dress code for today, but that's no surprise – they never include me in anything.

Karen is wearing a long piece of red tinsel like a feather boa. When she spots me walking into the office she hurries over to me with a plate of mince pies.

'Hello, Sadie,' she says brightly.

'Erm, hi,' I reply. I narrow my eyes suspiciously.

'Mince pie?' she says.

'Oh, erm, thanks,' I say politely. 'But, it's strange, I've never really liked them.'

Karen looks almost offended, but she doesn't let her smile slip.

'How about you sit on Santa's lap?' Colin chimes in.

Oh, God, I'd like that even less.

I just laugh awkwardly.

'I'd, erm... I'd better get to work,' I tell them. 'Can't keep the boss waiting.'

I go to walk away but Karen steps in front of me.

'Oh, speaking of Damian,' she starts. Suddenly I realise she wants something. 'Any sign of our Christmas bonuses from him? He does like to give them in person...'

Oh, so that's why they're talking to me. Because they think I'll remind Damian about their Christmas bonuses. I could not feel less special right now – the only way this could have made me feel worse is if I were sitting on Colin's lap while she asked.

'I'll ask,' I say bluntly as I walk off.

Sure, they're not people I would usually hang out with in real life (although who is these days, apart from Damian and the occasional drink with Xara?) but it doesn't feel great to be excluded by them, to see them having a Christmas party without me, and somehow making things worse by trying to include me for a couple of minutes, but only so they can get their hands on their cash bonuses. I wonder if they treat Adam like such an outsider too. I can't wait to chat with him about it.

Thinking this just reminds me of how much I am looking forward to finally meeting up with him, so I hurry over to my desk, fling open the drawer and... nothing. There's nothing there. Not a card, not a Post-it, nothing. It's been a couple of days, and he did say something in his card about speaking again before we finished for Christmas so... oh God. Shit, I feel like such an idiot. He doesn't want to meet up with me – why would he? I'm just a girl he shares a desk with, someone he swaps Post-it Notes with to pass the time. Why did I ever think it was anything more than that? I'm so embarrassed I can feel my cheeks glowing red.

'Oh, Sadie, hi,' Damian says as he walks out of his office. 'Are you OK?'

'What? Yeah, I'm fine,' I reply, maybe a little too bluntly. I mentally remind myself I don't need to feel embarrassed in front of him; he doesn't know what a ridiculous weirdo I've been. 'Sorry, just... Christmas stress.'

'No worries,' he says. 'Did you see they're having a bit of a Christmas thing in there?'

'I did,' I reply. 'They made me a part of it for all of thirty seconds, while Karen offered me a mince pie and Colin border-line sexually harassed me, but only to remind me to remind you that they want their Christmas bonuses.'

'Those vultures,' he says with a smile. 'Well, I have them in here, but... can you step into my office for a second?'

'Yeah, sure,' I reply.

I can't help but feel as if my heart is heavy. The rejection hurts, even if it is someone I've never even met. Most of all I just feel so foolish. I'm usually so realistic and, what? Now here I am thinking I can fall for someone because we swapped a few notes? It just... I don't know, it sounds dumb now, but the connection just felt so real, as if it could go somewhere. But it wasn't going anywhere at all; it was just stationary.

My mood is immediately lifted the second I step into Damian's office.

'What's all this?' I ask.

The room is decked out with Christmas decorations and his desk is laid out with food. It's not unlike the celebrations going on in the main office, except the food looks much nicer here, and it's just me and Damian.

'It's, well, whatever they are doing out there, but in here and much better,' he says. 'I even stole some of their tinsel! Oh, and I know you hate mince pies, so these ones are just chocolate and caramel tarts. I've had two already – they're really good.'

'What's all this for?' I ask, still smiling.

'It's just like a "sorry I trapped you on a man-made island with a murderer" kind of thing,' he says.

'The pursuit of art,' I say with a shrug. 'This is lovely though, thank you. It's really cheered me up.'

'Are you sure you're OK?' he asks me as he points towards the sofa, gesturing for me to sit down.

'Yeah just... a weird day. I'll be fine,' I insist.

'Well, I'm trying not to be so stressed about work, so some Christmassy stuff seemed like a good idea. I'm thinking maybe if I just loosen up a bit, my creativity will come surging back.' Damian must notice the look on my face. 'I know, that sounds really lame and stupid, but anything is worth a try. And, before I go give that lot their bonuses, here is yours. Merry Christmas.'

'Thanks,' I say with a smile, opening the envelope. 'It's good to hear you so positive. Maybe that is what you need, to just forget about trying too hard, and let things come naturally. You're so brilliant and you have such a great ey— Oh my God!'

'Merry Christmas,' he says again with a big smile.

'Damian, this bonus is...' I stare down at it. 'This is a *bonus* bonus. This is so much – no wonder that lot out there are desperate for theirs.'

'That lot get nowhere near as much so don't go telling them,' he says quickly. 'But they don't work anywhere near as hard as you do.'

'I bought myself a really good Christmas present, like you told me,' I remind him. 'This is too much.'

'It's not even close to what you deserve,' he insists. 'So, you looking forward to Christmas?'

'I really am,' I say, my smile beaming even bigger now. With all this extra money I could stop at a few of the local shops back home and get some really fancy festive food to take with me. 'Are you?'

'I guess so,' he replies. 'What's the plan?'

'The plan?'

'Yeah, our plan,' he continues. 'What are we doing for Christmas?'

'Erm... *I'm* going home to see my family. What are you doing?' I reply. I'm so confused.

'Oh... I figured I'd be spending it with you,' he says, rather casually, given what he just said.

'Seriously?' I blurt.

'We do everything together,' he reminds me. 'Work together, eat together, hang out together.'

'Apart from when you have dates,' I remind him. 'Couldn't you get a Christmas date?'

'I guess everyone is with their families,' he says with a shrug.

I'm pretty sure we only eat together because we're usually still working together. It's not that I don't feel as if we're friends, I suppose we are, and I do really care about him but at the end of the day he does pay me.

'Aren't you going to see your family?' I ask. It was just after Christmas last year when I started working for Damian, so I don't actually know what he does to celebrate.

'Oh, no, I don't spend Christmas with them,' he replies. 'Didn't you send presents?'

He looks worried.

'I did, I just figured you'd be following them,' I reply. 'Why don't you spend Christmas with them? And I saw that invitation to their New Year's Eve party – I figured they were just being formal, sending you an invitation, not seeing if you'd turn up this year...'

'It's a whole thing,' he replies with a bat of his hand. 'Could I... could I not come with you? If not, I'll be home alone and we all know how that movie goes. I don't have any food in, any ability to cook...'

'Do you have any friends you could stay with?' I ask.

'No... but do single people in their thirties actually have friends in real life?' he asks. 'Is that not just a sitcom thing?'

'I have... a friend,' I say. 'Do you really not have anyone?'

I guess we're both always so busy. And as for Damian, he's so well known, everyone loves him, but he just doesn't trust people's motivation for being friends with him. I get it.

I watch Damian's face change. He must realise how seemingly ridiculous it is to ask your employee if you can spend Christmas with them... and how kind of sad it is too.

'Sorry, forget I said that,' he says quickly. 'That's crazy. I'll be fine on my own – I guess Christmas kind of snuck up on me. I'll be fine. I guess I just forget how much I rely on you, but I'm a big boy, I can spend a week on my own or whatever.'

It's more like two weeks but I don't point that out.

When I think about it, Damian's life is almost as empty as mine is. Maybe emptier. I suppose I'm so focused on my own that I don't stop to think about his. Sure, he goes on loads of dates, but the relationships never go anywhere, and his phone is always alive with messages, but I think even he is sick of the never-ending series of underwear shots he gets from hopeful models that have somehow got hold of his number. I used to think he gave it out, that he wanted all the attention that he got, but whenever I've been with him and he's opened a message, only to be confronted with a huge pair of fake boobs, he's always acted frustrated and wondered where they've got his number from. True or false, that's not the kind of girl who is going to take you home for Christmas with her family, is it? The kind of girl who would do something like this is... well... someone who feels incredible guilty over something.

'OK, well, why don't you come home with me for Christmas?' I suggest.

'What? Really?' he replies.

'Yeah, definitely, it will be great,' I insist. 'My mum is always cooking for a group of us anyway, there's loads of room, the Christmas activities are pretty intense but incredible fun. It's going to be great.'

That's twice I've said it's going to be great – I'm hoping if I say it enough times it will be true. God, what am I doing, inviting Damian home for the holidays with me? I don't know what I'm doing, but I know why. I feel guilty. So, so guilty. Not just at the thought of him spending Christmas alone, but also because I've been underplaying in my head just how much Damian does rely on me. I really am the only consistent person in his life, the person he's closest to. Sure, I'm just his assistant but I am always there. I was supposed to be giving my notice today and instead I'm inviting him home for Christmas! How could I give my notice now? After he's given me a huge bonus, a mini Christmas party, and he's told me he's going to be all alone for the foreseeable...

'That's amazing, Sadie, thank you so much,' he says, leaning over to wrap an arm around me, pulling me close for a half-hug. 'When do we leave?'

'I've got a train ticket booked for Sunday morning,' I tell him. It's Friday today.

'Oh, right, well, I'd better get ready,' he says, jumping to his feet.

Hmm. That's usually my job.

'OK,' is about all I can say.

I need to call my mum and explain anyway.

'Great, I'll just go toss this money to the vultures,' he jokes. 'Be right back.'

It's weird to see Damian so chipper and excited. He's never either of those things. He's usually quite dark and moody. It's good, I guess, I just feel bad. I tell you what, though, there's no way I can give my notice now, not until after Christmas. At least I can give him a good Christmas before I go, ending our working relationship on a high.

Anyway, I'm not just doing this for him, I'm buying myself some time too. Because I have absolutely no idea how I'm going to break the bad news to him.

18

The only thing weirder than Damian getting himself completely ready for our trip is the fact that he's coming with me at all, and that I'm talking about him as if he's a kid who just managed to tie his own shoes for the first time.

Still, I'm not about to knock it. I've packed so many bags for that man I was starting to think he didn't know how.

When Damian said he was going to pick me up from my flat I had a mini panic. Well, Damian lives in the posh bit of London, and my Chalk Farm flat in an old converted house has seen better days. Not old enough to look charming, but run-down enough to look like a poor man's haunted Disney attraction. The external white walls are covered with some kind of dried-up crawling plant, which almost makes it look like an abandoned building. Inside is super-fancy, it's just also super-tiny, and it's so, so expensive for what it is, but when Damian picks me up all he's going to see is the knackered old outside.

I did offer to meet him at King's Cross – being no stranger to public transport – but he insisted on picking me up at home so I said I'd meet him at the end of my road.

When Damian did turn up he was being driven – as usual – but this time he was in a massive Range Rover. His driver loaded my bags into an already pretty stacked boot before opening my door for me.

'Morning,' Damian said brightly. 'I brought you a coffee.'

I can smell the Starbucks wafting from the cupholder where the middle seat would usually be.

'Thanks,' I replied. 'Erm… are you really taking all that on the train?'

I asked as though they would even let him on a train with that much. He'd need extra tickets just for his luggage.

'Nah,' he said casually. 'I don't like trains. I figured we'd drive.'

'Drive?' I practically squeaked.

'Yeah, well, Martin is going to drive us,' he said, as though I hadn't already figured that out. 'And then he's going to go home to his family, with one hell of a Christmas bonus, and he's going to pick us up when we're done, whenever that is. It's way easier than the train.'

'For everyone but poor Martin,' I corrected him, well aware he can hear our conversation. 'And it takes much longer but… OK… sure.'

'It will be fun,' Damian insisted. 'I thought about a helicopter but, after we got back from the wedding, I'm pretty sure I heard you muttering something about "never-a-fucking-gain" as I pulled your fingernails out of my hand.'

He smiles. At least I'm amusing when I'm terrified.

* * *

Do you know what? Damian was right: it has been fun. We've been on the road for hours now, but it's been lovely. Sure, it takes more than double the time the train does, but it's nice to be so relaxed. Just having room to sprawl out, comfortable seats to snooze in – heated seats, no less. We stopped multiple times for bathroom breaks and bites to eat. We listened to music and played games and chatted in a way we don't often get chance to, just about everyday stuff – like what a kind of unusual year it's been for both of us, and how it's simultaneously felt really long and also gone in what feels like a heartbeat.

'We're nearly there,' I tell him. 'Less than fifteen minutes.'

'Why am I nervous?' he asks with an awkward laugh. 'I've never met anyone's parents. Well, I'm sure I've met parents before, but not *someone's* parents.'

'Hmm, you've never met an employee's parents before?' I say sarcastically. 'How odd this must be for you.'

Damian laughs.

'You've never brought a boss to meet your family before?' he asks.

'I've never taken *anyone* to meet them,' I say. 'And the problem with that is that I don't know if they're weird... I don't think they're weird. No weirder than me.'

'You said they take Christmas pretty seriously,' Damian says. 'Dare I ask a little more about that?'

'Christmas in the Kirke household is like a military operation,' I tell him. 'We have our traditions, our weird quirks, and then there's all the neighbourhood stuff...'

'Neighbourhood stuff?' Damian interrupts.

'Well, to be honest, it's the whole town,' I say. 'Everyone takes Christmas very seriously. We even have our own Winter Wonderland – although it's nothing like Hyde Park's, it's much smaller, and much more... local.'

'Local,' Damian echoes. 'What do you mean lo—?'

'Erm,' we hear Martin say from the front of the car. That's never a good noise to hear from a driver, is it?

'What's wrong?' Damian asks.

'The satnav, I think,' Martin says. 'It's telling me to drive out into the sea...'

'Oh, gosh, are we so close already?' I say, looking out of the window. 'Sorry, I didn't think. I guess because I was supposed to be arriving much earlier. The causeway is closed.'

'The what?' Damian says. 'The causeway?'

'Yeah, sorry, I didn't think to mention it,' I say as I mess with my phone. 'I grew up on a tidal island.'

'A tidal island?' Damian says.

'Is there an echo in this car?' I joke. 'You know, a tidal island. As the tide comes and goes it cuts us off from the rest of the town.'

'I have never heard of that,' Damian says firmly. 'Is that real?'

'They're definitely real,' Martin says with a laugh. 'I just didn't realise we were going to one. I just keyed the postcode in earlier but I can see it now – we're at Hope Island.'

'We don't have to wait long. It says here it should be open in the next thirty minutes,' I tell them. 'We just need to hang tight until then.'

'I reckon the Range Rover could get through that water, you know,' Martin reasons. 'Shall we chance it?'

'Oh, God, please don't,' I insist. 'Seriously, it is such a big deal here.'

'How deep can it be?' Damian asks.

'You'd be surprised,' I tell him. 'At high tide the water can be six-feet deep. The road is a mile long, which doesn't seem far, but people get stuck in the middle all the time – maybe every couple of months.'

'What happens when someone gets stuck?' Damian asks curiously.

'The coast guard has to rescue them,' I tell him. 'It only takes a couple of feet for cars to float.'

'You know so much about this,' Damian points out, almost amused.

'Seriously, they taught us all about it at school, so we always took it seriously, mostly because the school is on the mainland side, so many of us would have to cross it multiple times a day,' I tell him. 'They even taught us this cringey rhyme to remember the key facts.'

'Obviously we need to hear it,' Damian insists.

'Oh, God, no,' I say quickly. 'Small-town school is so weird. The headteacher, Mrs Snowball, used to come up with these awful, embarrassing rhymes for everything.'

'Your headteacher was called Mrs Snowball?' Damian says in disbelief.

I nod. I could tell so many stories about Mrs Snowball – she isn't as wholesome as she sounds. I remember, back when I was at school, she seemed like a giant. Her short, sharp, dark bob put me in mind of Cate Blanchett's Irina Spalko character from *Indiana Jones and the Kingdom of the Crystal Skull*, but with *big* Miss Trunchbull from *Matilda* energy. She was so sickly sweet but so blatantly evil. I was so pleased to see the back of her when I left primary school, but even more delighted as a teenager when a photo of her as a student did the rounds. She was protesting something – and getting arrested – and most notably she didn't have a bra on. You can't put a price on discovering that kind of dirt on the teachers who terrorised you.

'Come on, we've got half an hour to kill – tell us the causeway rhyme,' Damian begs. 'Martin wants to hear it, don't you, Martin?'

'I kind of do,' he admits sheepishly.

'Ergh, OK, let's see, how did it go?' I babble. I'm only pretending I don't remember it as a stalling technique because I absolutely don't want to do this. I do remember it though – I remember it perfectly. It's weird, isn't it, how we can be so forgetful in so many ways about such important things, but we can recall every dumb song they taught us at school? I'll tell them; they might get a kick out of it.

'So it went something like... Six foot at the highest part of the tide. Five is the minutes it takes for the drive. Four-by-fours still find it hard. Three thousand pounds it costs the coast-guard. Two times a day is when we see the tide. One life would be wasted if you surely died.'

'Shit, that's dark,' Damian says through his laughter. 'And awful – does it really cost the coast guard three thousand pounds?'

'Two thousand pounds for a sea rescue, four thousand pounds for an air rescue... I suppose that's what the rhyme was getting at with three thousand pounds,' I reason.

'Well, yeah, let's just wait it out, then,' Damian says, still laughing. 'God, that's made my day. I can't believe it. I'm spending Christmas in *The Wicker Man*.'

'You asked to spend Christmas in *The Wicker Man*,' I remind him.

'Yes, I did,' he says. 'And I can't wait.'

As we turn onto the street where my parents live it is just starting to get dark out. This means that everyone's Christmas lights should be switching on right... about... now. Wow, I didn't think that would work. As predictable as ever, the entire street's joint Christmas-lights effort has come to life, like clockwork, and right as we are driving along it – what a fantastic way to see it for the first time.

'Is this for us?' Damian asks with a laugh, his faced pressed up against the glass, with all the excitement of a child at... well... Christmas.

'I'm worried you didn't quite believe me when I said that my family takes Christmas very seriously,' I say. 'Every year everyone on this street works together – and yet still low-key competes with each other – to have these epic Christmas-light displays in their garden. It's all for a good cause though. Tourists and locals all come to see the displays. There's even a secure collection box at the end of the road, so that people can donate money – last year they were raising funds for a local hospice.'

'I can't believe this is someone's real life,' Damian says.

'You literally left your multimillion-pound bachelor pad to chill out at a five-star sea resort with a serial killer and a bunch of models. You definitely have the least believable life.'

'Maybe,' he says with a laugh. 'But this is pretty cool too.'

'That's my parents' house over there,' I tell Martin.

'The one with the Santa Claus statue outside?' Damian asks.

'Erm, not exactly,' I say, feeling just a little awkward. Maybe my family *is* weird. 'That's not a Santa Claus statue, that's my dad.'

'Ho, ho, ho,' my dad bellows so loudly you can hear him from inside the car. He's ringing a big golden bell – one that is older than I am but still packs a really loud chime. My dad would always dress up as Santa Claus when my sister and I were kids. As we got older, even long after we stopped believing in Santa Claus, he would still dress up in his trusty old red suit and welcome us home as Old St Nick. I don't think he was showing any signs of growing tired of it but now that Selena has Ben, well, he'll definitely keep doing it until he's old enough to stop believing. Not that I mind. It's quite the welcome home.

'You know that Christmas song that's about stepping into Christmas?' Damian says.

'Erm... "Step into Christmas" by Elton John? That one?' I reply.

'That's the one,' he says, either not detecting or completely ignoring my sarcasm. 'I feel like I just did that.'

'Ho, ho, ho,' my dad says as Martin helps us up the driveway with our bags – most of them are Damian's and God knows what he's got in them. 'Did you boys and girls get caught by a closed causeway?'

'We did indeed,' I say as I reach forward to kiss him on his cheek. His plastic beard makes my face itch.

'So, two extra for Christmas, is it?' my dad asks, finally breaking character.

'Oh, no, I'm not staying,' Martin insists quickly. Yes, because *that* would be weird.

'Dad, this is Damian. Damian, this is my dad, Eric,' I introduce them.

The two of them shake hands in that manly way men do.

'Great to meet you, lad,' my dad says. I swear he always sounds more northern when he's talking to other men.

'You too,' Damian replies. 'That's a great suit you've got there. You've even got the fake belly.'

My dad's face falls.

'That's… that's not a fake,' my dad says sadly.

'Oh, shit,' Damian blurts. 'Shit, sorry, I…'

'I'm just joking,' my dad says, putting him out of his misery. 'Of course, it's fake. Although, I suppose it is my belly – I did pay for it.'

You can practically see the relief surging through Damian's veins.

'Oh, my God, you had me there,' Damian says as he exhales. 'I thought I'd offended you and sworn at you within thirty seconds of meeting you.'

My dad laughs to himself as he grabs a few bags and heads for the front door.

'Don't worry about the swearing,' he reassures him. 'We're always shit-ing and fuck-ing in this house.'

'He doesn't mean that as bad as it sounds,' I whisper to Damian. 'I hope…'

'OK, boss, I'll be off,' Martin says with a big smile. You can tell he's amused by all of this.

'Yeah, sure,' Damian says, suddenly sounding a little uneasy. 'I'll be in touch after Christmas.'

'It's not too late to turn back,' I tell him. 'You could get in Martin's car and go home...'

'Nope, I'm here now. No turning back,' he says before taking a deep breath.

Honestly, I think he was less nervous about meeting the murderer.

20

'You actually got here just in time for dinner,' my dad says as he helps us up the stairs. 'Mum is just putting the finishing touches on it – Selena is probably putting out the fire.'

Damian knows that this one is a joke and laughs accordingly.

'I figure I'll show you to your rooms – just in case Sadie has forgotten where her room is. Then we can go get you introduced to everyone. See if you still want to stay.'

'Sounds great,' Damian says.

'Right, Damian, you're in our Selena's old room. Grandma is in the spare room and I didn't think you'd want to bunk up with her,' my dad continues – he *never* stops. When his mum died he cracked a joke during her eulogy. She would have loved it though.

'Oh, boy,' is about all Damian can say as he steps into Selena's old room. I don't think I've ever heard the words 'oh, boy' come out of his mouth but if Selena's room is how I remember it... yep.

'Sorry about all the eyes on you,' my dad says. 'She went through a bit of a phase.'

In the years before Selena moved out, probably when she was about sixteen to eighteen, she was absolutely obsessed with the boyband Blue. I was never a Blue fan; I always thought I was way cooler than that (I wasn't, I was going through a Marilyn Manson phase at the same time, but I had the good sense to take my posters down at some point), but honestly Selena was absolutely obsessed. She thought she was going to marry Lee Ryan – in fact, I bet deep down she probably still does.

Every inch of Selena's bedroom wall is covered with posters of Blue, so many, in fact, that I don't even remember what kind of wallpaper she had. As if that isn't creepy enough, she actually has a large poster of Lee Ryan on the ceiling above her bed.

'Dad, I really don't think Selena would mind if you took these down,' I say. 'She's married with a kid – I really don't think she's coming back.'

'Ah, but if I take them down that wouldn't be anywhere near as embarrassing for her, would it?' He chuckles. 'I don't want her forgetting, no matter how old she gets, or how well she's doing, that she glued a poster from *Top of the Pops* magazine to a dodo.'

Damian looks horrified until I turn him towards Selena's desk chair. Sitting on it is a stuffed dodo with a poster of Lee Ryan's face stuck on it. Still pretty bad, but it could be much worse.

'Are you going to be OK sleeping in here?' I ask.

'Ah, he'll be fine,' my dad insists. 'He's made his bed. Now he has to sleep with Blue in it.'

It's probably pretty weird that my dad is still fully dressed as

Santa Claus. Damian has been chatting away with him and still has no idea what he looks like.

'Are you going to ditch the outfit for dinner?' I ask him.

'And eat in the nip?' he shrieks. 'Yeah, will do. I'll just go get the rest of Damian's bags.'

'Oh, they're gifts for you guys,' Damian says. 'I didn't want to turn up empty-handed, so I picked up a couple of Harrods hampers. There's bound to be something everyone likes in them.'

'Oh, that's very good of you,' my dad says. 'We'll get stuck into them after dinner. For now, you two offload your junk, I'll get my kit off, and then we'll go eat dinner. How's about it?'

'Sounds great,' I say with a smile. It might be weird to have Damian here with me but it's so good to be home and I am still so impossibly excited for Christmas. I can't wait to see Damian's face when he sees what we've got lined up for him.

'Are you going to be OK sleeping in here?' I ask him once we're alone.

'I'm trying to remember... I think it was one of Blue who punched me at a Christmas party... or was that one of...' Damian thinks for a second '... Blazin' Squad maybe? Whoever it was it was long after they'd outstayed their showbiz welcome. Either way, yes, I'm fine sleeping with them watching over me. I probably won't hug the dodo though.'

'A wise choice,' I say. 'OK, well, I'll just ditch my stuff in my room and we can go get some food.'

'Can I get a peep into your room?' he asks curiously.

'Later,' I tell him. 'But you'll be disappointed. I took all the embarrassing stuff out of mine. That's the joys of being the second child – you get to see what to do, what not to do, and so on.'

'I know that's right,' Damian says. 'I was the eldest. Everything was a battle for me. I paved the way for Si to have it easy.'

'Who did Si have on his walls?' I ask.

Damian really doesn't talk all that much about his family – especially not his brother Simon – and now, with him not wanting to spend Christmas with them, he's got me wondering.

'Oh, it will have been some Aston Palace player,' he says with a tone that suggests he got that wrong on purpose. 'He's a lads' lad.'

'And what are you?' I ask curiously.

'I think my dad thinks I'm some soft creative who doesn't like to get his hands dirty,' he says. 'Anyway, dinner.'

'Yes, dinner,' my dad interrupts as he reappears in the doorway, suddenly looking like himself again.

Eric Kirke is sixty-three years old and still gets mistaken for a man in his late forties – something he is incredibly proud of. He's tall, slim, and doesn't appear to have a grey hair on his head. My mum always makes jokes about him dying it but I don't think he does. It was so annoying, growing up, with all my friends thinking I had a hot dad. And yet he's this big nerd who cracks terrible jokes.

'I know what you're thinking – is this her dad or her brother?' my dad jokes.

'You're going to need to brace yourself for a lot of dad jokes,' I tell him. 'My dad wrote the book on them.'

'My dad cracks a lot of dad jokes too,' Damian replies.

'No, my dad literally wrote the book,' I say. 'He writes joke books.'

'That's pretty good, darling,' my dad says as he pats me on the shoulder.

'Cheers,' I reply with a smile.

His dad jokes might be relentless but I'd much rather he

bring this job home than his previous gig – he used to be an army sergeant.

'OK, I'll say it again,' my dad says with a big old dad clap of his hands – the kind that makes your ears ring for a few seconds. 'Dinner time.'

We arrive in the dining room just in time to find everyone already sitting at the table and my mum placing the last piece of best china down. Dinner is already on the table, in the fancy white dishes with the lids. We never get the lids, not unless we have company. Selena and I chipped one when we were kids (there is some disagreement over whose fault it was but, if we get into that, we'll argue until the new year) and my mum decided then and there that we could never be trusted with them for the rest of our lives. Watch, I bet she won't let either of us touch them today.

'Oh, hello,' my mum says brightly, whipping off her pinny as if she's in a Bucks Fizz tribute band. Actually, she wouldn't look out of place in the line-up, with her voluminous bright blonde hair. Unlike my dad, my mum has had a little intervention from the hairdressers but I honestly don't know many people over sixty who aren't grey. I'm pretty sure I've got a few already. 'You must be Damian.'

'No, it's your daughter, Sadie,' my dad tells her slowly and loudly.

He... does... not... stop.

My mum has learned to completely ignore his jokes. She's managed to engage some part of her brain to just straight up filter them out.

'Welcome to our home,' my mum says, 100 per cent putting on airs because she knows that Damian is a big deal, in art circles at least.

'Thanks so much for having me,' he says.

'Please, take a seat,' my mum insists. 'Eric will get you introduced to everyone while Sadie and I grab the gravy.'

'Erm, OK,' I say, following her to the kitchen.

Once we're alone my mum hugs me.

'So good to see you, my darling,' she says. 'I just can't believe you brought your boss.'

My mum knows everything. She knows how much I've been wanting to change my job, how much Damian can drive me crazy. She also knows that I'm quitting, that I chickened out of giving my notice, and that I felt so guilty I invited my boss home for Christmas. To be honest, when I told her I was bringing him, she just sounded excited.

'I always thought if you brought someone home for Christmas it would be a boyfriend.' She laughs. 'Or a girlfriend. Just not, you know, your boss. Then again, if I had such a good-looking boss, I'd take him everywhere with me too.'

'I don't take him everywhere with me,' I insist. 'If anything he takes me everywhere with him.'

'Maybe he has the crush on you,' she teases.

'Hardly,' I reply, perhaps a little too loudly. I quickly lower my voice. 'If he did he wouldn't have me intervening in all his dates.'

'Or maybe he would,' she says with a wink. 'Anyway, let's go back through.'

'Do you need me to carry the gravy?' I ask, noticing two fancy jugs of gravy on the worktop in front of her.

'Of course not,' she replies firmly. 'You're mad if you think I'm letting you get your hands on my jugs.'

We head back into the dining room where my dad has just about finished introducing everyone to Damian.

'And this beautiful creature is Susie, *my wife*,' he says. He says 'my wife' in Borat's voice, which is either a seriously dated reference that needs retiring, or so out of touch it's actually even funnier to say now.

Damian is sitting next to Ben, my nephew.

'What's your best turnip price?' Ben asks him.

'Five hundred and thirty bells,' Damian replies. 'Yours?'

'Four hundred and eighty bells,' Ben replies.

I know kids like to talk gibberish, but I never thought I'd hear Damian humouring a six-year-old. My face must show how confused I am.

'Animal Crossing,' Selena tells me by way of an explanation as she reaches to lift the lid off the dish in front of her. My mum lightly slaps her hand with a slotted spoon, stopping her in her tracks. Selena just rolls her eyes. 'I didn't think you'd be bringing someone here who could talk video games with Ben.'

'Saves me pretending I know what I'm talking about,' her husband, Mark, chimes in. 'I'm pretty sure my son has a mortgage from a racoon.'

I'm sure that makes sense to someone, somewhere. It clearly makes sense to Damian because he laughs.

'Can I visit your island?' Ben asks him.

'Of course, you can,' Damian replies. 'I didn't bring my Switch with me but I'll invite you as soon as I get home.'

'I've got mine,' Ben tells him. 'I'll show you mine after dinner.'

'Can't wait,' Damian replies. Then he looks at me and laughs. Probably at my face – I don't know what it's doing but this is honestly all so surreal.

'You doing all right, sis?' I ask.

'Yeah, you?' she asks with a cheeky smile. She also knows everything. I think everyone might know everything, to be honest... everyone but Damian.

'Dinner smells great,' Damian says.

'Thank you,' my mum replies as she removes the lids from the serving dishes. 'We always have a Christmas dinner dry-run before Christmas.'

'But we have sausages, instead of turkey, so we don't completely ruin the main event,' I joke.

'It's Susie's practice run,' my dad says. 'So she doesn't muck it up on the day.'

'I have never mucked up a dinner in my life,' my mum insists. 'But I do like to have a go at the vegetables, make sure my timing is right.'

'A dry-run so we don't get dry spuds, if you like,' my dad says.

'Well, two Christmas dinners sounds better than one to me,' Damian enthuses.

'Let me serve you,' my mum says. 'Carrots? Peas? Potatoes?'

'Yes, please,' Damian replies.

'Yorkshire puddings? I know not everyone thinks they belong with a Christmas dinner, but we are *in* Yorkshire. What about parsnips?'

'Do I like parsnips?' Damian asks me.

'Does she chew your food for you too?' my dad jokes.

Damian looks a little embarrassed. I don't think he thought it was weird that his assistant would be doing a better job at keeping track of what foods he does and doesn't like.

'Yes, you like parsnips,' I tell him with a smile and a friendly nudge of my elbow.

My mum serves everyone – which I think is a combination of trying to seem fancy because Damian is here and of course the lifetime ban on my sister and me touching the crockery – as we make small talk among ourselves.

'Have you told Damian all about how we celebrate Christmas?' my mum asks right before popping a carrot into her mouth. You can see the look of relief on her face when she realises it's perfect – she shouldn't worry so much. My mum has been a housewife for at least the past thirty years. It's safe to say she's amazing at everything.

'Yes, I've told him how intensely we celebrate Christmas,' I say. 'But I haven't got into the ins and outs.'

'We have lots of weird and wonderful traditions for what we call our Five Days of Christmas,' my mum explains. 'On day one we go for a walk around the island, and the town, delivering Christmas cards. We split up into teams, take a pile of cards each, and the winning team gets a prize. Day two is Dickens Day.'

'Dickens Day?' Damian says.

'The less you know about Dickens Day, the easier it will be to go through with it,' Mark reassures him. Poor Mark, roped into all our weird family traditions. At least Damian only has to do all of this once. Mark has married into it.

'Day three is preparation day. We make sure everything is ready, all presents are wrapped, all food is stocked up, and so on. Day four – which is Christmas Eve – we visit the Winter Wonderland during the day, and in the evening we go to the cinema.'

'We've got this gorgeous old cinema on the seafront,' I tell him. 'Every Christmas Eve they screen *It's a Wonderful Life*. The place absolutely packs out. And everyone is invited to go in their pyjamas, so it isn't weird to see lots of people walking around ready for bed on Christmas Eve.'

'Oh wow,' Damian blurts. 'When you said there was lots going on you really meant it. What happens on Christmas Day?'

'Oh, Christmas Day is just Christmas Day,' my mum says.

'We exchange presents, have dinner, play games. Do you have any family traditions?'

'Erm, not really,' Damian replies awkwardly. 'Just all the usual stuff.'

'Do you have any non-English heritage?' my dad asks curiously. 'You know how lots of us, if you go back enough, usually have family from somewhere else. Different cultures have some fascinating traditions.'

'My dad wrote the book on that too,' I tell him. 'Christmas traditions around the world. He writes all kinds of novelty books.'

'Christmas is so different in so many places, as you'd expect,' my dad starts. 'In Italy, traditionally, their presents are brought by a witch, not Santa Claus. My favourite story – and, you know, take these things with a pinch of salt, of course – a particularly dark Christian tale... La Befana was just a normal woman whose child died. Then, when she heard about the birth of Jesus, mad with grief she convinced herself that he was her child.'

'Dad,' Selena shrieks. 'Not in front of Ben!'

'It has a happy ending,' he insists. 'She met him, gave him gifts, and in return he made her the mother of every child in Italy. So La Befana brings the presents. There are a few versions but that's my favourite.'

'I think I had a great-great-great-granddad who was from Iceland,' Damian says. 'Maybe even a couple more greats, actually. My mum did one of those family tree things online.'

'Ah, Iceland,' my dad says excitedly. 'Have you heard of the Yule Cat? Another traditional Christmas folklore character that is really quite dark. The Yule Cat is a huge, vicious creature that lurks in the snowy countryside, just waiting to devour people who haven't received new clothes to wear for Christmas. In some rural societies, employers would reward members of their household with new garments and sheepskin shoes. So really, if you didn't do good work in the run-up to Christmas, you might get devoured by the Christmas cat.'

'Well, I'd be in big trouble,' Damian says. 'I'm way behind on my work.'

'You've got your cameras with you, right?' I remind him. 'Maybe just going through the motions will inspire you.'

'And if not, it's the cat,' my dad says menacingly.

'OK, enough talking about witches and vicious cats over dinner,' my mum insists.

A perfectly normal thing to say over practice Christmas dinner.

I don't even think Ben is listening to us, he's too busy playing with his food. I do love to hear my dad's weird stories – and his terrible jokes, if I'm being honest – I find it all so fascinating. Damian seems to be really fascinated by them too but that doesn't surprise me. I've always known that he's just a massive dork hiding beneath a cool exterior.

I really thought this was going to be weird, and awkward, and kind of embarrassing for me on both sides but everyone seems to be getting on really well, and Damian seems to be on board for anything.

Just wait until he finds out what Dickens Day is…

21

There is something so strange about waking up in your childhood bed. It's a real mixture of feelings, some good, some bad.

On the one hand it all comes flooding back from my school days. Waking up, seeing the faint outlines of the glow-in-the-dark stars on my ceiling, and either dreading going to primary school where I knew Mrs Snowball would make us all sing 'You Are My Sunshine' until we got it perfect, and throw our Lunchables in the bin because she didn't deem them healthy enough, right through to high school where worries shifted to how do I get out of PE today and did I revise enough for my science GCSE exam? But then there's the comfort of all the nice memories too. Being around my family, my mum bringing me boiled eggs to eat in my bed on a Saturday morning while I watched *The New Adventures of Superman* (I think Dean Cain in his spandex might have been my first crush) and *Live and Kicking*. I don't think I've ever had a bad Christmas here. Then again, I've never brought my boss home for Christmas, so this could be the first. Adam will not believe this, when I tell him about it – if I get the chance to tell him, that is. Thinking about Adam reminds me how spectacularly I have embarrassed myself. What's the best I can hope for, if we do get to swap a few more notes before I leave? Probably if we both pretend I never asked him out.

I pull myself out of bed and grab my dressing gown. Every Christmas my mum buys us new matching pairs of festive pyjamas and a big, fluffy dressing gown and leaves them on our beds. They are always impossibly Christmassy – perfect for wearing to the cinema on Christmas Eve – but this year, oh, boy, my mum really has gone for something dorky: elf pyjamas, and, no, not pyjamas with elves on them, but pyjamas that make you look as if you are dressed like an elf.

I'm slipping my robe on when I remember that Damian is here. I'm not about to go and have breakfast with him when I'm wearing pyjamas that make me look like an elf. Never mind that it feels kind of unprofessional, it's just completely weird.

Instead I take the time to get dressed and put on some make-up. Some boundaries need to be kept in place for this to not be too odd.

When I walk into the dining room everyone is already sitting at the breakfast table – including Damian, who is wearing a pair of elf pyjamas. The moment is so surreal I feel frozen on the spot. My boss... at my parents' table... in pyjamas... because he's here for Christmas...

'Good morning,' he says brightly through a mouthful of crumpet.

'Morning,' I say as I sit down next to him.

He washes it down with a swig of tea from a mug that says 'I'm on Santa's nice list' on it.

'How are you?' he asks.

It's so weird; there's this glimmer in his eye that I don't think I've ever seen before... It's as if he's right at home, relaxed, comfortable in a way I've never seen. I suppose what I'm trying to say is that having Damian here isn't weird at all, and *that's* weird. God, I need a cup of tea.

'Yeah, I'm good,' I say. 'You?'

'I'm great,' he replies. 'Slept really well, even though, even with the lights off, the lights outside were bouncing off Lee Ryan's face above me.'

'Such a relatable problem,' I reply with a smile.

'Anything you want for Christmas?' my mum asks me.

'Dial-a-Date,' I say in perfect synchronisation with my dad. They both knew I was going to say that.

'What's a Dial-a-Date?' Damian asks curiously.

'Dial-a-Date was a board game I wanted in the nineties. I asked Santa for it every year but he never brought me one,' I explain with a faux frown.

'Santa didn't think it was appropriate,' my mum says. 'It was basically like Guess Who? but instead of chaps with moustaches and glasses, it was hunky men in their twenties and thirties – in a game aimed at young girls.'

My mum shakes her head to herself as she dashes back to the kitchen.

'It had these cards with it, with different men on, and this fake phone that would give you details about your dream date. The aim of the game – like Guess Who? – was to try and narrow down who it was. The first player to guess right was the winner.'

'Well, you've got Matcher for that now,' my dad points out.

Yes, my dad knows what Matcher is. My dad knows all about dating apps because he compiled a book of dating app fails. It was a particular high point for me when he called up and asked if I had anything to contribute.

'Excited for the walk today?' my mum asks upon her return,

changing the subject as she puts another plate of Christmas-tree-shaped crumpets on the table. My dad immediately grabs one and starts flooding it with butter.

'You know it,' I reply. I mean, I'm not that excited. It's a walk – how exciting can it be? But my mum loves it, so I love it. 'I'll bet Dad is looking forward to being teamed up with his favourite child.'

'Well, with Damian being here, I thought you could team up with him this year,' my mum suggests. 'I'm putting your dad with Ben. Maybe he'll stand a chance of winning without you slowing him down.'

My dad and I exchange a brief, subtle knowing look. The reason we never win is because we would always get bored halfway through and sack it off for an hour to go to the pub.

'I'm quite competitive,' Damian says. 'Maybe I can help you win.'

'Maybe,' I say with a smile, although I doubt it. I've always preferred a leisurely walk taking in the scenery, rather than dashing around jamming cards through letterboxes like Postman Pat on speed.

'Darling, I know you've just sat down, but your sister should be here any second – can you go unlock the front door and give her a hand in? She's bringing Grandma.'

'Sure,' I say as I pull myself to my feet. 'Pop the kettle on for me coming back.'

I make my way from the dining room to the hall, admiring the Christmas decorations as I go. While outside may be a barrage of Christmas lights, inside is way more to my taste. Subtle shimmers of gold, delicate twinkling lights, and then there are the family portraits. All year round the walls in the hallway are decorated with framed family photos but, when Christmas comes along, my mum takes them all down in favour of the annual family Christmas group shots my parents have been taking since before Selena and I were born. It's nice, to be able to look back at Christmases over the years. First it was just my mum and dad, then a few with grandparents, then Selena pops up, then there's me. Other than a few teenage boyfriends the line-up stays pretty solid until Mark married into the family – then the grandparents start disappearing. It's sad to see my dad's parents, and my granddad on my mum's side no longer in the pictures but I'm so grateful for the pictures we do have with them, and all the good memories attached to them. I only need to look at the family portrait with my granddad George with a full jug of brandy butter all over his Christmas jumper to remember the incident with the skateboard that I'm sure you don't need me to spell out for you.

Selena is already knocking on the door by the time I get to it.

'Grandma,' I squeak excitedly the second I lay eyes on her.

I lean forward and hug all 5'1" of her.

'All right, all right,' she says. 'You'll squeeze my teeth out.'

My grandma Winnie is maybe the grumpiest lady you will ever meet but it's all a front. She likes to play it all moody and disapproving but I know that she's happy and that she loves us all – even my dad, although the two of them do love to pretend they're at war sometimes.

'You're walking good,' I tell her as she passes me.

'I'm knackered,' she replies.

'She and Mum are going to sit the walk out today,' Selena says. 'She's a bit achy today.'

'I'm achy every day,' she says as she heads for the dining room. 'I'm excited to meet this fella of yours though.'

'She knows the deal, right?' I ask Selena once we're alone.

'She does but she is completely convinced otherwise,' she says with a laugh. 'But she doesn't know about your Post-it boy.'

'Oh, God, let's never talk about that again,' I say quickly and quietly.

'Ooh, did something happen?' she asks. 'You have to tell me if something has happened because everything you've told me about it so far has been so incredibly dull.'

I glance over her shoulder to see if anyone can hear us.

'Mark and Ben are down the road looking at Gerry's inflatable snowman,' she assures me. 'Come on, spill.'

'Well, given that I was giving my notice and I knew we wouldn't be able to talk any more, I invited him out for a drink with me,' I admit.

'I can tell from the look on your face that you're not happy with the way things went...' she says with a wince.

'He didn't even reply, and I know that he was in the office, because he told me he would be,' I say. 'He just wasn't interested.'

'Do you know his last name?' she asks.

'I don't...'

'Well, try and find it out from Damian,' she suggests. 'We could look him up on Facebook and send him a message, see if he's OK – maybe he was off sick?'

'It's a good job you're married,' I tell her with a laugh. 'You'd be terrible at the dating game now. Doubling down and sending another message would be a terrible idea, and even more embarrassing. I could peep at his profile to see if he's married or has a girlfriend though – that might explain why he's ghosting me all of a sudden.'

'Speaking of Damian, how is he doing?' Selena asks. 'He's very good-looking – better than the pictures I looked at online. Hey, I saw you in one, from that wedding you went to.'

'Oh, really?'

'Yeah, you're in the background, sitting at a table, looking moody. Totally on-brand for you,' she teases.

'Har-har,' I say sarcastically. 'Anyway, Damian is great, just great. He's sitting at the table, dressed like an elf, eating crumpets with Mum and Dad like it's the most normal thing in the world.'

'And how is he finding sleeping in your room with the glow-in-the-dark stars?' she asks through a grin.

'Oh, Dad didn't put Damian in my room, he put him in yours,' I say.

I watch as the colour drains from her face before it comes rushing back bright red.

'Wait, what? He's... he's in my room?' she babbles.

'Yup,' I reply.

'I was fifteen when I put those posters up – does he know that?'

'I'm fairly sure you were seventeen,' I correct her. 'Don't worry, he found all the Blue stuff funny. You should talk to him. I'm pretty sure one of them punched him at a Christmas party.'

'God, so he's cool *and* hot,' she says with a sigh.

'Yes, it is both so cool and so hot to be punched by a boyband way past their best,' I say as seriously as I can.

'Does he look hot as an elf?' she asks.

'Selena, come on,' I say.

'I'm going to look,' she says excitedly as she dashes off to the dining room. She steps inside before poking her head back out. She nods wildly as she mouths the word 'yes'.

I follow her to find my grandma sitting next to Damian, smiling in that big, bright, beaming way she usually reserves for the likes of Des O'Connor.

'I like this one,' she calls over to me.

I just smile awkwardly. Damian laughs. He's loving the attention.

'Do you two want to grab the tea and some more cups from the kitchen?' my mum asks.

'I hope by "this one" she doesn't mean as opposed to Mark,' Selena whispers to me as we do as we're told.

'Except Mark was your boyfriend when she met him and we all know Damian is just my boss,' I whisper back.

'OK, but no one brings their boss home from Christmas,' she insists once we're alone in the kitchen. 'Who does that? No one does that.'

'Someone who feels really bloody guilty about leaving him in the lurch when he pretty much relies on her for everything,' I point out.

'I think maybe you like how much he depends on you,' she says. 'I think he likes it too.'

'Erm, you're a recruiter, not a psychologist,' I point out. 'Stop trying to make something out of nothing.'

'OK, but you did have a huge crush on him when you first started working for hi—' she starts but I don't let her finish.

'Selena, can you not?' I insist. 'That was a long time ago, before I knew him. I fancied the idea of him – just like everyone else does – but I know better now.'

'OK, fine, fine,' she says. 'I'll stop. But I'm your sister – we're supposed to say stuff like this to each other, and borrow each other's clothes...'

'Oh, God, if you start banging on about your black and red fishnet top from Tammy Girl from 2002...'

'*Did* you borrow it though?' she asks me with an irritated seriousness the conversation absolutely doesn't deserve.

'No, Selena, burglars with big slutty teenage girl energy

broke in and stole it, then broke in again and put it back. Of course I borrowed it. You need to move on.'

'Oh, yeah? Mentioned Dial-a-Date to Mum and Dad yet?'

'Just once,' I admit with a laugh. 'Come on, let's go back through. I'm desperate for a cup of tea. We'll be heading out delivering the cards soon.'

'I hear you're paired up with Damian,' she says. 'You going to show him all the sights?'

'Some of them,' I say.

'I'll be interested to hear which ones later,' she says with a smile.

'No romantic ones, if that's what you're getting at,' I reply as I follow her back to the dining room. Damian has one of his cameras with him now – an instant one that pops the pictures out of the front. He's taking my grandma's picture while she poses. Honestly, that smile. She never smiles like that.

'I was just telling Damian about the family Christmas portraits we take every year,' my mum tells me. 'Damian says he'll take it for us this year. Imagine – a genuine Damian Banks family portrait.'

'Imagine that,' I reply.

I smile at him, puzzled. I guess shooting that wedding must have softened him up a little because Damian has always been adamant that he isn't an event photographer, he's an artist, and he's always made a really clear distinction between the two.

Selena is right about him – he does look strangely attractive dressed as an elf. I suppose it's not so much the outfit itself, because that would be so very weird, but more how he looks in it. It's such a ridiculous, dorky outfit and he wears it as if it's a limited-edition Gucci suit. He isn't embarrassed or awkward; he's wearing those elf PJs with attitude. That's what's sexy about it.

I can't believe Selena called me out on having a crush on him before I really knew him. That's not cool – we all make mistakes. But as I watch him with his arm around my gran, showing her the snap he just took of her, seeing that smile on her face... Bringing Damian home for Christmas certainly wasn't a mistake. At least I can say that.

22

The Kirke family Christmas-card-posting race is nothing if not fair. Well, fair-ish.

My mum writes the cards and then separates them into two piles: on the island and on the mainland. Everyone gets the same number of cards for each location. Rumour has it she's been known to add or remove people from her Christmas-card list to keep the game fair, but I can't actually verify that.

Teams are normally me and my dad, my mum and my gran, and then Selena, Mark and Ben all work together. Today things are different. My mum and gran are sitting it out, Selena and Mark are going it alone, and my mum must deem Ben old enough to be paired with my dad – although he isn't old enough to sneak off to the pub. Maybe my mum is on to us. And there's me and Damian.

When you grow up in a tourist town almost everything about it is totally wasted on you. None of it seems remarkable. A tidal island is a true wonder of nature but, when you grow up on one, it just makes you annoyed that you can't just go over to play at your friend's house because the bloody sea has cut you off from civilisation.

Now that I'm an adult though – and an adult who lives in a big city – coming home is a genuine treat. Everything captivates me. And it's nice having Damian with me, and showing an interest. I'm having fun talking him through all the sights.

We're over on the mainland, at the top of the main street that leads down to the coast.

Damian climbs onto a wall, looking out to sea.

'What's that, over on the island?' he asks.

I follow his gaze.

'The Hope Island abbey ruins,' I tell him. 'I can take you there – it's great for taking photos.'

'You never told me you grew up somewhere so perfect,' he says.

'I guess we don't usually talk too much about our personal lives,' I remind him. 'And you didn't strike me as the kind of guy who likes wholesome village-y stuff.'

'I like you, don't I?' he jokes. 'And you're technically wholesome village-y stuff.'

'I guess I am.' I laugh. 'Or maybe I used to be, before city life corrupted me.'

'Nah, you've always seemed a little different to everyone else, to me at least.'

I'm not sure if he's complimenting me there or if I should be offended.

Damian raises his camera to his eye to snap a picture of the scenery. I'm trying to encourage him to take loads of pictures to try and reignite his passion in the hope it will inspire the last-minute change of direction he is in desperate need of if he's going to go ahead with his preview in February.

'Oh, quick,' I say, noting the couple sitting on a bench

across the road. 'We can shave ten to fifteen minutes off our time.'

Damian hops down and dutifully follows me across the road where Clara and Henry – a couple in their late sixties who I've known all my life – are wrapped up nice and warm, sitting on the bench.

'Hello,' I say brightly.

'Sadie, hello,' Clara replies. 'Home for Christmas, without fail. And with a handsome man too?'

'Oh, this is Damian,' I say. 'He's just my—'

'Just her friend,' Damian interrupts.

I smile at him. That's probably a much better thing to start telling people.

'How modern,' she says. 'Anyway, how are you, love?'

'I'm doing good, thanks. I have your Christmas card from the Kirkes,' I say as I hand it over.

'Trying to win the race this year, huh?' Henry says with a wink.

'Nah, just make it end faster,' I admit.

'That's a fancy-looking camera,' Henry says to Damian. 'You take a lot of pictures?'

'Damian is a really good photographer,' I tell him.

'Oh, yeah? Fancy taking our picture?' Henry asks.

'Oh, leave them alone,' Clara says.

'I'd love to,' Damian insists as he lines up his shot. Even though it's just a snapshot for a couple on the street he treats it with all the care and attention he would a serious photoshoot. He lines up the shot, messes with the settings on his camera, twists the lens to focus, and then... snap. Lots of photographers like to take multiple shots and pick the best one. Damian almost always likes to take just one. He likes his photos to capture the moment. Not the moment after the moment.

'That looks great,' Damian says as he checks the picture. He holds up his camera screen for them to see.

'Oh, wow,' Clara says. 'You can tell a professional took it.'

'I can send you it, if you like?' Damian suggests. 'Do you have an email address?'

'Certainly do,' Henry replies proudly before telling Damian what it is so he can type it into his phone.

'I'll get this sent over to you later,' he tells him.

'Thanks,' Henry says. 'It's been years since we had a good picture together.'

'Well, we'd better get back to posting these cards,' I tell him. 'Don't tell my mum we didn't put it through your door.'

'Your secret is safe with us, love,' Clara says.

'It really is a great shot.' Damian shows me as we walk down Main Street. 'With the Christmas arch behind them and the way they just look so happy together.'

'Wow, that is great,' I tell him. 'Just keep taking great pictures until you get those feelings you get when you know what you want to do.'

It's such a weird process to explain but Damian hates everything he does until he doesn't.

'Yeah, well, I need to get a move on with my work,' he starts. 'Or I'll be getting a visit from the evil Christmas cat.'

I laugh.

'The Yule Cat,' I remind him. 'Don't worry, if the worst comes to the worst, I'll get you a new coat to keep the cat away.'

Damian smiles and then looks down at his camera screen again.

'They really are a cute couple,' he says. 'I can't quite put my finger on what it is, but I love this photo.'

'They're both so lovely,' I tell him. 'They own a cafe. I would always love going when I was younger because their chicken nuggets were the closest thing you could get to a McDonald's locally. They've actually had a really difficult life. They were boyfriend and girlfriend when they were at school, until Henry's dad, who was in the army, moved the whole family somewhere else. They moved back just in time to become teenage sweethearts – right before Henry joined the army. They had years of almost being together. Henry got quite badly hurt and wound up moving back here to be close to his family – and who was the nurse they hired to take care of him until he got back on his feet? Clara. They finally got together, gave up their jobs to open the cafe they'd always talked about, got married, started a family and the rest is history.'

'That's what it is,' he says. 'That's what I can see in the pictures. Their history. They wear it in their smiles and their scars and look how happy they are. When I looked into Mackie's eyes in the photos I took I just saw a dark, empty void. There was nothing to see but darkness – and I still wanted to look away. But in this picture... there's love.'

'Well, love is easier to find than an interesting portrayal of a wife murderer,' I point out. 'Mackie is just a dark hole – whether he did it or not, there's nothing to see when you look at him.'

Damian stops on the spot.

'I should be capturing love,' he announces. 'Not hate, not poverty, not abuse. I've done enough of that. Maybe it's time I showed people something new? Maybe that's why I'm struggling. I need something fresh. Oh, come on, don't laugh at me, Sadie.'

'I'm not laughing at you,' I tell him. 'I'm laughing at one hell of a coincidence.'

'Oh, yeah, what's that?' he asks.

'The date your preview is due to open,' I say, but it doesn't trigger anything.

'What's the date?'

'February 14th,' I remind him. 'Valentine's Day.'

'OK, that's it, it's a sign. I'm doing it. I'm capturing true love – and not just romantic love; I want families, people with their dogs, people doing things that they love, so long as it's real.'

'I like it,' I tell him. 'No, wait, I love it.'

Damian shuffles on the spot a little.

'Is it too much of a departure?' he asks. 'Will people think I've gone soft? That I've lost my edge?'

'Look at that photo again and you tell me.'

'I love it,' he says.

'Well, there you go, the Yule Cat isn't going to be eating you this Christmas,' I say with a smile.

I'm not only happy that Damian has found an idea, but I'm also so relieved I'm not going to be leaving him in the lurch, struggling with work, with no idea what he's going to do. I am, maybe, just a little bit disappointed though. Well, in my year working with him, this was going to be my first show with him, and, annoyingly, I'm really excited about it now that it actually feels as if it's going to happen. I've never seen him this excited about any of his ideas yet; this one feels different. It's a shame I won't get to see it through.

'In fact, it sounds like you've done good work, so let's go try some clothes on,' I say, edging towards Pandora's Boutique.

'But what about the race? Don't you want to win?' he replies.

'The prize is a trap. The winner gets to dress the table for Christmas dinner. The prize is *work*! We usually let my mum win, because she thinks it's a genuine honour and way more fun than it is, but with her not joining in, the real winners will be the ones who don't arrive home first.'

Damian laughs.

I won't tell him that the last team to return home has to wear dorky Christmas accessories to the cinema on Christmas Eve. I'll just try and make sure we're not home first, but not home last either.

'Your mum is great,' he says. 'OK, sure, let's see what this shop has to offer.'

'I absolutely love it here,' I tell him as we head for the door. 'I get loads of my cool, vintage stuff here. Either when I visit home or through their eBay shop. They get some really amazing stuff – stuff I could never afford but, when I'm home, it means I can at least try on the things I can't afford. I suppose you won't know the joy of doing that.'

'Well, I'll try on a dress that I couldn't possibly wear with my manly, hairy legs – if that makes you feel better?' he jokes.

'That sounds fair,' I reply.

'Stranger,' Erin says the second she claps eyes on me. She hurries out from behind the counter to give me a squeeze. This is either because I'm her biggest customer, or because we're old friends. Probably the latter.

'Hello,' I say. 'How are you?'

'I'm great, I'm great,' she replies. 'Ugh, this girl never lets me down, in here every Christmas, putting food on my family's table – and by family, I mean cats.'

Damian laughs. I don't think he knows what to say.

'Look at me, talking to you like I know you,' she tells him with a laugh as she runs a hand through her big, curly purple hair.

Erin, who owns the shop, is probably somewhere in her forties. She's a petite 5'3" but what she lacks in height she more than makes up for in accessories. Looking exactly as you would expect someone who owns a vintage boutique to, Erin is so cool, with a style that is completely her own. For Erin it's all about intentional clashing. Mixing gold with silver, patterns with completely different patterns – basically breaking all of the rules we're told we are supposed to follow.

'This is Damian,' I say. 'Damian, this is Erin.'

'And is he with you or did you bring him for me?' she asks with a wiggle of her eyebrows.

'He's with me,' I reply, but then I catch myself. 'Well, he's here with me, but he's not with-me with me.'

Smooth, Sadie. Really smooth.

Erin just laughs.

'Well, you know where the good stuff is. I trust you alone up there,' she says with a wink. 'Ring the bell if you need me.'

'Will do, thank you,' I say before turning to Damian. 'This way.'

I lead him to the back of the shop where there's a doorway that leads up a very narrow staircase. The top floor is where Erin keeps the good stock – the things she doesn't display on the shop floor because they sell online. Also up here is all the new stock, so I can have my pick of all of it before she puts it out, which is like a dream come true. Shopping is one of the main things I miss the most about living here. Oh, after my family, obviously...

The large attic room is a series of shelves and rails. In the centre of the room there is a rail for a curtain, allowing a little privacy for trying things on. Up here the rails are sorted by decade so I start rifling through them, one at a time.

'Why do I feel like I'm in your wardrobe?' Damian asks with a laugh.

'Oh, I wish,' I reply. 'I couldn't do what Erin does for a living. I'd just want to keep everything.'

'Good job your job is to hold my hand or you'd be skint,' he replies.

'I might be anyway, there's so much good stuff here today,' I say as I grab a few more items. 'You can see the sea through that window.'

As I point out where to get the best view I pull the curtain closed between us.

'I'll just try a couple of things on,' I say. 'Don't worry, I'm such an efficient clothes shopper.'

'Take your time,' he replies. 'I could probably look out of this window all day.'

I cycle through a few items before deciding which two to get. Obviously I want to buy all of it but I need to show some restraint.

As I whip the curtain back Damian turns around.

'Oh, don't I get to see?' he says.

'Erm...' I laugh. 'I didn't think you'd care.'

'Are you buying anything?'

'Yeah, this lime-green 1950s tea dress, and a leopard-print Calvin Klein dress from the nineties.' I hold them both up for him to see. 'Let it never be said that I'm not versati... oh my God.'

'What?' Damian asks. 'What is it?'

I peer down into the cabinet next to me. It's an old wooden cabinet with a glass top that is locked shut with a padlock.

'This is my dream handbag,' I blurt. I realise how stupid that sounds – who dreams about a handbag? But bags like these are precisely the ones you do dream about, because normal people don't carry them. The way I see it, with designer handbags, is like this: some people can never afford a bag like this, some people could technically have the cash to pay for a bag like this, but, unless you are rich, you don't just have spare thousands of pounds to sink into a handbag. Never carry or wear anything you couldn't afford to lose.

'Ah, yes, the much sought-after black bag,' Damian says sarcastically. 'Nice.'

'Watch your mouth,' I joke with a fake gasp. 'This is a black Hermès bag, and the reason I love it so much is because it's a handbag that turns into a backpack.'

'You gonna buy it?' he asks.

'Ha!' I cackle. 'That is maybe two grand of handbag right there. I don't think so. I'll stick to my dresses.'

As we head back towards the winding staircase I notice a mannequin with a flat cap on.

'We should get you that for tomorrow,' I tell him. 'That's not so bad.'

Damian stops in his tracks in front of me.

'Why would I need that for tomorrow?' he quizzes me.

'Erm, let me pay for these and then we'll take the scenic route home,' I tell him. 'You and I need to have a chat about Dickens Day.'

'Oh, God, Dickens Day… everyone is making me think I am not going to like Dickens Day.'

I can pretty much guarantee that he's going to hate it but, if you come for the Kirke family Christmas, this is all part of the package. And, hey, I should look on the bright side. If he hates it as much as I think he's going to, he'll probably sack me. Then I won't even need to give my notice. For some reason the thought of doing so gets harder every day.

23

When I say that my family take Christmas traditions seriously, I really can't stress just how seriously that is, and when I say that my home town goes all out at Christmas, again, I don't think I'm doing justice explaining just how full on it can be.

So, when you factor these two things together, what do you get? My boss, standing in front of me, the moodiest I have ever seen him, dressed in the best spare Victorian outfit my mum had to offer him – because of course my mum has spare Victorian outfits.

'This sucks,' he says like a moody teen. 'This sucks so much.'

Damian is decked out in the works: a suit – complete with a waistcoat and cravat – finished off with a top hat that, I swear, is pushing down on his face, making his frown seem even more apparent.

'You're lucky the fake mutton chops wouldn't stick on over your real beard,' I tell him. 'And that you're not wearing a corset.'

I rejig my outfit in an attempt to make my boobs feel less as if they're being absorbed into my body – in a way that is most unbecoming of a lady from Victorian times.

'I figured Dickens Day would just be, I don't know, the day your family got together to watch *A Christmas Carol*,' Damian says. 'Not... this.'

Damian raises his arms up by his sides, gesturing to our surroundings, just in case I haven't noticed we are standing in the middle of the annual Dickensian Christmas Festival.

I have attended the festival every single year of my life. Sure, it's dorky, especially with the fact that everyone dresses up for it and that almost no one breaks character, but you can't get much more Christmassy than everyone gathering on Main Street, dressed in their Victorian best, to eat roast chestnuts and drink mulled wine.

Main Street is alive with people from the past. I'm looking around but I can't see a single person in their regular clothes. Well, in a world with so much to worry about, what's not to love about dressing up as something else, pretending you're in a different time?

The street is overflowing with people – a mixture of locals and tourists who travel for miles just to attend. It's strange but plenty of people travel here, to spend the Christmas period in Marram Bay. Then again, I grew up here, in this Christmas-crazy town. There's nowhere I'd rather be.

To say my outfit is complex would be an understatement – chaotic is what it is. But there comes a time in a young woman's life when her mum buys her the dress she's going to wear to the Dickens festival every year, and this is the grown-up one my mum bought me when I finally stopped growing. What it lacks in comfort it makes up for in authenticity. A dress tightly corseted on top, with a rounded bell shape from the waist down. I don't know how many petticoats I'm wearing – I always stop counting at four. They're definitely keeping me warm. The icing on the cake for me, though, is surely the bonnet. But, boy, do I wear the heck out of this bonnet. As someone who is always experimenting with fashion – and who is used to doing this dance every year – I don't mind it so much. Poor Damian though, he looks so uncomfortable... in more ways than one.

'You don't have to wear it for long,' I tell him.

'Good,' he replies quickly. 'You look sexy, I look stupid.'

Damian telling me that I look sexy makes me feel self-conscious all of a sudden.

'I say, is that a frown?' one of the storytellers asks as he slinks up alongside Damian.

The storytellers are people employed by the festival to walk around, fully in character, and tell people tales about the man himself.

The storyteller in question is dressed as a chimney sweep. He's tall and skinny, with black soot all over his face – well, I imagine it's face paint really, but if he were to admit that they would probably take him to the town hall and hang him.

'He's not really into it,' I tell the chimney sweep, hoping he'll take the hint and leave us to it.

'Oh?' he replies. 'How so?'

'It's a bit lame, isn't it?' Damian says pointlessly. Of course, this guy is going to disagree.

'You think Charles Dickens is boring, do you?' the chimney sweep asks. He sounds almost offended. 'Well, let me tell you something about Dickens and see if we can't change your mind. On 9th June, 1865, a fifty-three-year-old Charles Dickens was travelling home from France with his lover – and her mother – when the train they were on derailed while crossing a bridge. The carriage he was travelling in was hanging off the tracks, and others had fallen into the river below, but Dickens did his bit to save his fellow stranded passengers. Then, when he was done being a hero, he climbed back into the carriage to retrieve a recently completed instalment of *Our Mutual Friend*. Now, tell me, sir, is that *lame*?'

Damian just stares at him, blinking a couple of times until the chimney sweep drops his shoulder and goes off to talk to someone else.

'I think you just ruined his day,' I tease Damian.

'You know I hate street performers and party entertainers – the ones who bother you, even when you don't want them to, when you're clearly not into it,' Damian admits once we're alone again.

'I know, I remember dragging you away from that magician at that party.' I laugh. 'Still, at least you can take lots of pictures for your real people exhibition.'

Damian cocks his head thoughtfully.

'Real people... I like that. I could call it Real People – what do you think?'

'Sounds great,' I tell him. It really does. I'm so sad I'm not going to get to see this one through with him.

'Well, lame as this may be, it is great for photos so I'll do a quick lap, see if anything catches my eye.'

'OK, well, I'll go find my mum – maybe if I tell her we have work to do we can duck out early,' I suggest.

'OK, sure, I'll find you,' Damian calls back to me as he dashes off eagerly, camera in hand.

Top hat aside, I think he's having more fun than he's letting on.

I'm about to try and locate the rest of my family in the sea of top hats and bonnets when the mulled wine stand catches my eye. Perhaps if I...

'Sadie?'

I turn around.

'Oh my gosh, Ivy, hello,' I say as I pull her in for a hug. 'How are you?'

'I'm great, thanks. How are you?' she asks. 'It's so lovely to see you.'

Ivy and I were friends all the way through school – such good friends, in fact, that I can only remember us falling out once, and even that was a misunderstanding caused by the causeway making me late for the Steps-themed birthday party she was having, but didn't really want.

We both had such clear ideas about what we wanted to do when we grew up. Of course, things never work out how you want them to when you're a teenager, do they? I knew that I wanted to work in the art business, I wanted to marry my high-school boyfriend, have some babies, live happily ever after. It didn't occur to me, at the time, that elements of my particular plan were never going to play well together.

For Ivy it was all about cooking – mostly baking. She would absolutely smash it at food tech every time, which made everyone want to work with her, but she always chose me. Ivy's dream was to open up a cute little cafe where she could sell her creations.

'How are things?' she asks. 'Was that a handsome south-erner I heard you talking with when I walked over? I have one of those – he's over there, by the chestnuts, frowning. He hates stuff like this.'

'Mine too.' I laugh. 'Well, he's not mine... my southerner, I mean. The southerner that is here with me.'

Ivy looks confused.

'Oh, is he not your boyfriend? Sorry,' she says. 'I just assumed...'

'He's my boss,' I tell her. 'He's taking pictures here.'

I realise I'm being quite creative with the truth but, well, at this stage I think people are starting to feel more embarrassed than I am when I try to explain what we're doing spending Christmas together.

'At least it sounds like you got your dream job,' she says with a smile.

'Actually, I'm quitting,' I say with a really dorky laugh. 'I'm leaving for another one though – a better one – an assistant curator, which is definitely a foot on the ladder I need to be climbing. How are things at the shop?'

Ivy runs the local Christmas shop, Christmas Every Day. There's something so fascinating about a Christmas shop that is open all year round. Luckily Ivy loves all things Christmas, and always has. I'm not sure I'd have the stomach for listening to 'Jingle Bells' every day.

'Oh, haven't you heard? We've branched out. I have my own cafe now. Finally, after years of slaving away in the shop, my dreams have come true! I had a lot of help from my fiancé over there but, well, that's the perks of being a team, right?'

'I didn't know you were getting married! Congratulations,' I tell her. 'Have you set a date?'

'We were thinking Christmas,' she says excitedly. 'We've made a few preliminary plans but, honestly, I'm so tempted to back out of them now and just get hitched at a register office somewhere. You know what it's like living here – even though we don't know many people, you kind of know everyone at the same time. But we want something small and I just really can't wait to start a family. Not getting any younger back here.'

That last part was clearly Ivy's attempt at a joke about her biological clock, but the implication makes her cringe.

'You know what I mean,' she says. 'Are your family keeping well?'

'Yeah, all good. I was just going to find my mum – tell her we probably need to go home and do some work. It was lovely to bump into you though.'

'You too,' she says. 'Good luck with the job change.'

'Thanks,' I reply. 'If I don't speak to you before, I hope you have an amazing wedding!'

As soon as I'm walking away from Ivy, I allow my face to slip a little. I'm happy for her, of course I am, but that conversation was my ghost of Christmas past, present and future right there. Past, because Ivy and I had the same start in life; we both had dreams we wanted to follow, and the plans to do them. Present, because she looks amazing, has a handsome fiancé, and she's finally opened her cafe. And future because, well, look at everything she has to look forward to. A wedding, kids, a career she clearly loves. I might be changing my job but I can't help but feel as if I'm starting at the bottom. I'm heading for my mid-thirties, I'm single, I'm not having any kids any time soon... Don't get me wrong, I'm not having a pity party, I'm just stating the facts. My life isn't going to sort itself out, just because I want it to. Now is the time to make changes, to shape my future. The only problem is, right now, I have no idea what it's going to look like.

24

This morning I have woken up with a real post-Dickens Day hangover. It's not so much that I drank too much – although all the mulled wine I drank at the festival and then all the wine that Damian brought that I put away probably didn't help – it's from having so much fun last night.

For the second part of Dickens Day we take things back to basics. Well, not entirely, we don't shun all technology and go outside when we need the loo, but we do have an evening without the television for entertainment in favour of all playing board games together.

What very much feels like a hangover I think is actually just from having a good time, staying up until three a.m., laughing until my face hurt.

We played classics like Cluedo before turning to more modern games like Cards Against Humanity – which is kind of awkward to play with your family, you have to feel so comfortable making controversial jokes. I was so relieved my gran had already gone to bed at that stage.

But it was when we played Articulate that we had the most fun because, it turns out, when you spend pretty much every day with someone for a year, you become so in tune with one another that team games like Articulate are a doddle. I would describe a celebrity, Damian would know who I meant. Damian would describe an object and within seconds the answer would just fall into place for me. We won by an absolute mile. In fact, the first game went so quickly we played again, and we won that round too. It turns out we make one hell of a team, but Damian said he already knew that, given how well we work together generally. I'm sure it's much easier for him than it is for me though.

I definitely haven't slept enough, my face still aches from laughing, and I'm in desperate need of a cup of tea. I pull myself up from my single bed, extending my neck to peep out of the window. Ever since I was a kid I've always been obsessed with the idea of it snowing on Christmas Day, just like it does in the movies and the songs, but the Dickensian scene of widespread snow lying on the ground on Christmas Day is unfortunately rare. If this were a movie, I would wake up on Christmas morning, peep out of my window, and there it would be – delicate little flakes dancing down, settling on the floor, just waiting for me to run outside in my dressing gown to make a snow angel. Ahh, that's never going to happen, is it? I'll just have to settle for it looking cold.

I figure, now that I've seen Damian dressed as an elf, and he's seen me in a corset and a bonnet, I don't need to worry too much about dressing for breakfast. If you can't spend the festive period in a state of near-constant undress, when can you? I throw on my dressing gown and head to the bathroom to wash my face and brush my teeth. I notice that Selena's bedroom door is closed, which makes me wonder if Damian is still asleep. It's still closed by the time I'm out of the bathroom and heading downstairs.

Sitting at the breakfast table there's my mum, my gran, and Selena.

'Morning,' I say as I pull up a seat and grab the teapot.

'Good morning, darling,' my mum says. 'Sleep well?'

'I'm knackered,' I say, yawning right on cue.

'I think we all are,' she says. 'Last night was fun though.'

'At least you didn't have to travel home at three a.m. with a sleeping child,' Selena points out.

'You live on the island,' I remind her. 'That can't have taken you more than five minutes.'

'I suppose it would be quite a bit further, for you to travel home,' she jokes. 'Now you're a *London girl*.'

I laugh at Selena's attempt at a cockney accent.

'Never liked London,' my gran says with a bat of her hand. 'If I had my way we'd chop the south off at Birmingham, send 'em all to France.'

'Just give me a bit of warning,' I tell her. 'I'll make sure I'm on the right side.'

'Aye, I'll do that,' she tells me. 'And you can keep that Damian on this side too. I like him.'

'Given what you've said about work over the past year, I can't believe I'm saying this, but I like him too,' my mum practically confesses. 'We all do. And you both seem so excited about his new project, and I've seen all the amazing pictures he's taken so far, and, well... are you sure you want to quit?'

'You're quitting your job?' my gran says. 'In this financial climate?'

My gran's knowledge of the financial climate can't extend beyond the things that make her angry when she watches *Question Time*, but I can't help but feel touched.

'I have another job,' I reassure her. 'Don't worry. It's not just another one, it's the one I've always wanted.'

'But Damian won't be there,' my mum reminds me.

'And neither will Adam,' Selena adds cheekily.

'Wait, who's Adam?' my gran chimes in.

I reach out and drag the plate of biscuits in the centre of the table, so they're closer to me for easier access, because I'm going to need them.

'He's just some guy from work,' I say.

'Some guy she's been flirting with for a year,' Selena adds excitedly.

'Snitches get stitches,' I mumble under my breath. It might be annoying me slightly right now, while she's spilling the beans on my private life, but I can't help but love the way that as soon as you put siblings together in their family home, all of a sudden they regress to behaving as they did when they were kids.

'Oh, tell us everything,' my mum says.

'Yes, come on, give your old gran some excitement,' my gran joins in. 'I left my Mills & Boon in the hall at home.'

With the three of them all staring at me like this, all eagerly awaiting a bit of gossip, it's hard not to see the family resemblance.

'Well, I haven't actually met him,' I confess. 'We swap notes.'

'Oh,' is about all my mum can say. She looks disappointed.

'Reminds me of the war,' my gran says. 'Swapping letters with soldiers. Not that I was old enough, but your auntie Mavis was quite the goer.'

'You know how I said you should find out his last name and look him up online,' Selena says.

'Yeah, I'm not going to ask Damian what Adam's surname is. How would I explain wanting to know?' I reply.

'You don't have to,' she says with a grin. 'I looked up Damian's company on one of the work-based social networks we use at work...'

'Oh?'

'I've got your attention now, haven't I?' She laughs. 'Well, it allows me to look through different companies and see who has worked there, and I did find an Adam who listed Damian as an employer.'

'How can you be sure it's the right person?'

'Well, it didn't have any dates listed, and Adam is a pretty common name, but I clicked on his profile and he had a picture... and he is one handsome chap. Looked like the kind of bloke you could fall in love with over a Post-it.'

'Oh, let's have a look,' my mum says.

'He might have a common first name but his surname is Miracle,' Selena says. 'How many Miracles do you think are out there, huh? Look him up on Facebook.'

I grab my phone and punch in his name and sure enough, there he is, Adam from work.

'Oh my God, that's him,' I say as I scan his profile for info. I don't know what I'm looking for. Signs of life? Signs of a wife? Anything that might explain why he didn't reply. His profile is reasonably private – about as much as your average person's is, so I can see some of his basic info and his profile pictures – but as far as I can tell he is both alive and seemingly single. Obviously, without a deeper dive, I can't say for sure, but without being friends with him that's not going to be possible.

'Oh, come on, let's see,' my mum says curiously.

I open up his profile picture and hand over my phone.

'Oh, look at him,' my mum says as she flicks through his profile pictures. 'He is handsome. Mum, look at this.'

My gran pushes her glasses up her nose before taking the

phone from my mum. She does that adorable thing older ladies do where, to get a better look at your phone, they hold it at arm's length and make a face.

'Not bad,' she says. 'He's no Damian, but he's not bad.'

As I watch her navigate his profile I wonder who has taught my technophobic gran, who is no stranger to trying to change the channel on the TV with the cordless phone that she hates, how to use a smartphone.

'Oh, I think I've done something,' she says casually as she hands the phone back to my mum.

That's when I realise... no one has taught her to use a smartphone.

'Let's see,' my mum says, taking the phone from my gran, holding and staring at it in the exact same way. 'You've just sent a friend request.'

'Wait, "just sent a friend request"?' I say as I reach out for my phone. 'To Adam?'

'Yes,' my mum says with a wince. 'Can you cancel it?'

'I can, but he'll probably still see it,' I say, hoping the ground will open up and swallow me. 'Crap.'

'Maybe this is a blessing in disguise,' Selena says. 'Maybe this is what you need, to get the conversation going again. Maybe, just maybe, he never went back into work before Christmas. If he accepts not only will you know that everything is fine, but you'll also have the Internet to message each other on, like normal people, not Post-its like sociopaths.'

'It's a miracle,' my mum jokes.

'You've been spending too much time with Dad,' I tell her with a chuckle.

'Speak of the devil,' my dad says from the doorway.

'Dad!' I jump out of my skin. 'How long have you been there?'

'There's the sign of a guilty conscience,' he says. 'What were you saying?'

'I was just pointing out how Mum has caught your terrible sense of humour,' I say. I notice he's wearing his coat. 'Where have you been?'

'Come to the kitchen and all will be revealed,' he says mysteriously. 'Come on, all of you.'

'I'll stay here,' my gran informs him.

'OK, misery, fine.' He chuckles. 'Everyone else, come on, come quick.'

We do as we're told and follow my dad into the kitchen where we find Damian, all dressed up in his warm clothes as if he's just got here, surrounded by shopping bags and boxes.

'Have you been out?' I ask him. 'I thought you were in bed!'

'No, I was up early, and your dad was going out to pick up the Christmas food, so I said I'd go with him,' Damian says. 'Sorry, I thought I'd let you sleep.'

'I thought I was letting you sleep.' I laugh.

'What's all this?' my mum asks as she peers into one of the bags. 'Have you picked up the right order? This doesn't look like ours...'

'You should see this one let loose in the farm shop,' my dad says with a beaming pride. 'A man after my own heart.'

I've been to the farm shop with my dad before. It's a miracle he makes it out of there without selling off organs to pay for everything he's bought.

'You've all been so generous, letting me spend Christmas with you, including me in everything. I just wanted to do something nice,' Damian says.

'It was like *Supermarket Sweep*, tell 'em, lad,' my dad says, sidling up alongside Damian to give him a friendly nudge. 'We were just grabbing whatever we wanted and, then, we get to the checkout and he goes… "It's on me"… It's on me! He paid for the lot.'

'Oh, Damian, that is so generous of you,' my mum says. 'You already spent so much on the hampers, I'm sure.'

'Just call it my Christmas present to everyone,' he says.

'Thank you,' my mum says again. 'Thank you so much. Selena, help me get all this food put away before it spoils. You too, Eric.'

'Can I borrow you for a sec, Sadie?' Damian asks, nodding towards the hallway.

'Sure,' I reply following his lead. 'What's up?'

'You know I gave you some money and told you to buy yourself a Christmas present from me?' he says.

'Yes…' I say cautiously.

'Do you have it with you?' he asks.

'Erm, yes,' I reply. 'It's a skincare set with some fancy moisturisers in. I haven't used it yet though, I'm making myself wait until Christmas Day, because I'm sad like that.'

'Perfect,' he says with a smile. 'Can I have it back? Well, not back, because I never had it, but can I have it to wrap up, so I can give you it on Christmas Day? I don't want to look like an arsehole in front of your family.'

'Sure,' I say with a laugh.

'Your dad said he'd get me some wrapping paper to use.'

'OK, sure.'

I head upstairs.

I did buy Damian a present, which I was going to give him before I left for Christmas, but then he invited himself to come with me before I had a chance so I hung onto it. At least I'll have something to give him on Christmas Day, although it won't be anywhere near as impressive as the face cream he (kind of) got me. I suppose it seems kind of thoughtless, that he has me buy my own Christmas present, but I think that he thinks he's doing the right thing. He probably thinks that, by giving me money and telling me to get whatever I want, he's making sure I get myself something nice, rather than him wasting money on something for all of his staff and hoping they like it. That's what everyone else in the office gets; I know, because it's my job. I just arrange for a Christmas hamper for everyone. Well, they don't talk to me, so I don't know them well enough to make an informed purchase. I just buy enough for everyone, wrap them, pop them in the main office and people take them. It's very heart-warming.

Weirdly, as far as Damian's family goes, I kind of do know what to buy them. I feel as if I know them quite well, because it's me who reads his emails for him, so it's me who sees the family newsletters. I like to read them. It feels like a peep behind the curtain, to see what the man from Oz is really like. His family seem so normal and down to earth. Not like Damian at all. Perhaps that's why he keeps his distance – not that it makes sense to me. Honestly, as annoying as they can be, and as ridiculous as they make the Christmas holidays play out, pump my family into my veins because I love everything about them.

'Damian,' I call into the kitchen. He meets me in the hallway where I hand him the bag with my present in.

'Thanks very much. Remember to look surprised,' he says. 'Oh, by the way, your dad and I passed a pub, down on the coast, just before we crossed the causeway,' Damian starts.

'The Ghost?'

'That's the one. He was telling me how great it is – the food, the drink, the live music. He also said that usually the two of you have already been at least once by now. Fancy going with me this evening?'

'Just me and you?' I ask. I don't know why I ask.

'Yeah... don't worry, I just squared it with your folks. There's nothing going on this evening. Susie says today is a preparation day and, since I paid for the food, your dad won't even let me help put it away.'

'Oh, OK... yeah. I'd love to,' I say. 'Good job I bought a new dress.'

'Which one are you going to wear?' he asks.

'You'll be the second to know,' I tell him.

I love them both so much, I might just throw them up in the air and see which one I catch.

'OK, well, seven o'clock?'

'OK, I'll be ready for seven,' I reply.

'It's a date,' he says. 'Right, make yourself scarce so I can wrap your present with your mum's help. I feel so out of my depth.'

'Fine, fine,' I say. 'I'll go try to get a smile out of my grandma – that'll kill an hour.'

'I find it easy,' he calls after me.

It takes me until I'm sitting back at the dining table for Damian's words to hit me. I grab a biscuit and bite down on it meaningfully. That's just a thing people say, right? 'It's a date'... It has to be because... I don't have a date with Damian, do I?

25

Stepping into The Hopeful Ghost pub is like meeting up with an old friend you haven't seen in years, but when you do meet up it's as if you've never been apart. Kind of like when I bumped into Ivy yesterday, only far less embarrassing for me.

It's a reasonably big pub/restaurant, with a large round bar at the heart of it.

I especially love it around Christmas time because they always have such gorgeous, classic Christmas decor, roaring fires and Christmas music. They often have live music here and tonight is no exception. There's a man with a guitar in the corner of the room, doing acoustic covers of popular Christmas songs. The thing I've always loved the most about the live music at the Hopeful Ghost is the fact that it's only ever intended to be background noise. Even though a real person is playing it, you could be forgiven for thinking they were just streaming something. It's always the perfect volume – just loud enough to hear but quiet enough for you to have a conversation.

After everything Damian has paid for today, I have insisted on buying his drinks this evening. We've had some local fruity ciders, sitting on a sofa by the fireplace, and we've chatted for a couple of hours now. For the last thirty minutes I've been petting a chocolate Labrador. I have no idea who he belongs to – I assume he's here with a human and hasn't just brought himself for a pint and an ear-scratching, but I'm giving in to his demands and messing with his ears.

'Everything up here has a sort of rustic charm, doesn't it?' Damian observes as he swigs his drink.

'I guess it does,' I reply. 'Wait, do I have a rustic charm?'

'Your family does, kind of – I don't mean that in an offensive way,' he babbles. 'You don't have a rustic charm. You're like a child of the world.'

'I'm not sure what that means but I'll take it.' I laugh. 'What are your family like?'

Damian's face falls.

'You tell me, you email them,' he jokes.

'Damian, come on, humour me,' I insist.

Damian puffs air from his cheeks.

'OK, fine, fine. What do you want to know?'

'Just tell me about them – pretend I haven't been emailing them as you for months,' I suggest with a cheeky smile. 'Pretend I'm a date, but instead of texting your assistant under the table, asking me how you get rid of me, actually talk to me.'

I don't know why I worried earlier, when Damian said, 'It's a date,' because it's absolutely not a date. For the first hour we were here all we talked about was work. He brought his camera with him, just in case something caught his eye. He's been showing me his pictures so far and, even on his small camera screen, they look fantastic. I love this new direction he's taking, and I think everyone else is going to love it too.

'OK, well... My parents are Ray and Gloria Banks. They live in Banbury, where I was born, raised and could not wait to leave.' Damian starts out kind of jokey but then he gets more serious. 'I have one brother – Si – who is six years younger than me. He works for the family business. I don't. He's married. I'm not. He has a baby called Stella, who really is the cutest baby to ever exist. The closest thing I've ever had is a goldfish and even he jumped out of his tank. Si isn't even thirty yet. I'm thirty-five. I shot Leonardo DiCaprio for a magazine cover and he invited me to his birthday party on a yacht... but Si took over the family business so he's the impressive one. Is this what you wanted?'

I think he's just realised he's ranting.

'Yes and no,' I reply. 'Don't worry, we don't have to talk about it.'

I don't want to make him feel uncomfortable. He's not exactly struggling to open up about it but it's clearly not his favourite subject to talk about.

'We should probably get going soon. The causeway closes at eleven,' I say. 'If we're getting a taxi we need to give the driver plenty of time to get back across here – I bet you didn't have to worry about that growing up in Banbury.'

'Sadie, it's eleven o'clock now,' Damian says.

I glance over at the clock on the wall.

'The clock behind you says ten...'

'OK, but my Apple Watch says it's 10:58,' he says, holding it up to show me.

'Shit,' I blurt. 'Shit, quick.'

We grab our coats and hurry down to where the causeway starts. I don't remember exactly what time it closed – it was just after eleven – but now that we're here, looking out into the darkness, there's no way anyone would attempt to drive us across, and obviously walking is out of the question.

'It's not an exact science, right?' Damian says, hugging himself to keep warm.

'I think it might be one of the most exact sciences there is,' I reply.

'OK, so what happens now?' he asks. 'I assume this has happened before?'

'This was the bane of my life growing up,' I say with a sigh. 'It's no wonder I moved to London, where pretty much everything is connected.'

'Back to the pub?' he suggests.

'It will be kicking-out time soon,' I remind him. 'I might have an idea – let's see if this still works...'

'What still works?' Damian asks as he follows me along the edge of the water.

'Wait and see,' I tell him. 'It might not even still be a thing.'

We pass the pub, following the water along until we hit a small dock. You can only just about see it in the dark.

'You might want your phone torch for this bit,' I say. 'The floor is kind of uneven and it's only going to seem darker as we get closer.'

'It's bloody freezing,' he tells me, as though I haven't realised.

As soon as we both have our torches on Damian can see clearly where we're headed.

'Is that a boat? Don't tell me you know how to drive a boat... Are you going to drive us across the water?' he asks.

'Shh, just, give me a second,' I insist. 'Wait here.'

I stand outside the boat, facing inland. I just need to remember the numbers...

'I take fifteen steps inland, turn left, ten steps, turn forty-five degrees...'

'This really isn't doing anything to dispel my Wicker Man fears,' he whispers.

I shine my torch at the tree in front of me. There it is, the rock I'm looking for, on the floor in front of it. I hurry back to Damian with it.

'Oh my God, Sadie, are you... are you going to steal a boat? Please don't steal a boat,' he insists.

I twist the fake rock to reveal a key hidden inside it.

'Did you seriously think I was going to steal a boat?' I ask with a laugh.

'It *is* pretty cold out,' he says with a shrug.

I unlock the door to the boat's cabin before we both step inside. I search around for the switches that bring everything to life. The lights, the heater – everything we could possibly need.

'Whose boat is this?' he asks.

'You know... I'm not sure,' I admit. 'Let's get comfortable and I'll tell you all about it.'

'OK, but only if this doesn't get me arrested,' he replies.

The cabin has a small living room with a little kitchen. The living-room area has a U-shaped sofa – perfect for two people to snooze on until the causeway opens again in four hours.

'Cup of tea to warm you up?' I ask.

'Erm, yes, please,' he says with a laugh. 'This is so weird.'

'So this boat has been here for as long as I can remember,' I tell him as I make our drinks. 'Everyone knows about it. It's a sort of port in a storm for locals who miss crossing the causeway and can't get home.'

'Does it move?' he asks.

'Nah, I don't think it's worked for years. The power, I think, is from the pub... The idea is that, if you use it, you bring something to leave in it the next time you're passing. That's why it always has teabags and long-life milk. Blankets, books, board games...'

'This might honestly be the loveliest thing I have ever heard of,' he says. 'Don't people abuse it?'

I hand Damian his mug before I wrap myself up in one of the blankets and sit down next to him. I cradle my mug in my hands to try and warm up faster.

'Small-town life is lovely,' I tell him. 'Everyone takes care of everyone in the hope that one day, when they need help, there will be a line of people waiting to do whatever they can. That said, yes, when I was a teen I used to come here with my boyfriend.'

'Sadie, I didn't know you were a bad girl,' Damian teases.

'Everyone is a horrible teenager – even you were a horrible teenager,' I remind him.

'I wasn't, I was an angel,' he informs me. 'I was a photography nerd. I didn't lose my virginity until I was nineteen.'

Wow, that was honest.

'And here you are, in your wholesome little town, sneaking onto this boat with boys...'

'Erm, boy,' I correct him. 'Just the one. Brian Swash. My boyfriend at the time.'

'There's no way that's his name.' Damian laughs. 'Brian? You dated a Brian?'

'I did,' I say. 'For a long time... but we grew apart as we grew up. We wanted different things.'

'Like what, he wanted to play Pokemon cards, but you wanted to play with Barbies?' he jokes.

'First of all, I'm going to take issue with the blatant sexism in that statement,' I tease him. 'But we were together until the day before my eighteenth birthday. I know that still sounds young...'

'Nah, I get it,' he says. 'I couldn't even get a girl to text me back, back then – people were fussy about who they texted on pay as you go.'

'And look at you now,' I say. 'You're not just getting texts, you're getting softcore porn.'

'What a time to be alive,' he jokes.

It's nice to see Damian taking himself less seriously.

It's warming up nicely on the boat now so I let my blanket hang down around my shoulders. I look out of the window while I sip my tea – not that there's anything to see out there.

'I always pretend I have to work through Christmas,' he tells me. 'This will be the third time I've done it.'

'Honestly, Damian, you don't have to talk about it,' I insist. 'There's Scrabble on that shelf behind you.'

'Is that what you and Brian did?' he asks. 'Played Scrabble?'

'Sometimes,' I say honestly.

Well, when you're a teen in love, sometimes all you want is a bit of time to yourself. Nothing dodgy, you just want it to be the two of you, with no adults breathing down your necks, making you feel like kids.

'I guess I just feel so pointless at home,' he says. 'It's why I visit less; it's why I don't read the newsletters. I've got fans, critical acclaim, endless opportunities – and I'm so proud of everything I've achieved – but... I suppose that isn't the kind of success my parents wanted for me. To them success is getting married, starting a family, joining the family business.'

'What is the family business?' I ask curiously.

'I don't want to tell you,' he says. 'You'll laugh.'

'Of course, I won't,' I reply.

'Maybe I'll tell you some other time,' he says 'All you need to know is that I'm the oldest son... So I was just supposed to want to join the family business, or, even if I didn't, I guess I was supposed to resign myself to it being my job and get on with it. I swear I used to be much easier to work with. You really did rock up at the wrong time. The pressure is mounting, my confidence is wavering. I'm finding it harder to trust people. Not you though, I know I can trust you. And I guess I just know that you'll always accept me as I am. There's a great deal of comfort in that. Not for you, obviously... you're spending Christmas with your boss.'

'Come on, we both know you're more than just my boss,' I tell him. 'You're my friend. We've braved a Dickensian Christmas festival together, in full costume – something like that binds two people together for life.'

I give him a smile, to let him know it's OK.

'Don't move a muscle,' Damian demands.

'OK... why not?'

'Because I have never seen you look so perfect. Can I take your photo?'

'Can *you* take *my* photo? You want to take my photo?' I ask, completely surprised.

'Yep, all of the above,' he says with a laugh. 'Please?'

'Sure,' I reply. 'I know what people do, to try and get you to take their picture. I'm not about to turn that down. How do you want me?'

'Just... exactly as you are,' he says.

With one click of the shutter Damian locks in this moment forever.

'OK, now we can play Scrabble,' he suggests with a laugh.

I smile but, honestly, even though Damian saying I looked perfect makes me feel like the most beautiful girl in the world, I could not feel worse about myself right now. Not because I'm quitting – although obviously I feel terrible about that – but for doing all of it behind his back. Even now, I keep it from him every single day. But wouldn't it ruin his Christmas if I told him now? And he does really seem to be enjoying it so, so much. I know I'm going to have to tell him but, the longer I leave it, the harder it seems as if it's going to be. Whether I do wait until after Christmas, or I tell him before, I know one thing for sure. I absolutely shouldn't tell him right now, not when we're trapped on a boat together for the next four hours.

26

To a recovering bumpkin like me there is something so impossibly cool and intimidating about Hyde Park's Winter Wonderland. Hyde Park is more than a third of the size of the island I grew up on – and that's before you add in the Winter Wonderland, which creates a disorientating festive maze in the large open space. Pretty much minutes after you walk through the gates, it only takes a couple of turns for you to lose your bearings. Sure, you can use some of the impossibly tall rides – each so different from the next, but all having in common the fact that I will never ever go on them – to figure out where you are, but only in the context of the fair. Life outside the walls, where bright lights turn to shadows, almost ceases to exist.

Our Winter Wonderland is nothing like that. Here it has more of a small-town vibe, highlighting all the festive goodness the town has to offer.

It's more open, for one thing. A series of stalls, rides and various other attractions all set up on a large grassy area down by the seafront on the mainland. It's a real mixture of everything but I always get excited about the same few things. The stalls that make up the Christmas market have all sorts of wonderful Christmas decorations, and the food stalls – God, the food stalls – offer all kinds of festive yummies. I'm a big fan of the street-food vendors too. You can usually find a pizza oven, freshly made doughnuts, marshmallows dripping with melted chocolate and covered in pretty much anything you can think of!

I do have one other favourite attraction – one that has nothing to do with food, surprisingly – and that is the Christmas tree maze. It's exactly what it sounds like – a hedge maze made from Christmas trees – but it isn't the walk in the park it you might think. It's big, with tall trees, and enough twists, turns and dead ends to keep you entertained for a while. The first time I went in it, when I was a kid, I was so excited I just charged away from my parents and my sister, determined to conquer it alone... Of course I got lost, and cried like a baby, and it takes someone a few minutes to rescue you because it is literally a maze. I waited a few years, before I tried it again alone. I used to think I could memorise it for the following year – I don't know how many years it took me to realise that was never going to work because they change the layout each time.

So every year I'm excited to find my way to the centre and back out again, but even to this day I'm always a little anxious about going in, just in case I wind up crying on the floor again. It's amazing, how much we hold onto from our childhood, just to avoid getting hurt.

It's not even lunchtime yet and the Winter Wonderland is overflowing with people. Men, women, children of all ages, dogs – it feels as if everyone is here today.

It's cold, but not too cold. It never really does feel all that chilly in the thick of the festivities though. Perhaps it's a combination of a lot of people gathered together, surrounded by heat-generating fairground rides and street-food vendors. It definitely makes a much nicer experience. It's better than shivering, clutching at hot drinks to keep warm, losing the feeling in your toes because they're oh-so cold. You get all the magic of a winter wonderland without any of the, you know, winter.

We have been walking around for an hour now, stopping so that Ben can go on rides, my mum can buy new Christmas ornaments, or so Damian can take photos. With each shot he takes that he thinks he can use, he takes down the details of the subject, so that he can let them know if he's going to use it.

Right now my dad and Mark are in the beer tent, my mum, Selena and Ben are on the big, old-fashioned carousel, and Damian and I are queuing outside a little hut to get gingerbread lattes. They are all I can smell right now. To say I was desperate for one would be an understatement.

'You've got me all whipped up for this maze,' Damian says, shifting back and forth on the spot like an excitable child. 'I've never been in a maze.'

'I've been in this one plenty of times,' I tell him. 'It's still my nemesis. Back again, just in a different form. Like a comic-book-movie villain.'

'Well, you've got me with you today,' he says with a smile. 'I'm the Pepper Potts to your Tony Stark.'

'Ooh, I like what you're doing with gender roles today,' I say. 'Is this because I teased you about your choice of boys' and girls' toys last night?'

'Maybe,' he says. 'Last night was, well—'

'Oh my God, that's Brian,' I blurt, spotting him over Damian's shoulder. 'Is it? I think it is... I don't remember him being so, I don't know, manly when I was with him.'

'Wasn't he seventeen the last time you saw him?' Damian points out as he looks over at him. Brian is currently playing that fairground game where you hit something with a sledge-hammer to see how strong you are.

'Oh, yeah.' I laugh to myself. 'I should go say hello to him, right?'

'Yeah, sure, why not?' he says. 'You go catch up with Brian, I'll grab our coffees.'

'OK,' I say, nervously excited.

Bumping into an ex is completely different from bumping into an old friend. Sure, it's easy to measure yourself against your old school friends, but with an ex... you were a team. You were two parts of one thing. And then there's the obvious fact that, if your relationship didn't work, and you're still single and they're not, well, was it you who was the problem?

Brian and I broke up because we wanted different things. I wonder if he ever got his...

There are so many ways I could approach this. I could call out his name, get in his eyeline and wave, heck, I could even pretend to bump into him. Somehow I just end up hopping in front of him and sort of popping up in front of his face.

'Brian,' I say brightly. Perhaps a little too bright. Blinding, I'd say.

'Sadie Kirke, look at you,' he says, pulling me in for a hug. 'Wow, your hair is so long.'

'Look at me? Look at you,' I reply. 'All tall and beardy.'

The last time I saw Brian he was seventeen, skinny, and baby-faced. Now he's much taller, with a trendy lumberjack beard, and wearing a long blatantly designer coat.

Brian has a genuine smile on his face – a twinkle in his eye, even. He really does seem so pleased to see me. It's great to see him too. It's easy to forget that the people from your past continue to exist outside your bubble.

'I can't believe it's taken us so long to cross paths again,' I say.

'I moved away,' he tells me. 'I pop back a couple of times a year but I live in Milton Keynes now.'

'Oh, really? I moved away too,' I tell him. 'I live in London.'

'I commute to London,' he replies excitedly. 'A couple of times a week.'

'Really? What do you do?'

'Have a drink with me tonight,' he says, changing the subject. 'I'll tell you everything.'

I'm a little taken aback by his offer. I wasn't expecting to see him – never mind him asking me for a drink.

'I... erm... it's Christmas Eve,' I say.

'Oh, so you'll be at the cinema, then? Do you still do that?'

'We do indeed,' I say. 'You know my mum.'

'OK, well, what about before? The Ghost is minutes from the cinema. I'll have you there on time,' he assures me. 'I wouldn't get on the wrong side of Susie – not at Christmas.'

'I'd have to turn up in my pyjamas,' I point out.

'Every man's dream,' he says with a smile. 'Five-ish?'

I feel my cheeks warm up.

'OK, sure,' I reply with a big smile. 'Sounds great.'

Everything around us sort of fades out of focus. Even the sound of the excitable crowds and the Christmas music tapers off. It's just me and Brian suspended in the moment.

'Here's your latte,' Damian interrupts. 'They were out of gingerbread, unsurprisingly, so I got you caramel. I didn't think you'd fancy cinnamon.'

'Perfect, thank you,' I say as I take it from him eagerly.

I look back up at Brian, who looks like a rabbit caught in the headlights. He glances back and forth between me and Damian.

'Hello,' Damian greets him warmly.

'Erm... hi,' Brian replies.

'Brian, this is Damian, my boss/friend,' I tell him. Because that sounds completely normal. 'Damian, this is Brian.'

'Good to meet you, buddy,' Damian says. 'Are you the sailor she was telling me about?'

Sailor? Oh, God, he's making a joke about the fact I told him Brian and I used to meet up on the old boat. I shoot him daggers.

'Erm, no, that's someone else,' Brian says, still a little awkwardly, before turning to me. 'OK, Sadie, well, I'll see you at five.'

'See you then,' I say.

Damian sips his coffee as he waves off Brian with a smile.

'You're seeing him later?' he says. 'But we're all going to the cinema to watch *It's a Wonderful Life* in our pyjamas – it's Christmas Eve.'

He sounds so disappointed, which is a big surprise.

'OK, Susie Kirke, calm down,' I tease, because that is exactly the kind of thing my mum would say. 'I'm meeting him at five p.m. for a catch-up. I'll be at the cinema by seven. I'll go in my pyjamas so I'm all ready for the cinema.'

'You're going for a drink with him in your pyjamas?'

'OK, now you sound more like my dad,' I say with a laugh. 'There's always loads of people walking around in their pyjamas just before the cinema opens. It's totally normal here. I'll wear a coat – I won't get cold... promise.'

Damian sips his coffee again.

'OK,' he says, immediately walking it all back. 'I suppose that will give me a chance to flirt with your gran while you're not around. I think I might be her favourite.'

'I think you might be too,' I say. 'But you do have the tactical advantage of being able to flirt with her. Has she told you that you remind her of a young Des O'Connor yet?'

'Only twice, but I do have a decent year-round tan and a winning smile,' he says. 'Come on, let's get in that maze. You need to make it out in time for your date with big Brian. I think I'm starting to figure out what your type is.'

'Whoa, hold up,' I say, stopping in my tracks. I laugh for a moment at the sheer absurdity of the conversation. 'There's so much to unpack there I feel like I'm moving house. I'll start with the fact that you can't possibly have figured out my type by briefly bumping into my ex from over fifteen years ago – and, like you said, he was a kid the last time I saw him. He certainly wasn't a "big Brian". I'm assuming you're also referring to Hunter, but that wasn't really anything...'

'It might have been, if I hadn't disturbed you,' he reasons.

'So, for that reason, I only sleep with big guys? But it's fine that you only sleep with models?'

'OK, now you need to hold up.' He laughs. 'No one said anything about sleeping with anyone. Your dirty mind! You know my sex life has ground to a halt because you're the patron saint of all my failed dates.'

'Well, whatever,' I say, a little embarrassed. I know that I shouldn't even be thinking about my boss's sex life, but it has occurred to me on multiple occasions, while he does go on a lot of dates, I never really notice women existing in his life outside them, and there are only signs of two women in his apartment – me and his cleaner. And I don't know why he feels as if he has to justify himself to me. 'The fact that you're even commenting on my type...! Also, I am *not* going on a date with him. Just a catch-up. OK?'

Damian just laughs. He's so gorgeous when he smiles,

which makes it all the more annoying when he's laughing at me. I check myself, for checking him out.

'Whoa, OK,' he says. 'I didn't mean anything by it. Come on, let's get lost.'

Back when I first started working for Damian, when I had an entirely physical crush on him – something that I had hoped I'd never have to think about again, that I am so embarrassed by now – there were a handful of things that I thought made him attractive. His smile and his laugh made me go weak at the knees. His perfectly groomed hair and beard were like something I'd only ever seen on actors and models. And then there were his eyes... his big, brown puppy-dog eyes. Looking into them was a delightful mystery because, as big as they were, they weren't letting anyone peer inside. Damian's eyes are still very much a piece of one-way glass. He sees you but you don't see him – not really.

Thinking about it, am I embarrassed that I used to have a crush on him? Pretty much every woman who meets him fancies him; I guess it would be weird if I hadn't noticed it, acknowledged it, and then got over it.

And while I'm thinking about things, perhaps Damian isn't the closed book he used to be. He's told me about his family, about his sex life – those are deeply personal things.

Realistically, he's probably only worried about me going out with Brian because he thinks I'll be bailing on the cinema tonight, leaving him alone with my family, in a public place, in his pyjamas. That's weird, right? That would explain why he's acting so out of character.

At least, for once, the Christmas tree maze isn't the most complicated part of my day.

27

'I still can't get over the fact you're here dressed as an elf.' Brian laughs.

Let's just say the pyjama situation has escalated.

Our annual Christmas-card-posting competition isn't something I give all that much thought to. Ordinarily I am teamed up with my dad, we do a rushed job, chill in the pub for a bit, and land home in that second place sweet spot that means we don't have to set the table and we don't have to wear the Christmas ties or the mistletoe headbands or whatever ugly Christmas accessories my mum decides the losers should wear. I got off lightly the last time we came in last – all I had to do was wear a flashing Christmas badge over my pyjamas, which I obviously had to switch off inside the cinema, so it was as if it were never there. But this year Damian and I came last... and this year the festive accessory is much worse.

'I hadn't anticipated the outfit being so embarrassing,' I tell him.

'I don't mind it,' he says. 'It's nice to see your mum still taking thing so seriously. And you. The ears are quite the commitment.'

Yep, that's what the losers have to wear this year. To match our elf pyjamas we have pointy elf ears.

'Well, there was a glue involved, so I had to have them stuck on at home,' I say. 'Damian too, so at least I won't be alone.'

'You said Damian is your boss?' Brian says. 'It's a bit unusual to spend Christmas with your boss, isn't it?'

For a while now we've just been making polite chit-chat, catching up, talking about how our families are doing, work – all the usual stuff. Now we're finally getting into it.

'We're friends too,' I tell him. 'Maybe it's weird but... I guess circumstances are weird this year.'

'Are you two a thing?' he asks, but immediately backtracks. 'Sorry, I shouldn't be asking you questions like that.'

'No, no, it's fine,' I insist. 'We get that a lot but, no, we're not a couple. He just needed a friendly festive family to spend Christmas with.'

'You guys are certainly that,' he says. 'I loved my Christmases with your family. Never managed to find a girlfriend whose family did it quite like yours.'

'Look at my ears,' I tell him, pointing at them both for emphasis. 'You got off lightly.'

'Perhaps,' he says. 'I'm single at the moment so... I'm going to have to rely on my lot to keep me entertained this year. Are you seeing anyone?'

'Only my boss,' I joke. Wait, that didn't come out right. 'I mean, he's the only person I see. I am single.'

Just when I think I can't sound any less cool I always find a way to impress myself.

'Maybe we could go out for drinks in London when I'm

there for work,' he suggests. 'It sounds like your social life is as non-existent as mine is.'

'Yep, my social life has been on the back burner for a while now,' I say, stalling for a few seconds. I'm a little taken aback he's inviting me for another drink, while we're still having this one.

'Well... what are your plans for New Year's Eve?' he asks. 'Will you be back in London?'

'Nah, I'll still be here,' I reply.

'That's a shame,' he says. 'I've been invited to a big, swanky party in the city. I have a plus one on my invitation, you could've joined me.'

'Aw, thank you,' I say. That's very sweet of him but we've only just reconnected – I'm not about to spend New Year's Eve with him. 'If I hadn't already said I'd spend it here... But I'm changing my job soon and I'm hoping that will give me more free time.'

'You're leaving Damian?' he says. He sounds surprised.

'Well, I'm not leaving him, I'm leaving the company,' I clarify. 'But yes.'

'He looked pretty chipper for someone who's employee/friend – the kind he's close enough with to spend Christmas together – is leaving him,' he says.

'That might be because I haven't told him yet,' I say sheepishly. 'I'm going to soon just... after Christmas.'

Brian smiles.

'You're such a sweetheart,' he tells me. 'Most people don't think twice about when they give their notice.'

I shrug.

We're sitting in The Hopeful Ghost – where thankfully there are other people in their pyjamas, grabbing food and drinks before they head to the cinema – in the exact same seats

Damian and I sat in the other night. I keep looking up at the clock, reminding myself that it's an hour slow, so that I'm not late for the movie. Hopefully I'll notice when all the other pyjama-clad people sleepwalk out of here and follow their lead.

'Do you believe in the universe?' Brian asks.

'Do I believe in the universe?' I repeat back to him, certain I must be misunderstanding him. 'The universe as in the thing we exist in?'

Brian laughs.

'No, not like that,' he says. 'The universe doing things. Course correcting. Bringing people together.'

'Oh, erm... I've never really thought about it,' I tell him. 'I met Zac Efron at a work thing earlier in the year and he didn't ask me to marry him. And then I met a man who maybe murders women and he didn't kill me. Maybe I'm on the right track?'

Brian just stares at me for a moment. I'm not sure my sense of humour is landing with him.

'I'm thinking, we just bump into each other after all this time, we're both in London, both single...' he muses. 'Do you ever wonder if things are meant to be?'

'You never know, do you?' I say tactfully. I'm not sure I subscribe to that.

I suppose you can put that kind of spin on anything if you want to, can't you? We bumped into each other – in our home town. We're both in London – but only sometimes, and also London is massive. We're both single, but I really don't think I can pin my lack of a love life on the universe. That's a stretch.

I look up at the clock again.

The weirdest thing about sitting in the same place as I sat with Damian is that I keep thinking about him. About being here with him. About snoozing on the boat together until the tide went out before creeping back into my parents' house like a couple of naughty teenagers. It's always going to be awkward, hanging out with an ex, but I can't stop thinking about how much more fun I would be having right now if I were sitting here with Damian instead of Brian. And I've just realised that the entire time I have been here, I haven't heard from Damian once, and he usually always interrupts me when I'm with other men; it's as if he has a sixth sense for it.

Brian is a great guy, with some very interesting ideas about the universe and, sure, he is tall now but... I'm scared to even say it, but I think I'm missing Damian. This has to be some sort of Stockholm syndrome kind of deal – I've spent so much time with him recently no wonder it feels strange being without him.

I look up at the clock again.

If I'm just used to being around Damian all the time, then why am I so excited to see him? To go to the cinema together, in our pyjamas, with our ridiculous elf ears glued on – and they are really glued on there. I'm terrified they're not going to come off.

I'm missing him. I really am. And if I'm missing him now, how much am I going to miss him when I'm not seeing him every day?

28

It's a different kind of Christmas this year, but a great one so far.

After my super-deep, super-weird catch-up with Brian I practically ran out of the pub and across the road to the cinema. The Kirke clan, plus Damian, were waiting outside for me. My heart skipped a beat when I saw Damian, in his elf outfit, the ears still glued to his head in solidarity with mine. I still find it hard to believe he's here, doing all this.

It's a Wonderful Life was magical, as always, and when Damian confessed that he'd never seen it I was even more excited. There's a real joy to be had in watching a movie that you love with someone who hasn't seen it before – you get to enjoy it again through their eyes and give them the gift of something great.

Then there's the fact that the Seafront Cinema is a truly magical place to experience a movie for the first time – especially an older one.

The Seafront Cinema is actually one of only a few remaining gas-lit cinemas in the UK. It's proper old school, with an external box office that looks out over the sea, towards the island. Over the years it has needed a lot of love. There have been many fundraisers and different owners, all making the necessary improvements. It's been modernised countless times over the years, but not so you would notice. With things like new seats being installed, and a concessions stand being built indoors, it is undetectable (unless you know) when you see everything alongside the old-school screen, the fuzzy red chairs and the retro lamps on the walls. Coming here to watch an old movie really does feel like hopping into a time machine. Last night we went back to 1946 and Damian absolutely loved it. It was already filling up when we got there, so Damian and I said we'd let the others have the seats nearest the front and – would you believe it? – we ended up sitting on the back row together. Still, we had a laugh about it, and it was nice to sit and watch the film together. I swear, at one point, I thought he was going to take hold of my hand, but I think he was just caught up in the magic of the scene where George offers Mary the moon. Well, it's hard not to get swept away by that, right? It's no wonder I started imagining things.

It's Christmas morning now and I'm spending it the only way anyone should spend it – sitting on the floor in a big pile of wrapping paper.

My mum, God love her, still makes up a Santa sack for all of us. She's even made an incredibly last-minute one for Damian, which makes it all the cuter.

Selena, Mark and Ben spend their Christmas mornings at home before coming over here for Christmas dinner so this morning it's just me, Damian, my parents and my gran.

We're drinking Buck's Fizz and eating panettone, taking it in turn to open presents.

I reach under the tree and grab my present for Damian. It's a small, light box so I toss it to him.

'Merry Christmas, gaffer,' I say.

Damian's eyes light up. He examines the small package but only for a second before he unties the ribbon and rips off the wrapping paper.

'Oh my God,' he says as his eyes light up. 'It's the knife.'

'The knife?' my mum says.

'The knife the murderer had,' he says by way of an explanation.

'It's from a TV show,' I reassure them.

'It's a Swiss army knife with a flash drive built into it,' Damian tells the room excitedly. 'But it only works with your fingerprint. There's a little scanner built into the USB.'

'I'm not fully sure what that means but it sounds good,' my mum says.

'Sounds very hi-tech,' my dad chimes in.

'You remembered that I really wanted one,' Damian says, as if I didn't know. 'Thank you.'

'You're welcome,' I say with a smile.

'I suppose I'd better give you your present,' he says, pulling out a box from behind the sofa, which I absolutely hadn't noticed him put there.

Damian places the beautifully wrapped box down in front of me.

'Merry Christmas,' he says.

'Oh, I wonder what this could be,' I say intentionally theatrically, because we both know that I chose this for myself. Damian flashes me a cheeky smile.

I pull off the bow and tear open the paper and...

'Oh... my... God! It's a Dial-a-Date,' I squeal in such a high pitch I'm sure only dogs and Mariah Carey can hear me. 'You got me a Dial-a-Date – where the hell did you find a Dial-a-Date?'

'Oh, God, she's finally got one,' my mum says, clapping her hands with joy. 'Is that what you had delivered here that you didn't want her to know about?'

Damian nods. He looks so proud of himself and he should because this is all I have wanted for Christmas forever.

'I can't wait to show Selena,' I say as I examine the box. It's bright pink and covered with nineties-issue hunks and I couldn't be happier with it. 'We should all play it later.'

As soon as I think about what the game entails I wonder if maybe it might not be my dad's sort of thing – finding a hunky man to go out with.

Damian pulls out another box.

'Another one!' my gran says. 'He's got her another one.'

'Thank you,' I say with a knowing smile.

It means so much to me that, not only did he go out of his way to actually buy me a present himself, but it's something so personal, that clearly shows how much attention he's been paying. And I still have no idea where he got it from!

'I wonder what this could be,' I say, doing the dance again as I rip off the paper and open the box. 'It's...'

I'm stunned into silence.

'What is it?' my mum asks, but I can't speak. I don't know what to say. I just stare into the box.

'Come on, spit it out,' my gran prompts me. 'I don't have long left. I'm not spending it watching you staring into a box.'

'Damian, I can't accept this,' I say. I want to, oh my God do I want to, but I can't.

'Well, I certainly don't want it.' He chuckles.

'What is it?' my dad joins in. Even he is on the edge of his seat now.

I wipe my potentially chocolatey hands on my soon-to-beretired elf pyjamas to make sure they are clean before carefully lifting my present out of its box.

'It's my dream handbag,' I say. 'A vintage two-way Hermès handbag that turns into a backpack.'

'Oh, it's lovely,' my mum says.

'It's practically a deposit on a house, coupled with the other presents, and the bonus you gave me,' I tell him, exaggerating a little, but not that much.

'Not in London,' Damian replies. 'Come on, you've earned it. I've been an ars... an especially difficult boss this year.'

'Thank you,' I tell him. 'Thank you, thank you, thank you.'

I can't contain myself. I get up and practically leap into his arms, squeezing him tightly. It's not that he bought me an expensive bag – and it is a bloody expensive bag – it's the fact that he listened, that he values me.

'Steady on.' He laughs. 'You don't have to thank me so hard. I told you, you've earned it.'

'And you've earned this,' I tell him. 'It's so thoughtful, thank you.'

I loosen my grip on him and look into his eyes for a second. He just stares back.

My dad clears his throat and suddenly I remember all of my family members currently sitting in the same room as us.

I let go of Damian and head back to my pile of presents, smoothing out my PJs as I go.

'So an old board game and an old bag,' my dad jokes. 'I wish your mum was so easily excited.'

'Oh, and here's your boring face cream.' Damian laughs as he places my third and final present down in front of me.

And to think, I was so excited for my fancy moisturiser, and getting to finally try it out today. Now I don't even care...

29

Whether it was down to the dry-run or my mum's exceptional cooking skills (I'm sure it was the latter) Christmas dinner was a big hit – the only thing bigger right now is my stomach, packed to capacity with turkey, stuffing, vegetables, cranberry sauce, and, just when it seemed as if I was done, Christmas pudding with brandy cream. I would say that I don't want to eat again until the new year but I know we'll all be craving turkey sandwiches later on tonight, just as we always do.

'Shall we get our comfies on?' my mum suggests. 'Play some board games?'

We always dress in our best for Christmas dinner. I think all families go one way or the other, either dressing in their Sunday best or keeping it comfortable in their loungewear.

'Sounds good to me,' my dad says. 'I need the loo anyway.'

'Ohhh,' my gran scoffs.

'Don't announce it, Eric,' my mum ticks him off. 'Shall we all meet back at the dining table in, say, half an hour?'

We all agree to reconvene – providing we don't play

Monopoly, because life is too short to spend it falling out with your family over a board game that lasts hours.

'Oh, we should take the family photo first,' my mum says. 'While we're all dressed nicely and Selena, Mark and Ben are still here.'

'Still want me to take it?' Damian asks.

'If you really don't mind,' my mum replies. 'Imagine, a genuine Damian Banks on my wall, with me in it…'

Damian smiles as he messes with his camera settings.

'OK,' he says, snapping into professional mode. 'Everyone gather together around the sofa.'

We all shuffle into position.

'Ready?' he says.

'Aren't you going to be in it too?' my mum says.

'Me?' Damian replies. I don't think he was expecting that.

'Of course,' my mum replies. 'This is a family Christmas portrait and this Christmas you are a part of our family.'

Damian looks at me.

'I saved you a space next to me,' I tell him, to let him know that, not only is it OK, but we all actually want him in the photo too.

'Well, in that case I'd love to,' he says.

Damian sets up his camera on the sideboard, piled high on top of a stack of DVDs, which he assures us is deeply unprofessional but he hasn't got a tripod with him.

He lines up his shot before setting the five-second timer going and hurrying into the frame next to me. He stands next to me, hooking his arm around my waist, leaning into the photo. When he shows us all, to see if we like it, I can't help but smile at how at home he looks in the picture with us. It just looks right.

Damian and I head upstairs at the same time. I remember what he said, the day we got here, when he asked to see my bedroom.

'You wanna come in?' I ask him.

'Erm...' He laughs awkwardly.

'Just to see, I mean – to see the room. You said you wanted to see my room...'

'Oh,' he says – almost with relief. 'Yeah, I'd love to.'

'It's nothing special,' I tell him as he follows me into the room. 'I didn't realise my dad's plan to keep the rooms as embarrassment shrines, so I took most of my stuff out when I moved out. I took down my posters; all my childhood stuff is up in the loft. There's just one bit of me left.'

I close my bedroom door behind us.

'Lie down on the bed,' I tell him.

Suddenly he seems a little nervous again.

'What?'

'Lie down on the bed,' I say again. 'And close your eyes. Don't worry, you're perfectly safe.'

Damian does as he's told, sitting on my bed before lying back cautiously.

It's dark outside now so I flick off the bedroom lights and lie down next to him.

'OK, you can open them,' I say.

'Aww,' Damian says. 'That's so cute.'

For a moment we just lie together, staring up at the glow-in-the-dark stars on my ceiling.

'I like that, even though you took everything else out, you left these up,' he says.

'I mean, technically they're still up there because I can't reach them to get them down,' I admit with a laugh. 'But I do like to fall asleep staring up at them every year when I sleep here. I doubt my dad even realised they're still up there – not unless he's had a row with my mum at some point and she's made him sleep in here. I can't imagine him sleeping in Selena's room, can you?'

'I don't know, it seems like a good room to sleep in if you're feeling blue,' he jokes. 'I swear, I'm used to them now. It's going to be weird, when I have to go back to sleeping alone, without walls covered with men who are staring at me.'

Damian sighs, but it sounds more like a sigh of relaxation than resignation.

'I think a family Christmas was just what I needed to chill out,' he says. 'Thanks so much for having me.'

'When were you thinking of heading back?' I ask, while we're on the subject.

'Erm, I'm not sure,' he says. 'Have I outstayed my welcome?'

'No, of course not – are you kidding? I'm pretty sure any one of that lot downstairs would swap me for you in a heartbeat,' I tell him. 'I just wondered if you had plans for New Year's Eve?'

'Oh,' he says. 'No, no plans at all... Did you have anything in mind?'

'Why don't you go see your family?' I suggest.

Damian doesn't say anything, and because we're lying here in the dark I can't even see the look on his face to try and figure out how he's feeling.

'I just think they would all be so pleased to see you, and I think it would do you good to see them,' I say. 'And you said it yourself, you're feeling less stressed, and you've loved being around a family... so why not give your own a go? I get that you have issues but – they're your family. And, honestly, if they're not making you dress up in Victorian gear or gluing elf ears to you so you can go watch a movie in your pyjamas... I *still* have glue behind my ears.'

I stop talking and retreat to minding my own business. In the darkness I feel Damian reach out and take hold of my hand.

'Will you come with me?' he says.

'Of course I will,' I reply.

30

Where do you think the great Damian Banks comes from? I know he grew up in Banbury but that's not what I mean. I mean, more specifically, what are the required conditions for creating someone so effortlessly talented? I'm curious about the house he grew up in, what he was like as a kid but, most of all, I'm so curious to see what his family is like.

After a week of Kirke family festivities, I'm almost looking forward to visiting Damian's family for a few days. Well, I've never seen how other families do the holidays and, while we might be through the festive bit, I'm excited about the New Year's party.

As well as being excited, I'm pretty nervous. I don't know why. This is the first and last time I'll see the Banks family. I suppose I just want to help Damian reconnect with them.

I glance into the front of the car to peep at Martin's satnav.

'Seven minutes away,' I announce. 'Did you tell them what time to expect us?'

Nothing.

'Damian?' I prompt.

'I didn't exactly tell them we were coming,' he admits. 'They had made clear that I was invited. I said I probably couldn't make it, because I do feel bad just saying I'm not going – but we all know I'm not – but the offer stays open so...'

'So you're just turning up?' I say. 'Just turning up for a few days, to spend New Year's Eve with them. With me randomly in tow...'

'Yeah... they'll be pleased,' he says but then he doesn't look so sure. 'They'll be pleased, right?'

'They'll be pleased to see you, for sure, but it's just... all a bit weird.'

No weirder than me turning up at home with my boss, I guess, but still. At least I told my family that I was bringing him. They were prepared – physically and mentally.

Martin chuckles quietly to himself. 'Here we are,' he announces. 'Weird Christmas number two.'

We've clocked some miles together now so I feel as if we can make jokes.

'Come on, it's going to be fine,' Damian says with a big smile. 'I'm weirdly excited to see everyone now.'

He gets out of the car with a real spring in his step.

'Don't worry, Martin, we can take our bags,' he says. 'Come on, Sadie.'

'I guess I'm going, then, Martin,' I say. 'See you in the new year.'

'Yeah, see you then,' he replies. 'And don't worry. No one takes someone to meet their family unless they really like them.'

I'm so glad Damian didn't hear him say that. Is that true? Is Damian only comfortable bringing me here because he really likes me? By that logic, did I only bring him home for Christmas with me because I really like him? Obviously I really like him, we're friends – and we feel closer now than ever – but is Martin suggesting something more? I don't need to worry about it. He's a driver, not Jerry Springer.

Damian's parents live in a perfectly typical semi-detached house on a completely usual cul-de-sac. I'd wondered if he'd been brought up by super-rich, ultra-eccentric arty types but I couldn't be looking at a more normal house. It just goes to show, once-in-a-generation talent can grow in any type of land; it doesn't need to be a purpose-built, crazy hi-tech greenhouse with perfect conditions.

We stand on the doorsteps with our bags. Damian tries the door, but it's locked.

'They're definitely here, right?' I ask as I turn around and watch Martin drive away.

'The latch will be on,' Damian says as he rings the bell.

'Don't look so nervous, they're going to love you,' he reassures me.

I smile. I hope they do. I don't know why, because there really shouldn't be any high stakes here, but I really hope they do.

'Rudolph's lit up,' Damian says, nodding towards a reindeer light in the window. 'My parents would never go out without turning that off because my mum would worry about fires and my dad would worry about the electricity bill.'

A light appears in the hallway and then it's only a matter of time before the door opens.

A sixty-something woman answers the door. If I didn't know we were at Damian's parents' house (which seems as if it could have been a possibility, given that they didn't know that I was coming) I would know, without a doubt, that this was Damian's mum standing in front of us. She looks just like him – or rather he looks just like her, technically.

She stares at him for a few seconds, then glances at me, then back to Damian. Then she bursts into tears.

'Damian,' she says. 'Oh, Damian! I can't believe you came.'

She hugs him tightly before sticking her head back through the front door.

'Ray,' she calls out. 'Ray, Ray, quick, come here.'

'Is it that bloody fox trying to tip the bin again, is it?' a man asks as he emerges from one of the rooms. He's wearing a pair of navy sweatpants and a zip-up hoodie. I thought Damian looked a lot like his mum but he is the double of his dad.

'Damo,' he blurts. 'Bloody hell, what are you doing here?'

'We thought we'd come for New Year's Eve,' Damian says, trying to sound enthusiastic. 'If we're still invited?'

'You're always invited, to everything, ever,' his mum insists. 'And you brought a girl, oh my God, no wonder you didn't tell us you were coming. I bet you thought we'd put a banner up or something.'

As Damian's mum hugs me tightly I look back at him. He nods wildly to suggest that a banner absolutely would have happened.

'Don't stand out here in the cold, come in, introduce us to your lady properly.'

'You asked for this,' Damian whispers to me as we head inside.

The living room is so homely and inviting. There's a real, roaring fire on the go, and delicious-smelling scented candles lit on the coffee table along with a glass of wine and a beer. I can see that we've interrupted them watching *Eastenders* because it's paused on the TV.

'Is Si not here?' Damian asks as we sit down on the cream leather sofas.

'No, he, Nikki and Stella are at Nikki's parents' house tonight,' his mum tells us.

Si might not actually be here, but there are photos of him, with his family, with his parents, all over the walls. Si's photographic prescience is overwhelming.

'So, come on, introduce us,' his dad prompts excitedly. He's literally on the edge of his seat, leaning into us.

'This is Sadie,' he tells them. 'Sadie, this is my dad, Ray, and my mum, Gloria.'

'Lovely to meet you,' Gloria says.

'You too,' I reply.

'Let me get you some wine,' she insists as she disappears into the kitchen.

'Bring Damo a beer,' his dad calls after her.

It's so weird, hearing him call Damian Damo. I can see Damian visibly cringe each time. My parents had a nickname for me when I was younger too. They used to call me Diddy, for a few reasons. First of all, I couldn't say my own name, when I first started talking, so I would just repeat the 'di' sound at the end of Sadie. They also liked to call me it because diddy means small. Not only did I eventually master the pronunciation of my own name, but I grew much bigger. I literally grew out of my nickname but it looks as if Damo is still alive and well and living in this house.

'How long has this been going on?' Ray asks, pointing a finger back and forth between us.

'Coming up to a year,' Damian replies. 'Oh, wait, you mean...'

'We're not a couple,' I say.

'Sadie is from work,' Damian tells them.

'W-what?' Ray stutters in disbelief. 'You're the boss, aren't you?'

'Most of the time,' Damian jokes.

'So... you've brought an employee with you?' Ray asks. 'Or is this like one of those court-ordered, she has to keep an eye on you, check your pee and that...?'

'No, Dad, she isn't my probation officer, if that's what you're saying,' Damian replies with a sigh.

'Who's on probation?' Gloria asks as she places a tray down on the table with a selection of drinks, crisps and nuts. 'Not Damian? No! Didn't I say there were drugs...?'

Gloria doesn't explain what she means by this.

'She's my assistant,' Damian tells them.

'You brought your assistant?' his dad says. 'For New Year?'

'Trust me, it was weirder for my family, turning up with my boss for Christmas,' I point out.

'I thought you said you were working at Christmas,' Gloria says, with the big, sad puppy-dog eyes her son so clearly inherited from her.

Shit.

'I was,' Damian says. 'I went to the crazy Christmas island where Sadie grew up. I'll show you the pictures later. I'm doing a show with real people, real stories...'

'That's nice,' Gloria says kind of dismissively. 'So you're just employer and employee?'

'And friends,' I add.

'No one takes their boss or their employee to meet their family,' Ray says under his breath before swigging his beer.

Eesh, this is a little awkward.

'Did you get your presents?' Damian asks, changing the subject.

'Oh, Damian, yes,' she replies. She almost sounds a little choked up. 'The patio furniture is wonderful. Just what we needed to go on the new flags. I can't believe you were so thoughtful. We're excited about summer now.'

I mentally take a bow. I saw the bit in the newsletter his mum sent him about the new patio so when I was doing Damian's Christmas shopping, I decided on the furniture.

'You're welcome,' he tells them, as if it were all him, as if he's always known all parts of this information. It's scary how unflinching he is when he's lying. I wonder if I'd be able to keep a lid on it so easily.

'We weren't expecting you, so your present isn't exactly ready,' Gloria says. 'It needs wrapping and so on. Can I give you it later?'

'Yeah, don't worry about it,' Damian says. I'm not sure he even believes they have anything for him.

'And Si and Nikki were really pleased with the restaurant voucher you sent them – now little Stella is one, they're going out on more dates. Leaving the baby with us, of course. A one-year-old can't stay home alone.'

Gloria laughs at her own joke in such an adorably wholesome mumsy way.

'So, you're staying for the New Year bash, then?' Ray says excitedly. 'Both of you?'

'We are indeed,' Damian says. 'We're here.'

There's a tone to his voice that I reckon might be for my benefit. One that echoes his earlier statement of 'you asked for this'. I did. And I do still think it's the right thing to do, but I can see why he's reluctant to be here. In this room, surrounded by pictures of Si, with his parents talking about his job – his incredible job that he is so talented at – as if he's just got in with a bad crowd, and showing such little interest.

'I take it my room is ready?' Damian says.

'Of course,' Gloria replies.

'OK, I'll show Sadie up, so we can put our stuff somewhere, then maybe I can plug my camera into the TV? Show you the pictures I've taken. It really is so gorgeous, where Sadie grew up...'

'Yes, after *Eastenders*,' Gloria replies.

'Yeah, you can show us properly when it's finished,' Ray says, quickly adding: 'Not that *I* want to watch *Eastenders*.'

'This way, Sadie,' Damian says, nodding towards the hallway.

He closes the glass-panel living-room door behind us.

'She's just his assistant but they're sharing a room,' we both hear Ray mutter with a scoff, clear as anything, through the glass door.

'We're sharing a room?' I double-check with Damian as we head up the stairs.

'Yep,' he replies. 'It's a two-bed house. Two up, two down. You could sleep on that leather sofa but I wouldn't recommend it. It gets so warm, you'll wake up glued to it.'

'Is it not a bit weird, if we share?' I start, wracking my brains for the best way to tackle the situation. It's already weird I'm in my boss's parents' house. It would be even weirder to sleep in his bed with him.

'Don't look so worried.' Damian laughs as he opens the door with his arm.

I follow him inside and breathe a sigh of relief. Oh, that's why he's not freaking out as much as I am. I smile.

'I didn't realise you had bunk beds.' I laugh. I mean, it's still weird, but it's less weird.

'Baggy top bunk,' he says, practically vaulting himself up there with an energy usually reserved for children. 'The top bunk was always mine, the bottom was Si's. I figure, if I had to sleep in your sister's bed, you should have to sleep in my brother's.'

'Sounds fair to me,' I say.

'Come on, let's ditch our stuff and go back downstairs. My mum buys enough Pringles at Christmas time to feed an army. Let's go eat them,' Damian suggests.

'OK,' I say with a smile. 'You feeling OK about being here?'

I'm proud of him for coming.

'Let's have that conversation tomorrow,' he suggests. 'Once Super Si has shown his face. That's when you'll see them in all their glory.'

I follow Damian downstairs. He bypasses the living room to head into the kitchen where, sure enough, there are supermarket stock levels of Pringles.

We sit at the kitchen table, eat crisps and chat about work but, now that we're here, I can't help but worry that I've talked him into doing the wrong thing.

31

Have you ever woken up and not had a clue where you were? Well, talk to me when you've done it in a bunk bed, because there's something so terrifying about waking up feeling as if you're in a wooden box. Honestly, it was like something fresh out of *A Christmas Carol*, waking up thinking I was in a coffin, then remembering my ghost of Christmas future hovering above me. Not that a life working with Damian would be all that bad, but I don't want to be an assistant forever.

You don't realise how much takeaway there is from the Christmas movies you watch as a kid. I'm not talking about learning home-protection tips from *Home Alone* – especially seeing as though I put my dad in A & E when I was nine, with some well-intentioned but unfortunately placed baubles on the floor by the living-room window. I'm talking about films like *A Christmas Carol* and *It's a Wonderful Life*. Films that take the most wonderful time of year and turn it into a time for taking stock of just what kind of shape your life is in. It's just a coincidence that my own deep-dive into the state of my life has occurred during the Christmas period, and that my fresh start will coincide with the start of a new year.

I can't stop thinking about the choices I'm making. Before Christmas I was so sure of what I should do. I wanted a fresh start with my dream job. Work I would enjoy. Hours that would allow me to have a life too. Damian was driving me crazy and I knew I had to quit for my own good but then... well, since Christmas, things have been different.

He seems more chilled out, softer. More fun to be around. Not only that, but he isn't disturbing me when I'm on a date or on the toilet – he's pretty much self-sufficient. Other than asking me to come here with him – which I really can't blame him for now that I've met his family – he hasn't asked anything of me. I didn't realise at first but now that I have, I can't stop thinking about how much he's changed. The Damian I have known for the past year has always been so wound up, always freaking out about work, no idea what direction he was going, so indecisive about so many things. And then there's his impossible-to-understand love life. All of these things seem to have just vanished. He's on track with his work, he loves what he's doing, he's having fun. He even looks different. Being happy suits him. His brooding look might be what attracts most women to him but his easy smile and the cheeky twinkle in his eye are so much more attractive to me. And that's a problem in itself because I've stopped looking at him as if he's an annoying boss; I've started looking at him as if he's a man again.

I was relieved when I woke up this morning and he was already up and out of the room – although I was slightly mortified about the thought of him seeing me asleep, because who knows what they look like when they're asleep? Maybe I look like an angelic beauty, maybe I look like an ugly demon. I'm just going to hope it's not the latter.

I headed downstairs where I found him sitting in a reclining chair watching TV with his mum. She was wrapped up in a fluffy dressing down, sipping tea from the biggest mug I have ever seen.

'Morning, babe,' she said brightly before her eyes snapped straight back to the TV. 'Help yourself to whatever you want for brekkie.'

Damian jumped up, saying he'd get me something, ushering me into the kitchen.

'Breakfast here is self-service,' he joked. 'My mum is not like your mum at all.'

His dad was already at work when I got up. It's been a long time since Damian paid a visit to the family business so that's where we're headed now.

We're walking down a street on what feels like a bizarrely warm day for December. Christmases just never seem to feel that cold these days, which is good, but probably not a great sign for the world.

'So keep in mind, this is the family business,' Damian says. 'My dad's dad worked there, so did his, et cetera et cetera. I was supposed to work there, but it never, ever appealed to me. Even if I didn't want to take photos, there's no way I would have ever wanted to work there.'

'What sort of family business could a person feel so strongly against?' I wonder out loud.

'That kind,' Damian says.

I glance across the road at Banks and Sons Butchers.

'I'm surprised he hasn't had the "s" removed from "sons", given my absence,' he says. 'Come on, let's get this over with.'

Banks and Sons Butchers looks exactly how a butcher's shop should look. A small, single-level, detached building with a red and white striped canopy outside. The window is part of the counter, displaying different cuts of meats, pies, sausage rolls – I could really go for a sausage roll right now.

Leaning over to pick something up is a tall, skinny man with the trademark Banks family looks. He's wearing the full butcher's gear but I can just about see short brown hair poking out from under his dorky white hat. I know he's younger than Damian, but he looks quite a lot younger. Maybe he's had an easier life – or one that is a lot less fun, at least. I'd heard Damian was quite the bad boy in his twenties but there's no sign of that man any more. Perhaps there never was – he does seem to be preoccupied with how he is perceived, so maybe he created that image, or maybe he killed it off. Maybe it's a bit of both?

As soon as the man sees us he starts waving wildly through the glass before beckoning us inside.

'That your brother?' I ask.

'That's Super Si,' he tells me. 'Oh, and that's Nikki and Stella at the counter.'

By the time we're through the door Si is on the customer side of the counter, waiting to give his brother a big hug.

'Damo,' he says. 'What a nice surprise! What are you doing here?'

'Didn't Dad tell you I was coming?' Damian asks.

'I thought I'd leave it a surprise,' Ray replies with a big smile. 'It was certainly a surprise for us.'

'And this must be your lady,' Si says, hugging me too, as if we're old friends.

'Nope,' his dad says with a chuckle from behind the counter. 'Just his friend.'

'It's 2020,' Si says with a shrug. 'Man, I can't believe you're here. Come see Stella.'

Damian is right, Stella really is the cutest baby I've ever

seen. She has the chubbiest little cheeks and the brightest eyes. She's smiling and making those cute little noises babies make.

'She's gorgeous,' Damian says. 'More like her mum than her goofy dad.'

'OK, Lothario,' Si says. 'And you know Nikki.'

'Hi, Nikki,' Damian says. He turns to me. 'This is Sadie. Sadie, this is everyone.'

'Lovely to meet you,' I say.

'Don't you mean meat you?' Ray laughs. 'M-E-A-T.'

God, Damian was right, his dad cracks terrible dad jokes too.

'Look at your hair,' Nikki says. 'It's so long. Don't you sit on it?'

'Oh, all the time,' I reply.

Nikki has a wavy brown-to-blonde ombre do that just passes her shoulders.

'I'd love to be able to sit on my hair,' she says with a sigh. 'The only thing I sit on is the occasional baby toy by mistake and, frankly, it's usually the highlight of my day.'

OK, I really like this one.

I glance around the room. There is a series of certificates and awards on the wall behind the counter. And then there's the big, framed photo of Ray and Si with an arm around each other, giving a big thumbs up outside the shop. It's not just a photo, it's a newspaper front page – must be from the local rag – with the headline: Like Father, Like Son. I catch Damian staring at it.

'So you're going to be at the New Year's Eve party?' Si says. 'Both of you?'

'We are,' Damian says.

'That's great, that's so great,' Si says before turning back to me. 'We never see this one. He thinks he's too good for us now, huh, Mr Big Shot?'

He's saying this in a really friendly, jokey way but it just feels so awkward, and I can see it's annoying Damian, even though he tries to laugh it off.

'Sadie, let me get you some things to try,' Si says. 'One of our award-winning sausage rolls maybe?'

Oh, he might be a bit of a dick to his brother, but he is reading my mind.

'That would be lovely,' I say.

'OK, I might not have had any plans for Christmas, but I could definitely be at some fancy New Year's party instead of taking passive-aggressive remarks from this lot,' Damian whispers to me. 'So could you. Don't you want to party with – oh, God, I don't even know who is cool any more – the Angels and the Hunters of the world?'

I wonder if he said it like that because it sounds good or if there's some other reason he's purposefully not saying Lottie's name.

'Oh, I'm not sure any of that lot want to see me ever again,' I say. 'And I doubt they have sausage rolls like that – oh my God, it's massive.'

'The biggest and the best for miles,' Si says.

'I'm going to show Sadie the park,' Damian says. 'Mind if we take it to go?'

'Of course not,' Si says. 'Loads to do here, haven't we, Dad?'

'Loads,' Ray says. 'We're a man down.'

'Oh, rea...' Damian's voice tapers off when he realises the man down is him. 'See you both later.'

'See you at the party, Sadie,' Nikki calls after me.

'Yeah, see you then,' I call back. I give Stella a little wave too.

We're only a few metres down the road when Damian starts.

'You know what, I'm glad we came, and I'm glad you're with me,' he says, not sounding all that glad. 'Because you can tell me if I'm imagining it. Do they make me feel bad or do I just feel bad?'

'Oh, God, I can't answer that,' I tell him.

'Can't or won't?'

'It sounds like there's a lot going on,' I reason. We wander into a cute little park and walk along the edge of a pond. It's beautiful here, with a really nice family atmosphere. The place is full of people walking off their inevitable Christmas weight gain.

'Like Si saying I think I'm better than them,' Damian says. 'I don't think that at all. So they're a little rough around the edges, so what? I'm not embarrassed about where I come from. I'm from a working-class family. But the system isn't made to favour us. And the art industry definitely isn't an industry dominated by the working class. I went to Oxford and I felt like I didn't belong there. I grew up down the road – it doesn't matter; I didn't feel like I sounded right, or looked right, so I changed… but not because I was ashamed. I just changed. I blended into my environment.'

'Hey, I get it,' I reply. 'I'm from Yorkshire, remember? Up there I have one of the gentlest accents but plonk me in London in a room full of art gallery employees and I sound like a farmer, unless I try really hard to keep it at bay. There's a little voice in my head telling me to strip it back, play it down even more, if I want to get hired over someone who has that same accent everyone else has – that you have.'

'Is that what you did? To get the job?' Damian asks.

Oh, God, how much have I said? I'm so comfortable around him I'm just chatting away.

'Hmm?'

'Did you do an accent in the interview to get the job with me?' he asks.

'Oh, yeah, I guess I did,' I reply, relieved I haven't put my foot in it. 'I didn't think you'd hire a bumpkin.'

'Well, I didn't think you were a bumpkin,' Damian says. 'To be honest, I thought you were pretty hot. An industrial tribunal waiting to happen, that's what Henrietta said. I guess she knew you were my type.'

Henrietta is Damian's agent-type person. When he interviewed me, she and Karen sat in and the three of them grilled me together. That's not what's important in that sentence though; what's important is, well, basically every other part of it. He thought I was hot? I was his type? The only thing making my mind race faster than what he just said is me obsessing over the fact he used the past tense.

'What are you thinking?' he asks.

'I'm just wondering if I want my pay-out in cash or a cheque,' I joke. 'I could take you to the cleaners for that.'

'Hey, I never acted on it, did I?' he says. 'I might be an arsehole at times but I'm a professional arsehole.'

I can't help but laugh.

'That came out wrong,' he says. 'How's the sausage roll? I'm too petty to try one.'

'Really bloody good,' I say through a mouthful. 'But not as good as your photos.'

'Well, at least there's that,' he says with a smile, but then he sighs.

I don't know where we are exactly but we're walking through a park. It's starting to get a bit chilly now but there are plenty of people around, walking with their families, playing with their dogs.

'I actually had a bit of a crush on you when I started working for you,' I confess, not wanting to leave him out on a limb on his own.

'You did not,' he says.

'I really did,' I reply. 'So if you hadn't been professional then, I guess I wouldn't have either... but that probably would have ruined everything and we wouldn't be here.'

Damian stops in his tracks.

'That's interesting,' he says. 'Really interesting.'

I probably shouldn't have said that, should I? I've probably just made things incredibly awkward.

'It's just one of those things,' I say with a bat of my hand before wiping my lips with the back of it, because I'm suddenly paranoid I have pastry flakes all over my face. 'We know better now.'

'I don't,' Damian says, before he places one hand on the small of my back and his lips on mine. As he pulls my body up close to his, he runs the other hand through my hair, up the back of my head. We kiss for a few seconds before our lips part again, but he only pulls away far enough to whisper to me.

'Take me to a tribunal – that was worth every penny,' he jokes.

I can still feel his warm breath on my cold cheeks. I'm about to move in for more when a dog barking causes me to jump out of my skin. I'd kind of forgotten about all the other people in the park. We instinctively put a bit of distance between us, to try and cool off. But, honestly, I just want to do it again.

'Ah, crap,' he says.

Oh, God, he regrets it already. What was that, twenty seconds?

'I… erm…' I don't know what to say.

'I technically just tasted one of those bloody sausage rolls,' he says. 'They're pretty good.'

He really had me going for a second then. I thought he was going to say it was a mistake.

I laugh but reality is nipping at my heels.

'Do, erm… do we need to talk about that?' I ask.

'Nah,' he says. 'It's New Year's Eve tomorrow. Let's finish this year off before we start worrying about the next one.'

'OK, sure,' I say with a smile.

'Let's head back to my parents' place,' he says. 'I'm sure my mum will be waiting with baby pictures to show you – all of them will be of Si.'

I laugh.

'Can't wait,' I reply.

Damian takes hold of my hand and holds it as we walk through the park. As soon as we reach a bin, I throw the rest of my pastry away. For some reason my appetite has completely changed and, no, that's not me being saucy, I'm just not hungry now. If there's one thing worse than kissing your boss, it's kissing the boss who doesn't know you're leaving him…

32

Damian wasn't wrong when he said that his mum would be waiting for me when we got back. She really was, and with a box full of embarrassing childhood photos that make me feel a bit better about Damian seeing every embarrassing haircut I ever had as a child and every ill-advised fashion phase I went through as a teen chronicled through the family Christmas photos on the walls.

Damian was a seriously cute baby – way cuter than his brother, which I only point out because everything seems to be a competition between them. Despite what Damian said, there are a fairly equal number of photos of him and Si. I suppose it's as they grew up that Si became the firm favourite.

Damian didn't look how I expected him to when he was a kid, or a teenager for that matter. He was quite chubby and he had a big gap between his two front teeth – which his mum and his brother have, so he must have had some cosmetic intervention there.

'He managed to get a prom date, at least,' Gloria tells me, showing me a photo of a young Damian in a seriously ugly tux.

He's standing so far from his date – who is also wearing an ugly but completely of its time prom dress – that you'd think they were practising social distancing. 'I think it was more of a friends thing, or she was making someone jealous or something.'

'He looks so cute,' I say. 'And he's certainly got better at wearing suits as he's got older.'

'I almost wouldn't know,' Gloria says. 'Si's wedding was the last time I saw him in a suit, if you don't count the cuttings.'

'The cuttings?'

'Yeah, just a sec,' she says.

Damian actively didn't want to see his childhood pictures so we left him in the kitchen to go upstairs and look. I didn't realise I'd be climbing a stepladder into the loft but here we are.

Gloria pulls out a different plastic box and undoes the lid.

'Pictures from newspapers, things Ray printed out off the Internet, some postcards and bits of his work – they're a bit too weird to put on the walls, but we like to keep a box,' she says.

'Can I have a look?'

'Go ahead,' she says.

I have a quick peep through the box that is absolutely full to the brim of all things Damian Banks.

'He's a big deal, isn't he?' Gloria says.

'He really is,' I reply. 'Does he know you have this box?'

'Oh, no,' she says quickly. 'You know what he's like. He doesn't like a fuss from us.'

To anyone outside the family it's widely obvious what is going on here. Damian doesn't think his family are proud of him, and his family think that Damian has risen up through the classes to something beyond them. Neither statement is true.

'You should show him,' I tell her. 'I think he worries he's letting you down.'

'Letting us down? He's Damian Banks,' she says. 'Why would he think that?'

'I think he feels bad about not joining the family business, not having a family of his own...'

I wonder if I should be sticking my nose in like this...

'Can you imagine Damian covered in offal?' she says. 'Not a chance. He's always been too squeamish. He doesn't even like cooking meat, never mind hacking up a carcass. He's exactly where he should be.'

Too much information about the meat industry always makes me want to eat less of it.

'And as for him not having a family, well, Damian has always done everything in his own time. I'm sure he'll do this in his own time too. Still, I had high hopes when I saw him turn up at the door with you...'

'Sorry about that,' I say.

'Oh, it's fine,' she replies. 'Not that you wouldn't make a lovely couple. It just surprises me that he'd bring you here if you're just someone from work. That doesn't sound like him at all.'

I feel as if Gloria is tapping into some sort of mother's intuition, or that my face is giving away more than I would like.

She shows me the prom picture again.

'Debbie Hall never got to sleep in his bunk bed,' she tells me. 'He always kept girls at arm's length. But that's my Damian – he doesn't do anything until it's worth doing, and when he does do it, he does it right.'

She's not wrong about that. That kiss earlier, oh my God. I've never been kissed like it. He certainly doesn't kiss by halves.

I almost wish he did because that would mean he owed me the same again.

'I'll show him the box tomorrow,' Gloria says, snapping me from my thoughts. 'Maybe it will help us go into the new year with... I don't know, something better. You should always try and start the new year on a high, or it's all downhill from there.'

I would love for me and Damian to go into the new year with something better, although for us I'm not sure what that looks like. I want to kiss him again, I really do, but I can't, not until I'm honest with him. Perhaps tomorrow is the day I have to tell him that I'm giving my notice. I can't keep it from him any longer – I just really hope that after I do tell him, he still wants to kiss me again.

33

'I can't stop thinking about that kiss,' Damian says from above me.

It's 1 a.m. and we're both tucked up in our bunk beds. The room is pitch black, and it must be twenty minutes since we politely said goodnight and turned the lights off, and yet here we are, both thinking the same thing.

'Me too,' I whisper back.

'You don't know how long I've wanted to do that,' he continues, still in hushed tones. 'And now that I have...'

The sound of Ray coughing through the paper-thin walls stops him in his tracks.

'Now that I have...'

More coughing.

'Shh,' I say softly with a giggle. 'They can probably hear you.'

'Can I come down?'

I take a sharp breath. I wasn't expecting him to say that.

'Sure,' I reply. I want him to but I'm scared.

I can just about make out Damian's silhouette as he climbs

down from the top bunk. I don't really know what he's intending to do but I scoot up closer to the wall and whip the covers back.

It's an old, soft mattress so as Damian gets on the bed next to me he causes it to sink, which pulls me towards him. As my bare shoulder brushes against his bare chest I feel a shiver run through my body.

'Sorry,' he says. 'Shall I...?'

'No, no, it's fine,' I assure him.

Damian relaxes in place with his arm around me.

Single beds sure are small, aren't they? We sleep in them when we're kids but as soon as we're adults, even if we're single, we never look back. It's at least a double from there on out, home or away. It's been a long time since I was in a single bed. I don't think I've ever been in one with another person.

Damian and I are close. So close our bodies are touching from our toes right up to our shoulders. So far we've managed to keep our lips apart.

'You were saying,' I prompt him, still whispering. 'Before...'

'Oh, right,' he says. It takes him a few seconds to recall. 'I was saying, I've waited so long to kiss you and now that I have... I can't believe it's taking me so long to do it again.'

This time it's me who makes the first move. I still can't really see him in this dark room but my lips find his and that's it, the gentle kiss from the park is long behind us now. Things have kicked up a notch and it's all happening so quickly. In a few seconds, with some fancy manoeuvring, Damian is on top of me, but as we continue to kiss the bed frame knocks against the wall. And then there's that coughing from next door...

'Can you... do anything in a bunk bed without making a noise?' I ask, although I don't know why I'm being so subtle. Maybe it's because he's my boss, but he *is* on top of me, and my legs *are* locked around his waist. I don't think anyone is under any illusion what is happening right now.

'You definitely can't,' he says. 'Trust me.'

'You'd know, would you?' I tease.

'Only because I tested it, for logistical reasons, when I was a teen, just in case I ever needed to know,' he jokes. I think he's joking.

I grab him and kiss him again. I can't stop myself. I don't know what's happened. It's as if all this time I've had this lurking deep down inside me and now that the genie is out of the bottle, there's nothing I can do to get it back in. So to speak.

'Right, that's it,' he says before jumping out of bed. 'Grab your coat, you've pulled.'

'Are you serious?' I ask.

'Grab your shoes too,' he says. 'Come on.'

I think he's serious... Whatever he is, I'm here for it. I am on the hook.

'OK...'

I grab my shoes and throw my coat on over the vest top and knickers I was going to sleep in. I am so, so grateful I decided to leave my elf PJs at my mum and dad's or I am sure I'd be wearing them right now.

Damian takes me by the hand, leading me downstairs, into the dining room and then...

'Are we going outside?' I ask him as he messes with the patio doors.

'Yep,' he replies.

'To where?' I whisper.

'You know your boat?' he asks me. 'The one you and big Brian used to sneak off to?'

'Yes,' I reply, somehow managing to make my voice even quieter now that we're outside in the moonlight.

'I had this...'

He nods towards a shed at the bottom of the garden.

'A shed?' I say in disbelief.

'It's not as bad as it sounds,' he whispers back.

We creep across the lawn and down the path to where the shed is. Damian quietly finds the right key on the set and opens the door.

Once we're inside with the door closed behind us Damian twiddles the blinds closed before switching on the light.

'Oh, OK, this isn't a shed at all,' I say. 'This is...'

'My dad's man cave,' he replies.

'Your dad really likes The Beatles,' I point out pointlessly – I'm sure he already knows that his dad loves The Beatles and, if he didn't, the man cave full of Beatles memorabilia would be tipping him off too.

'He does,' he replies. 'He also likes sofa beds.'

I can't help but laugh as Damian pulls a handle that turns the sofa into a bed.

'Wait, you knew this was here?' I say.

'Yeah...'

'So I didn't have to sleep in your bunk beds with you.'

'No...'

Now that we're in here, with the light on, staring at each other in nothing but our underwear, coats and boots, it's as if we're being given the chance to put the brakes on again. He isn't just a sexy voice in the dark any more, he's my boss. I can see him, clear as day, and I do still need to tell him everything...

Damian kicks off his shoes and flings his coat into an armchair.

'Are you sure this is a good idea?' I ask as I approach him cautiously. There's a voice in my head telling me that it isn't and yet here I am, getting closer and closer.

'I'm not wild about that massive poster of John Lennon watching but I guess it beats Lee from Blue,' he jokes.

Oh, there's that cheeky smile. I can't resist that smile.

Screw it.

I whip off my coat and practically leap into his arms. Damian falls back onto the sofa bed. It lets out a big, creaking noise but it holds steady beneath us. The whole reason we're in here is to be sneaky – breaking a sofa bed would be a huge giveaway.

Any worries I had about whether finally getting together with Damian would be awkward fly out of the shed window because this just feels right. It's as if the whole year of working together, hanging out together, teasing each other, was all foreplay for this moment right now. Suddenly every moment of it seems worth it.

* * *

'Phew,' Damian says as he lies back on the sofa bed.

He scoops me up with one of his arms. I lie with my head on his chest.

That... was... amazing.

Damian pulls the covers over us to keep us warm.

'How long do you think we've been out here?' I ask him.

Damian glances around the room.

'I'm looking for a Beatles clock,' he says with a laugh. 'I can't believe there isn't one. At least we know what to get my dad next Christmas.'

The briefest mention of next Christmas sends me crashing back down to earth.

I need to talk to him. Now more than ever, but every single time it always feels like the absolute worst time to say anything.

Before I have chance to say anything the shed door opens.

'Oh, Jesus Christ, it's just you two,' Ray says.

He's standing in the doorway brandishing a fire poker.

I feel so lucky Damian had already pulled the covers over us. Still, I pull them up higher.

'What are you doing up?' Damian asks him.

It's so funny, Damian asking his dad what he's doing when we're the ones up to no good.

'I needed some water – I saw the light on from the kitchen,' he says. 'What are you two doing?'

He knows what we're doing – or what we were doing, at least. Once again, so relieved we were just lying still when Ray walked in.

'We're just… we were just…'

Damian doesn't know what to say and I'm not exactly helping him, just lying here in mortified silence.

'Well, I'll leave you to it,' Ray says.

As he pulls the door closed behind him we can just about make out him chuckle to himself: 'Didn't I say no one brings "just a friend" to meet their parents…'

34

Waking up in my bottom bunk I can't help but wonder if last night might have been a dream.

'Morning,' Damian says as he places a tray with a cup of tea and some biscuits down next to me. He leans forward and kisses me on the lips, anchoring me in reality. Last night did happen.

'My mum and dad have gone out to get the shopping for the party tonight,' he tells me. 'I'm going to jump in the shower. You just chill out there, drink your tea. I'll be back before you know it.'

'OK,' I say with a smile. 'Thank you.'

As Damian heads for the bathroom, with a real spring in his step, I grab my phone from the bedside table. I open my inbox to check my emails and notice one in Damian's inbox – the one that I manage.

My heart sinks when I see who the sender is: lottie@lottieloves.com. Subject: Here we go. And it's an email with attachments too. I don't want to open it about as much as I absolutely need to open it.

Misplaced your number but here's that Christmas present I
promised you. See you in the New Year. xxx

I can only see the top of the image included with the email
but it's obvious what it is. I can see Lottie – doing that stupid,
vacant look she does in every single picture, with the pout and
the stare. Her shoulders are bare. Do I really need to scroll
down?

Of course I do and the inevitable soft porn turns my stomach. Not because the sight of boobs offends me – truth be told
it's a sight I'm kind of indifferent towards, given that I have
some of my own – but because of what the message said.
Misplaced your number. Here's that Christmas present I
promised you. This was all agreed upon back at the wedding.
Why wouldn't he tell me, if he had something going with someone? If he knew these photos were coming? Why would he
make plans with her? He made out to me as if he didn't even
like her...

I jump out of bed and throw on my clothes because
whether I do or I don't confront him with this the second he
walks back into the room, I don't want to be nearly naked when
it happens.

I angrily stuff my things into my case as I think about what
a mug I've been. I'm just putting on my boots when Damian
walks back in. He's only got a towel around him and he was
probably expecting to find me still in bed, so the fact I'm
putting my boots on seems all the more obvious.

'What's wrong?' he asks as his face falls.

'You got an email,' I blurt immediately, so I guess that's the
route we're taking. 'From Lottie.'

'Oh, God, what did she want?' he asks. 'Was she offering to
give me a reference for my CV?'

He laughs but I don't find it funny.

I pull up the email on my phone and hold it up in front of him. The photos catch his eye for a second before he looks away hurriedly.

'Oh, boy,' he says. 'She's not shy.'

'Neither are you, by the sounds of it,' I say.

His eyes shift from looking in any direction but the phone to meeting my gaze instead. I'm still holding the phone out in front of me but he looks beyond it.

'What does that mean?' he asks.

'"Misplaced your number,"' I start reading, doing my best, exaggerated take on her super-squeaky voice. '"Here's that Christmas present I promised you. See you in the New Year. Kiss, kiss, kiss."'

Damian laughs.

'This isn't funny, Damian,' I say.

'It is,' he insists. 'She's full of it. I never gave her my number. I certainly never asked her to send me anything or made any plans with her. She's just trying her luck.'

'You must have given her your email address,' I point out.

'Yeah, the one you check the messages on,' he reminds me. 'I figured you'd tell her to piss off for me.'

'Oh...' I don't know what to say now. 'I'm sorry. I guess it takes a lot of trust, to navigate stuff like this.'

Damian grabs his phone from the desk. He unlocks it, taps the screen, and then tosses it to me. I look down at it to see his open photo gallery.

'Go through my phone,' he insists. 'Check my emails, my WhatsApp, Instagram – scroll through my pictures. There's nothing in it but you and me and Christmas. I've hardly touched my phone this past couple of weeks.'

I can see from his camera roll that it's all just pictures from the last couple of weeks. Selfies of the two of us, pictures of my family, all of the dumb Christmas stuff we did...

'I don't need to look,' I insist, tossing it back. 'I'm sorry, I overreacted because this is all new and weird... I guess we just need to trust each other.'

Damian scoffs. Not exactly the reaction I was expecting.

'You're one to talk about trust,' he says. He actually sounds annoyed at me now.

'Look, I overreacted, I'm sorry,' I say. 'Please don't be offended. It's more my issue than yours.'

'I'm not talking about that. I'm talking about trust,' he says. 'You're gunning for me, over something that didn't happen, weeks before we got together. But you're the one who can't be trusted.'

I just stare at him for a second. I don't know...

'You're not being honest with me,' he says.

I still can't make any words come out.

'I know that you're leaving me,' he says.

Oh.

'I know that you've got a new job – when the hell were you going to tell me? You've had weeks now,' he says.

Now I can think of a million things to say but none of them feels right.

'I was going to tell you,' I insist. 'It was just... wait, how do you know?'

How could he know? Did the gallery contact him for a reference? Did someone let it slip at home?

'You told me,' he says.

'I told you?'

'Yep.'

I'm pretty sure I didn't. I've been agonising about it for weeks, feeling worse and worse about it as we've been growing closer, so unless I've been babbling about it in my sleep...

'When did I tell you?'

Damian puffs air from his cheeks.

'You told Adam,' he says.

'So... Adam told you?'

'*I'm Adam*,' Damian says slowly and clearly.

'What do you mean? You're not Adam. I've seen a picture of Adam and he isn't you...'

'The Adam you swapped notes with is me,' he says.

'Damian, I am so confused,' I say as I sit down on the bed. 'His photo was on the desk – Selena found him online, it said he worked for you...'

'He did work for me,' Damian says. 'He quit. You took his job.'

'So... you sent me that first note? About yourself?' I ask. It sounds as if that's what he's saying but that can't be right... I have to be misunderstanding him...

'Adam's parting shot, when he quit, was to call me an arsehole, and a nightmare—'

'You are an arsehole,' I interrupt him.

'So, when you started, I thought it might be a fun welcome prank to leave you a note... but then you replied, and you agreed. So the next few were just to see how you were honestly finding things, and then I just liked swapping notes with you. We got on so well and everyone in that office treats me like the boss, just the source of their income who they have to keep sweet, so the two of us chatting in such a normal way... I really liked it.'

'Damian, that's so weird... You kept a picture of him on the desk,' I say.

'Technically I didn't,' he says. 'Adam just left that behind when he stormed out. By the time I realised things were already out of hand. You'd put your picture up. So I led you to believe Adam worked in the office on the days you didn't...'

'But it was always you,' I say, as if we aren't both crystal clear on that. 'How did you even...?'

No wonder the real Adam never accepted my friend request. I did wonder why he always wrote in block capitals – it was Damian trying to keep his handwriting under wraps.

I don't suppose I ever thought to ask any questions about my predecessor. Well, the contact address is supposed to be a direct line to Damian, so there were never any names in there, and I was given my own personal email address when I started. And no one ever mistook me for my predecessor on the phone because, well, Adam is a man, I'm a woman. As soon as I introduced myself as Damian's new assistant, why would anyone mention Adam to me? I feel like such an idiot.

'I'd always be in the office before you,' he says. He doesn't seem proud of himself at all. His shoulders are hanging heavy by his sides and he's looking at the floor in front of him.

'So that's why, when I told "him" I was quitting and asked him for a drink he didn't reply – because he was just you, and that's why he didn't add me on Facebook.'

'You tried to add him?'

'My grandma did,' I say. 'But don't be coming at me like I'm weird for striking up a connection over notes with someone when you were the other person and you were sending them as someone else. I feel so betrayed.'

'You feel betrayed? OK, I hold my hands up, I apologise for the way I've gone about things. I didn't know how to talk to you as myself, for the longest time, and it felt shitty trying to get to know you in one breath and then asking you to buy the office toilet roll in the other. But you're not completely innocent either, are you? Like, inviting me home for Christmas with you...'

'Oh, come on, you invited yourself,' I say.

'Because I was freaked out about you bailing on me and not telling me,' he reasons. 'I thought, if I could just spend some time with you, as myself, the real me, not the me freaking out over work or nagging you with work shit twenty-four hours a day... And when your dad asked me that question, about whether you chew my food for me, that was it, I could see where I was going wrong and I bucked my ideas up. For you.'

'So all that was just for my benefit?' I ask angrily.

'You say that like it's a bad thing,' he replies. 'I had feelings for you so I changed.'

'You had sex with me knowing you'd lied to me,' I snap.

'Yeah, well, so did you, the only difference is I stopped lying to you before I had sex with you. You weren't going to tell me you were leaving,' he says angrily.

We're both so angry, perhaps justifiably, but I feel so manipulated. The furious storm brewing inside me is too much. I'm not doing this any more.

'Damian, I quit,' I announce. 'Get yourself some other mug to run around after you and swap creepy little notes with them. Alternatively, learn to look after yourself like a man.'

'Oh, come on, you loved me being dependent on you,' he replies. 'You lived for it. At first you would offer to do more, to ease the burden, then you just started doing more, and suddenly you're the gatekeeper to everything.'

'I was doing my job,' I stress.

'Well, you don't have to do it any more, do you?' he replies. 'And, here's your leaving gift: you don't have to work your notice. This is it.'

His hostility wounds me even deeper. Does he really think he has the right to be annoyed at me right now?

'Fine by me,' I say. 'I can't wait for my fresh start.'

I stand up and put on my coat as I rant.

'Honestly, I have been counting down the minutes to when you are no longer my problem,' I say. I grab my bags. 'Good luck finding someone else willing to put up with your shit.'

'Yeah, and good luck getting a reference,' he calls after me as I head for the bedroom door.

I feel the anger bubbling up inside me. How is he mad at me right now? Sensible conversation is out of the window – all I can think about is saying something to hurt him. I want him to feel as horrible as I do.

'Ha, I don't even need one,' I reply. 'Because working for you for a year without winding up in a padded room is clearly proof to everyone else that I'm hireable. So, in the words of my great friend Adam The Fucking Imaginary, I quit. You're an arsehole and a nightmare to work for. All the best.'

I slam the door shut behind me and head downstairs. I storm outside and I walk as fast as I can, terrified that he's going to come after me, but he doesn't. Once I'm clear of the house I take out my phone and start punching in directions to get home. It's too late to head home to my mum and dad's because, not only will it be hard to get a train, but it would be so expensive. To go home to London is much easier; it just means spending New Year's Eve alone... Unless...

35

It turns out it takes a train, a bus, and a grand total of almost two shitting hours to get from Banbury to Camden, and trekking between various forms of public transport isn't exactly living it up in a Range Rover but, do you know what, I am a woman on a mission, and petty revenge has fuelled me every step of the way.

Am I still on the bus, staring sadly out of the window feeling sorry for myself? Nope. Am I moping in my tiny two-room flat, crying into an almost empty bottle of prosecco while I wait for *Jools' Annual Hootenanny* to start? Absolutely not.

I have put on my tightest, shortest dress – and I am not usually a fan of (un)dressing to kill, but these are extenuating circumstances – my highest pair of heels, and I'm meaningfully marching through the doors to The Marjorie Hotel.

It's a big, fancy five-star London hotel that just so happens to be hosting a spectacular New Year's Eve party in the ball-room, and I am invited. And there's my date, over there, by the indoor fountain in the lavish reception: Brian.

Not only will being here tonight – and plastering it all over my Instagram – show Damian that I don't need him to get into fancy parties, but he'll absolutely hate that I'm here with Big Brian.

'Sadie, I was worried you weren't going to make it before midnight,' he says, glancing at his watch before greeting me with a kiss on the cheek.

'Better late than never,' I announce, perhaps a little loudly.

So I might not have been crying into an almost empty bottle of prosecco while I waited for *Jools' Annual Hootenanny* to start, but I did drink quite a bit of fizz while I got ready to head out.

It's after 11 p.m. so I'm not surprised he was worried I wouldn't show. But by the time I got back to Camden, got all dressed up, and raced over here in my slightly tipsy state it was unsurprisingly pretty late in the evening.

Brian is wearing a tux with a black bow tie. His hair is neatly slicked down, leaving it flat to his head. He looks super-smart but at the same time he probably feels about as uncomfortable as I do.

'I look like a bloody penguin,' he says. He must be able to tell I'm looking at his outfit. I always think I'm so subtle, but I don't suppose I am, especially not when I'm drunk. 'It's a work do, and there's a dress code, so I didn't have much choice.'

It's amazing how much more northern we sound when you stick us in the city. Even the voice in my head feels as if it sounds more northern right now.

'You look great,' I assure him. 'Like a real adult.'

'So do you,' he tells me. 'That dress... wow.'

The fact I'm here, now, wearing this, might actually be me at my most immature but, you know what, I'll take it.

'Thanks.'

'Shall we head inside?' Brian suggests.

'Sure, just let me...' I wobble on my heels a little. 'Oops. Just let me snap a picture of the fountain.'

I hate that I can hear Damian's voice in my head giving advice on how to frame the shot. No matter how hard I try I can hear 'rule of thirds' ringing in my ears. He's always done this, everywhere we've been, and it's always driven me mad... It has always produced amazing photos though.

'OK, got it,' I say. 'Let's go.'

Walking into the ballroom is like walking into a dream – well, of course it is: I'm nearly naked and my ex is here. The ceiling is covered with fairy lights, like twinkling stars over our heads. I don't know what the walls usually look like because they're covered with cream, silky curtains, and I don't imagine I'll remember what they look like tomorrow because I've had a few.

As stunning as the room looks, the party is closer to the end than the beginning, so things aren't quite as perfect as I'm sure they looked when everyone arrived. I'll bet everyone looked gorgeous and had such high hopes for the evening. Now that it's nearly over, the tables are messy and people are starting to look a little worse for wear too, either because their make-up is fading and their curls are dropping, or because they've had way too much to drink. A New Year's Eve party is a pretty good metaphor for the year ahead, when you think about it. Everyone goes into it with resolutions to have the best one yet, but somehow, by the end of it, everything is just a mess. Still, there's always next year.

'Can I get you a drink?' Brian asks.

'I'd love one,' I say a little over-enthusiastically.

'OK, I'll be right back,' he says. 'It's nearly midnight anyway.'

I inflate my cheeks with air before slowly pushing every last drop out again. Oh, boy, I really did turn up late. Still, I'm here, and I've got my game face on, and that's what counts.

With Brian at the bar I take out my phone again. I hold it up at a high angle and strike my best Instagrammer pose. Head tipped, cheeks sucked in, pouting, looking as if I can't tell the difference between the home secretary and my eight times tables. A proper vacant Lottie face, except I'll probably keep my top on for the picture, thanks very much. Ergh, I can still see the pictures she sent Damian. I'll never be able to look at a Christmas bow the same again.

I snap a few pictures – because that's what you do, right? You take a bunch and then use an app to edit the best one until what's left is someone who looks nothing like you, with nonsensical facial features and skin so smooth it no longer looks like skin.

Brian rocks up alongside me as I'm taking a selfie. He sticks his face into the shot and poses with me. I can see my eyes light up in my screen because I know that it will annoy Damian so much, seeing a photo of me out with Brian, and that's what I want. I want to annoy him, because what he has done has absolutely horrified me. I can't believe it. I honestly can't believe it. Damian was Adam *the whole time*. Every single note was from him. Every note I wrote – complaining about Damian – was read by bloody Damian. OK, I might not have been honest with him about quitting but, my God, all this just goes to show that I have definitely made the right decision.

'I brought you some champagne,' Brian says. 'Seeing as though the countdown will be starting before we know it.'

Brian sounds a little bit drunk too. I guess he's been here all night and not swigging from a bottle in his flat while blasting Dua Lipa and piling on make-up.

'Thank you,' I say, taking the champagne flute from him as carefully as possible. I can feel the concentration on my face.

'So, did you have a good Christmas?' I ask him.

'Yeah, great, thanks,' he says. 'It's always nice to see the parents, isn't it?'

'I don't know, yours don't make you dress up,' I remind him as I post one of the pictures I just took to my Instagram story. Being a cool, artsy, fartsy blah blah blah – I usually try and keep my grid pretty carefully curated, with an overarching theme, and I basically never post to my story. I certainly don't rapid-fire drunken content like this.

'Hey, did you give your notice?' he asks curiously.

'Oh, boy, did I,' I say with a laugh. 'I mean yes, yes, I did. Officially free as a bird.'

'That's good,' he says. 'It's always nice to end things on a good note.'

'It is,' I agree. That's not what I did, but I do agree.

'It's nice, that we can both meet up here like this,' he continues. 'We should do it more often. I still can't believe we both work in London.'

'What do you actually do?' I ask. 'I don't think I know...'

'I'm an underwriting controls analyst,' he says.

I still don't know.

'What does that mean?' I ask.

'It means I'm really good with Excel,' he replies.

'Uh, I love it when you talk dirty,' I joke, fuelled by my drink.

My dirty joke catches Damian off guard. No, not Damian, Brian. I am not thinking about Damian.

The DJ takes a break from playing nondescript party beats to announce the countdown to midnight. I join in, shouting out the numbers with everyone else. When the clock finally does strike midnight there are some loud popping noises above us before gold, sparkly confetti rains down over us.

I've always found New Year's Eve so depressing. Something about the idea of a new beginning just really bums me out. On the one hand, the idea that the first day of a new year gives us a sort of second chance, an opportunity to change, sounds good on paper. On the other, don't we always say we'll do better and never actually do it? New Year's resolutions were made to be broken. That January diet you swear you're going to go on is a knee-jerk reaction to all the pigs in blankets you ate over the festive period and it's probably not going to be sustainable for long. I know, I sound like a moody little black cloud on an otherwise perfectly sunny day but people should change because they want to be better, not because it's New Year's Day, and certainly not because they want to stop their assistant from quitting by charming them into the sack – not even the sack, the shed. Ergh, it's no use, I can't stop thinking about him. Damian is in my head and he's not going anywhere. I could call him? But I'm so mad at him. And he's mad at me too. And I don't see my phone lighting up with calls and messages from him, so why should I have to make the first move?

I miss him though. I miss him so much. So much, in fact, that the whole Adam thing hardly seems worth falling out over, and yet I just can't let go of my anger. I suppose I'm angry about a lot of things.

Brian leans in and pecks me on the lips.

'Happy New Year,' he says. 'Do you want to get out of here?'

I sigh heavily.

'Absolutely,' I reply.

I knock back the rest of my drink, hand him my glass, and walk away on my own. Brian doesn't even call after me – or I don't hear him if he does. This was such a terrible idea and, if the new year really is the best time to change for the better, then the best thing I can do is go home. I'm about to embark on a new journey and I absolutely can't take any of my old baggage with me.

36

Is January the longest month of the year? I know, it's thirty-one days, like a bunch of the other months, but it's the one that feels the longest, isn't it?

Today, which is technically only the 31st January, feels more like the 78th January. It's been such a strange month and I sure will be glad to see the back of it.

To celebrate the end of the month my lovely friend Xara is coming over and she's bringing wine. Not only am I finding that I have much more free time to hang out after work, but I see Xara at work all the time too now that we work together.

I'm just putting the pizzas in the oven when I hear my phone ringing. I close the oven door and dive for my phone on the sofa, answering it just before it stops.

'Hello, Mum,' I say. 'How are you?'

'All good here, thanks, darling,' she says.

'Hi, Sadie,' I hear Selena call from in the background.

'Selena says hi,' my mum tells me.

'Say hi back,' I reply.

'Up to anything nice?' she asks.

'I'm actually just waiting for Xara to arrive,' I tell her. 'We're having a girly night.'

'Oh, London is going to run out of wine tonight, then,' she jokes. 'Listen, I won't keep you, I'm just calling about the post I got today.'

'Oh?'

'I figured you would know what I was talking about,' she says. 'Did you get any post today?'

'I haven't had chance to check,' I tell her. 'Hang on, I'll do it now.'

I slip on my shoes and head out to my post box.

'I have loads actually,' I tell her.

'Any invitations?' she persists.

'Erm, the one on the top looks like my smear-test reminder,' I say. 'So unless they're inviting you to that too...'

'Keep looking, Sadie, come on.'

I head back inside and dump the pile on my table.

'Erm, let's see... oh, yeah, this one looks like an invitation,' I say.

I tear open the envelope to see a piece of white card that says simply:

Do you believe in real love?

I turn it over to see the heading:

Real Stories, Real Lives, Real Love.

That's when I realise what it is. It's an invitation to Damian's preview on the 14th February. Valentine's Day.

'Oh,' I say.

'Are you going?' my mum asks.

'Erm, it's Valentine's Day,' I point out. 'What if I have plans?'

'If she's saying she has plans, she's lying,' I hear Selena call out.

'Do you have plans?' my mum asks.

'No,' I say simply. 'Hang on, why is he inviting you?'

'He's invited me and Dad,' she tells me. 'With Dad being in one of the pictures.'

'Wait, Dad is in one of the pictures?'

'Oh, yes,' she says. 'Well, I suppose they didn't tell you at the time when they took it because it was when they popped into Pandora's to get your bag. But he got a lovely picture of Dad, wearing a hat and holding a cane – he says your dad is a modern-day clown.'

'Damian is the clown,' I say.

I told my mum that we fell out. I didn't get into exactly why. I just let her believe that it was all to do with me quitting my job.

'Still not friends, I take it,' she says. 'He did invite you though.'

'It will be a professional obligation and nothing else,' I tell her. 'I'm not going to go.'

'Would you mind if we did?' she asks. 'Your dad is so excited about his picture.'

'Oh, no, you definitely go,' I say. 'I'll see it another day, when the man himself won't be there. Maybe we could go for dinner afterwards?'

'That would be lovely,' she says. 'Listen, I'll let you go. Have fun with Xara. We'll talk plans nearer the time.'

'OK, speak soon,' I say.

'Love you, darling.'

'Love you, Sadie,' Selena sings.

'Love you both too,' I reply. 'And tell Dad congratulations.'

Once I'm off the phone I look at the invitation again. The envelope is addressed to me but the invitation is just a general invitation. I wouldn't be surprised if Damian doesn't know I've got one; it was probably sent by someone in the office. I'm definitely not going.

My doorbell rings so I toss the invitation to one side and go to answer it.

'The wine lady is here,' Xara announces, holding up a bottle in each hand.

'Oh, God, you don't know how much I need a good friend and big drink,' I tell her.

'Uhh, I can smell the pizza, and I am starving,' she says. 'You get the food, I'll pour the drinks and meet you on the sofa.'

'Deal,' I say. 'Corkscrew is already on the coffee table.'

I serve up our food and join Xara on the sofa.

'What is it about pizza?' she asks. I wait for more but it never arrives. 'Just generally. What is it about pizza?'

'It's just one of those perfect things,' I reply. 'They say even when it's bad, it's good.'

'Like sex,' she says.

I pull a face.

'OK, not at all like sex,' she says with a laugh.

'Still enjoying the new gig?' she says. 'Three weeks in, it's hardly a new gig any more, is it? You're well and truly one of the team now.'

'It's great,' I say. 'Everything I hoped it would be.'

'Are you sure?' she says through a mouthful of pizza. 'You don't sound so sure.'

'I'm sure, sorry, I'm just thinking about Damian,' I admit. I didn't mean to sound so unenthusiastic; I really do love it.

'You still think about him?'

'Oh, you know, only every day,' I reply. 'Especially today though – he sent me an invitation to his preview.'

'Are you going to go?'

'God no,' I say. 'I haven't seen him since New Year's Eve and I plan to keep it that way. He didn't call me at midnight, and I put a bunch of dumb stuff on my Instagram story, all for his benefit, and he didn't even view it... He probably doesn't even think about me now. I doubt he sent the invitation.'

'Do you want to talk about it?' she asks. 'Or do you want distracting?'

'Distracting,' I say. 'Distracting for sure.'

'OK, well...' Xara takes a moment to swallow her mouthful of pizza and dust her hands down on her trousers. 'How about we play some games? Do you still keep them under here?'

Xara reaches under the coffee table, and of all the board games she could grab, the Dial-a-Date that Damian got me for Christmas is the first one she gets hold of.

'Oh my God,' she blurts. 'You have Dial-a-Date? This was all I wanted for Christmas when I was younger. My mum refused to buy me it because she said all the men were too old for me. I tried to tell her, "Mum, you don't actually call them up..." Where on earth did you get this?'

I let out a little laugh.

'Damian got me it for Christmas,' I tell her.

'Ergh, OK, well, that doesn't mean we can't play it,' she says. She clears some space on the table and opens up the box. 'It's still in such amazing condition... like new... it's... oh...'

'What?'

'Nothing,' she says. 'Let's do something else.'

'No, come on, what's wrong with it?' I ask.

She sighs before handing over one of the date cards. It isn't even in my hand yet when I notice what's on it.

I imagine, when Damian gave me this game, he figured I would either make him play it with me, or that he would still be in my life when I did. What he's done is taken one of the date cards and stuck a picture of himself on it. He must have done it at Christmas, with one of his instant photos. He's even doing a hunky pose, like the other men in the photos. I peel back his picture just enough to see that he's placed himself over the date card that looks the most like him, meaning that it's still a playable card.

I try to put him out of my mind, I really do, but he just keeps popping up. My ghost of Christmas past.

'OK, let's not play this,' she says. 'None of this, no talking shop – why don't we watch a movie?'

'Great idea,' I say.

I keep the card in my hand for a second, staring down at him – the Damian I spent Christmas with. Somehow this feels like my Damian. I mentally pinch myself, handing over the card so that Xara can put it away.

As she messes with my remote, looking for something for us to watch, I beat myself up. I wish I could forget about him. I don't want to keep thinking about him. I am so much happier with the work at my new job. I really hope Xara doesn't think I'm not. It's everything I want to be doing, and I actually feel as if I'm on the right path to achieve more with it.

I don't actually miss my old job at all. I do miss my old boss though. I really miss him.

37

I'm staring right into Damian's eyes. Not his actual eyes – that would be weird. I'm looking at the gigantic poster of him hanging in the entrance of the gallery where his preview is taking place right now.

It's been going on for a while now, I guess. Everyone will be in there, falling all over him, cooing at his art – my parents included.

My dad is so happy about his photo being included. I'm sure it's going to be all I hear about when we go for dinner after they're done – which is hopefully going to be soon. It didn't seem worth travelling home after work, only to head back in this direction to meet my mum and dad, so I'm just loitering outside like a weirdo.

And, no, it hasn't escaped my attention that I'm currently spending Valentine's Day starting at a huge photo of the man who broke my heart, and the most exciting plans I have this evening involve dinner with my parents – probably in a restaurant surrounded by couples, which, I'm sure you'll agree, is not especially romantic.

I look up at the poster again. If there weren't security guards here, I'd probably take an eyeliner from my bag and draw something offensive on his face. Actually, I definitely wouldn't, I'm such a baby, but I like to pretend I would.

My phone buzzes with a message from my dad. I'm hoping it's to say they're on their way out but it isn't, it's to tell me to go inside and see this photo. I do want to go in and see it, I really do, I just don't want to see Damian. Another message comes through telling me they haven't seen Damian for over an hour; they think he's already left. Hmm. What are the chances that's true? I guess it would be like Damian, to not hang around for too long...

I take a few steps closer to the door before turning around and walking away from the building again. Almost immediately I turn around again and this time I march straight inside. Screw it.

I follow the signs to the room where Damian's preview is and when I get there I walk in with my head held high. Well, after I give my name for the guest list, which annoys me because I don't want Damian knowing I was here. Then again, there's no way he's going to look at the list. I'm sure his new assistant compiled it anyway.

It's a big white room, with Damian's photos in large frames dotted around. His pictures are all in black and white, and in big black frames. I would say, at a glance, that half of the photos are bigger than I am.

I'm weaving through the adoring crowd, looking for my mum and dad, when I happen upon a picture that stops me in my tracks. There's a bench right in front of it so I plonk myself down, still just staring up at it. It's me. It's the photo of me that Damian took on the old boat. I'm snuggled up in a blanket, cradling a mug of tea, and I look so, so happy. It takes me right back to that evening, and to Christmas, and it makes me feel so happy and so devastated at the same time. Up until Damian and I fell out it might have been the best Christmas I've ever had... just with the worst ending. I had no idea he was going to use it – to be honest I forgot it existed. Seeing myself so happy makes me so sad. How did things manage to go so wrong?

I quickly wipe away the annoying tear that has escaped from my eye. I'm not going to cry here; I am a grown woman... I'll cry at home, alone, later.

'They say you're not supposed to have favourites,' I hear a voice say behind me.

'That's kids,' I reply, my eyes still firmly fixed on the photo.

'These are my kids,' Damian replies as he takes a seat next to me.

'So my dad set me up, huh?'

'He honestly took absolutely no convincing at all,' Damian replies. 'I really wouldn't trust him, moving forward.'

I laugh.

'I don't remember signing a disclaimer for this,' I say. 'Your new assistant is shit.'

'I don't actually have a new assistant,' he says. 'So, if anything is amiss here, it's all on me.'

I finally turn to look at him. He's looking great, in a pair of black trousers with a white shirt. His hair is perfect, but isn't it always? He's smiling and I do really miss his smile.

'It looks great,' I tell him. 'Seriously. You've done an amazing job.'

'Well, the critics seem to think so,' he says under his breath. 'So that's a relief.'

'I should probably go find my mum and dad,' I say.

'Wait, don't go yet,' he replies. 'My mum and dad just left, but they've been here since the doors opened. I had a long chat with my mum after you left. She told me that you'd told her to talk to me. We figured a lot of things out so thank you – we're in a much better place now.'

I laugh.

'What's funny?' he asks.

'I was just about to say "honesty is everything" but that seems almost sarcastic given everything that has happened,' I say.

'I am sorry, about all of that,' he says. 'I know a few words aren't nearly enough to explain what the hell went wrong but last year was a weird year. I know that I messed up. I backed myself into a corner with you. The first note was a misguided attempt at being funny – I didn't think you'd reply. Then I figured I'd use the insight to make things easier at work... and then I just loved the way you chatted to me. I know everyone in the office hates me and I suppose it just gave me a chance to chat to you, not as your boss, and get to know you but... I shouldn't have.'

'I'm sorry too,' I reply. 'I guess we both made such a mess of things.'

I don't have to agree with what Damian did to understand why he did it. I know what it's like to keep a secret and then get in too deep to tell the truth.

'The thing that I can't stop thinking, though, is that we made a mess of things before we got together... but everything after we left for Christmas was great, wasn't it?'

'I thought so,' I say. 'But that's exactly why I didn't know how to tell you I was quitting. I didn't want to hurt you.'

'How is the new job?' he asks.

'I love it,' I tell him. 'But I miss you.'

After months of lies and a messy fallout, what harm could the truth do now?

I feel a lump in my throat, as if my heart has just jumped up into my mouth. If he doesn't say something soon, I'm going to throw up.

'Maybe now that we're not working together, we could tolerate hanging out together sometimes?'

I smile.

'Yeah, I'd like that,' I reply.

I feel as if we've both made such a mess of things. Perhaps a fresh start – one where I don't have to answer to him – is just what we need.

'Would you like that tonight?' he asks. 'Because before your mum and dad lured you in here under false pretences, they invited me for dinner with you all.'

I can't hide my smile. I feel as if before, when I was working for him, there was this barrier that stopped us from ever moving forward. Now that it's gone, who knows what could happen? I'm excited to find out though.

'I bet they did,' I say. 'Sure, why not?'

'Phew,' he says. 'I'm so glad I didn't just write "I'm sorry" on a Post-it and stick it to your forehead.'

'Yeah, it's definitely too soon for anything like that,' I tell him. 'I'm not sure I'd find that funny... yet... But dinner with me and my parents sounds like a good way to get things back on track.'

Ordinarily you have to be pretty serious with a man before you'll invite him for dinner with your parents but, seeing as though Damian and I started out by having Christmas dinner with them, the three of us having regular dinner together doesn't really seem like a big deal.

'It's just great to have a second chance, to try and make it up to you,' he says. 'It's been weird, not seeing you for over a month.'

'Same,' I reply. 'But I did finally find your photo in my Dial-a-Date box a couple of weeks ago.'

'Oh, God, I completely forgot about that,' he says with a laugh and a gentle cringe. 'I thought it would be funny.'

'Oh, it was,' I assure him.

'Did I get a date, when you played it?'

'I didn't actually get around to playing it,' I say.

'Well, maybe we can play it with your mum and dad tonight?' he suggests.

'Did you just invite yourself back to mine?' I ask in playful disbelief.

'Only to play with myself,' he says. 'Wait, that came out wrong. But it is Valentine's Day, and it's the closest thing I'll be having to a date.'

'OK, fine, you can play Dial-a-Date with me and my parents. Is that the Valentine's Day you hoped for this year?'

'It really is,' he replies.

38

It's been a long time since I walked up these stairs. So long that I am either completely out of shape from not walking up and down them often, or I just don't remember their being as knackering as they feel right now. But don't we often have a habit of looking back at things and remembering them in a better light?

Sometimes it feels like only yesterday I was pulling myself up these stairs, with a latte in one hand and high hopes there would be a Post-it Note waiting for me to brighten my day up. But it wasn't yesterday, it was five months ago. May is almost over and by the time June is done it will be half a year since I worked for Damian.

I do love my new job. Not least because I don't have to climb a mountain of stairs to get to it, but that does help. I love working in a gallery and in a way it feels as if I've always worked there. I don't feel like a newbie any more, I'm just so comfortable.

Five months isn't really all that long, in the grand scheme of things, so Damian's main office hasn't changed much at all, which I find a little disappointing, but what did I expect? The only improvement, as far as I can tell, is that it's empty of all the co-workers I never really liked all that much, but that's more to do with the fact that the office closed fifteen minutes ago.

It feels both nostalgic and completely alien as I head for my old office – which actually was my own office, it turns out, and not a desk share. And then, when I'm inside, and I see her – the new me – it feels even more as though I were never really here.

'Hello,' she says brightly. 'He'll be right out.'

She's not unlike me in type. Tall, long hair, the sort of fashion sense that almost definitely looks as if you've tried hard but often confuses people. She seems friendly, and sharp, and she's got a good eye if her vintage coat is anything to go by. If he was going to have anyone, other than me, I'm happy that it's her. But that's why I suggested he hire her.

'How are you, Nadia?' I ask. 'How are you finding it here?'

'I'm loving it,' she says. 'Damian is such a dream to work for.'

I smile to myself, because I know that he didn't used to be.

'That's great,' I say. 'It seems like you're doing an amazing job. Damian is so happy with you.'

'Aww, that means so much, especially coming from the boss's girlfriend,' she says proudly. 'I feel like you must have such an honest, unique view into what he really thinks... If you can make sure he knows I'm really happy here.'

'Of course,' I reply.

Damian pokes his head out of his office door.

'Nadia, it's Friday, what are you still doing here?' he says. 'Go home!'

'Yes, boss,' she says with a giggle. 'See you both later. Have a good weekend.'

'You too,' I tell her.

And then it's just me and Damian, just like old times, except so much is different now.

'I just have one last thing to finish,' he tells me. 'Then I don't have any work to do for the whole weekend.'

'Sounds great,' I reply.

'Why don't you take a seat at your old desk, in your old chair?' he says. 'For old times' sake.'

'Oh, yes, that sounds fabulous,' I joke. 'But hurry up, I'm starving!'

'I'm on it,' he says, dashing back inside his office.

Sitting down in my old chair feels more like it. The way it wobbles a little, the way the arms knock the desk if you don't pull it out enough, even the smell of the material. It all feels so familiar.

And would you look at that? There's even a stack of Post-it Notes and a pad on the desk. Perhaps Nadia really is a lot like me.

I reach for the pad and pop the top off the pen. Maybe it's being back in the chair, with Damian in the other room, but I can't resist writing a note.

The boss is amazing.

I open the desk drawer, toying with the idea of sticking the note in there and calling Damian in to see it – we did always say that Post-its would be funny one day. Maybe that day is today? But when I look down and see that there's already a note there waiting, my heart jumps into my mouth. I snatch it up and I'm so relieved when I realise that Damian isn't up to his old tricks again – the note is addressed to me.

Sadie, come into my office. x

I smile at the note. Not just because it's cute, but because he must have known I would look. And the fact I was going to leave a note in there for him just goes to show we are on exactly the same wavelength.

'I thought you were never going to find it,' Damian says as I walk into his office. 'I thought I was going to have to come and get you, ruin the surprise.'

His desk is clear of anything that remotely resembles work. Instead it's laid out with Chinese food, from my favourite local takeaway, along with a bottle of champagne on ice with two glasses.

'What's all this?' I ask.

'I thought I'd surprise you,' he says.

'You certainly have,' I reply. 'Oh my God, is that always there?'

I've only just looked on the wall next to me, where there's a giant print of my photo from Damian's latest collection.

'Yes,' he says very seriously, before his face slips into a massive smile. 'Of course, it's not always there. It's part of the surprise...'

I slowly but cautiously walk around to Damian's side of the desk, eyeballing him every step of the way. What on earth is he up to?

'You're going to New York,' he tells me. 'Your photo is. All of them are. A gallery in Manhattan wants to show my work later this year.'

'Oh my gosh, Damian, that's amazing,' I say, grabbing him, hugging him tightly. 'Oh my God, my dad is going to go crazy when he finds out he's going to be in a gallery in New York! I can't believe it. I'm so proud of you.'

'I couldn't have done any of it without you,' he tells me, loosening himself from my extra-tight hug, just a little, so he can look me in the eye. 'Honestly, I owe all of this to you. That's why I'm so pleased that, even though you don't work for me any more, I can take you with me.'

'They'll never let you on an aeroplane with that,' I say, nodding towards my photo.

Damian places his hands lightly on the sides of my face and kisses me.

'I love you,' he tells me.

'And I love you too,' I reply.

'That's why I'm taking you with me, not just your photo, and don't worry, we'll figure it out around work, it's not going to get in the way of your job, but you deserve to be there just as much as I do,' he tells me. 'Honestly, Sadie, I *really* couldn't have done any of this without you. I'm not just saying that thing that people say. I can't even put it into words.'

'I guess you don't have to,' I say with a smile. 'That thing over there is worth a thousand, apparently.'

'Well, there is that.' He smiles.

'Do you think, if I hadn't decided to quit, or if you hadn't found out that I was quitting when you did, that we'd be here, like this, today?'

'Absolutely not,' he says. 'I would have put off telling you how I felt forever. And if you had told me you were quitting, I would have kept making up excuses to have you around more right up until the last minute... Then again, I don't think I could have let you go.'

'Lucky for us, everything turned out all right in the end,' I say, snatching up a spring roll from the desk. Well, I did say I was starving.

We might have had a rocky start but we've found our way through a maze of work politics, Post-it notes, and family Christmases, and, now we've come out at the other side, I can't wait to see what the future has in store for us. If we're starting as we mean to go on, well, it doesn't get much better than New York, does it?

Damian opens up his desk drawer and grabs one of the Post-its he used to use when he sent me notes as Adam.

'We did say Post-its would be funny one day,' I remind him.

'We did,' he says as he peels one off and sticks it to my forehead. 'This is why we have to stick together.'

Oh, God, a dad joke.

'*Hilarious*,' I reply.

ACKNOWLEDGMENTS

Thank you so much to Nia (the best editor on the planet), Amanda, and the rest of the team at the brilliant Boldwood Books.

As always, thank you to everyone who takes the time to read and review my books, it means so much to me that you enjoy them.

Massive thanks to my family who I couldn't do any of this without. My parents - especially my mum, Kim, and Aud, who have all always given me so much love and support. Thanks to James and Joey for always being there for me - I'd be lost without you both.

Finally thank you to my fiancé, Joe, for being nothing short of incredible. I love you all so much.

MORE FROM PORTIA MACINTOSH

We hope you enjoyed reading *Stuck On You*. If you did, please leave a review.

If you'd like to gift a copy, this book is also available as an ebook, digital audio download and audiobook CD.

Sign up to Portia MacIntosh's mailing list for news, competitions and updates on future books.

http://bit.ly/PortiaMacIntoshNewsletter

Discover more laugh-out-loud romantic comedies from Portia Macintosh:

Honeymoon For One

My Great Ex-Scape

The Plus One Pact

ABOUT THE AUTHOR

Portia MacIntosh is a bestselling romantic comedy author of 15 novels, including *My Great Ex-Scape* and *Honeymoon For One*. Previously a music journalist, Portia writes hilarious stories, drawing on her real life experiences.

Visit Portia's website: https://portiamacintosh.com/

Follow Portia MacIntosh on social media here:

- facebook.com/portia.macintosh.3
- twitter.com/PortiaMacIntosh
- instagram.com/portiamacintoshauthor
- bookbub.com/authors/portia-macintosh

ABOUT BOLDWOOD BOOKS

Boldwood Books is a fiction publishing company seeking out the best stories from around the world.

Find out more at www.boldwoodbooks.com

Sign up to the Book and Tonic newsletter for news, offers and competitions from Boldwood Books!

http://www.bit.ly/bookandtonic

We'd love to hear from you, follow us on social media:

facebook.com/BookandTonic

twitter.com/BoldwoodBooks

instagram.com/BookandTonic